I0640311

Their Somewhere Safe

The Rayne Falls Ranch Collection
Book 2

Sinful Grace

If you purchased this book without a cover you should be aware that this book is stolen property. It was reported as "unsold and destroyed" to the publisher, and neither the author nor the publisher has received any payment for this "stripped book."

ISBN- 978-1-7349328-2-9
Their Somewhere Safe
Copyright © 2020 by G&T Publishing.

All rights reserved. Except for use in any review, the reproduction or utilization of this work in whole or in part in any form by any electronic, mechanical, or other means, now known or hereinafter invented, including xerography, photocopying, and recording, or in any information storage or retrieval system, is forbidden without the written permission of the publisher or author, G&T Publishing, Sinful Grace.

This is a work of fiction. Names characters, places, and incidents are either the product of the author's imagination or are used fictitiously, and any resemblance to actual persons, living or dead, business establishments, events or locales is entirely coincidental. This edition published by arrangement between Sinful Grace and G&T Publishing. For questions and comments about the quality of this book, please contact us at gt.publishingbooks@gmail.com or visit www.gt-publishing.com for publishing and author contact information.

The horse and fox logo is a Trademark of G&T Publishing and its author affiliation. Use without written consent to publish, photocopy, or by any other means distribute this logo knowingly or unknowingly, without written consent, is forbidden and may face legal actions. **Printed in the U.S.A.**

Dear Reader,

I hope this book is as exciting as my first one was. Being my second book in this collection, it was a joy to complete for all of you. I would like to dedicate this book to my family. Without them life would have been much harder growing up. I would also like to give recognition to the friends and authors I have had the pleasure of getting to know from the writer's espresso book group. They are truly extraordinary and if you are new to publishing, check them out. They are always willing to help.

A bit about myself: I am a married mother of four. I work with several rescues both in the states and overseas. I work from home, yes with all my kids, as a medical professional, and have a great understanding of imagination. Romance is not only what I write about but am passionate about. There is an art in the languages of love, affection, compassion, kink, erotica, and romance in general. I find all of it to be enchanting and I hope you can see some of that within my work.

When I am not working, corralling kids, or writing, I am trying to play with animals or crafting. I am not only artsy in writing but other projects too. I cannot sit still.

I hope that within this book you find some romance that inspires you. Romance can be all consuming at times and I revel in the feelings it creates. I hope you enjoy those feelings as well.

Finally, if you feel you are in a bad situation, please reach out to someone. Information is at the end of this book. If you wish to check out more of my work, contact me, or provide feedback, please visit:

www.gt-publishing.com

https://www.facebook.com/Sinfulgraceromanceauthor/

https://www.facebook.com/georgia.grace.50702

http://chatstory.crazymaplestudios.com/page/msgstory/5e87fb9ee0bd5532268b461b/2/16348705

http://chatstory.crazymaplestudios.com/page/msgstory/5e7f68f7d1f9fac93b8b460f/2/16348705

https://writersespresso.com

https://writersespresso.com/Sinful-Grace

Instagram: Sinful_Grace

Twitter: @Sinful_Grace

Remember,
You can't have history without a story in it!

Sinful Grace

Lupus dentis, taurus cornis.

The wolf with his teeth, the bull with his horns.

-   Latin Proverb

Prologue

"You sure you want to drive yourself? My offer still stands to fly with me?" Reed yelled from the bathroom. His oldest brother always liked to arrive in style anywhere he went. "No, I'm good. I have been flying around so much I'd rather stick to the ground for a while." Kent replied. He had just gotten back from his second tour; this one was in Egypt and he took a month's leave to attend Austin's wedding. His younger brother was getting married to Annette, a mother of a little girl. From what he understood she had a lot of problems with her ex-husband, the birth father of her little girl, and domestic abuse. It all came to a head when he attempted to harm both of them and was shot dead. Now Austin has stepped up and is officially adopting the little girl, who already calls him Daddy and marrying the woman he loves in nine days.

The fridge door slammed shut hard when he used his foot to close it after grabbing a cold one and a package of pepperoni. It must have been louder than he thought when he heard his brother again, "Don't be breaking shit in my house!" He chuckled opening the package and taking a handful into his mouth. The bold flavor exploding over his tongue had his mouthwatering. It was still early, around seven in the morning but he planned on getting a move on since it was a 33-hour drive and he wasn't sure yet if he planned on driving the whole way or if he was getting a hotel for a break. Also, he planned to make a few stops along the way. Finishing his snack and his drink, he walked over to the window and gazed out at the sprawling city below. Reed lived in a penthouse condo overlooking central park in Manhattan. His brother had money and had no problem spending it on the finer things. He couldn't blame him though. This view was amazing and he knew he would never get tired of looking at it. It was just everything surrounding it that had him homesick.

Nothing but skyscrapers and tall buildings surrounded the green patch of land. People that looked like ants roamed around everywhere and the slight fog of the air had his heart aching for open land and blue sky. He missed his military family and their banter but his heart was also torn towards his home town. He left to serve his country with his friend, Jason, who died in a desert from an assault on their convoy. Jason had thrown himself in front of him and another soldier and got hit in the chest. The bullet went through him and hit Kent in the collar bone. It took their medic team 2 hours to retrieve the bullet from the bone. He still had pain from it every once in awhile, but he would never get over the loss of his friend. The bullet severed a coronary artery right near Jason's heart and he bled out internally before the medic team had shown.

"Bro, you listening to me," snapping of Reed's fingers in his face had Kent turning his head to his brother. Confused for a moment, Kent shook his head to bring him back from his memories. After the fog in his head cleared enough, "what is it?" His tone coming out a bit harsher than he meant it to but if Reed noticed he didn't say anything.

"Man, where was your head at?" His older brother ran a hand over the short stubble of a beard on his chin. Reed had started to show some signs of greying, which Kent teased him for when he got back but in all honesty, it suited his brother. Reed had always been the more mature one out of all three of them.

"Nowhere," Kent replied. Not wanting to get into it right now. Shrugging, Reed turned and went to the kitchen Island. Kent watched as he lifted a glass of tea and took a sip. *When had he gotten that*, Kent wondered? He must have really been out of it not to hear the fridge.

Reed spoke between drinks, "I am still surprised you don't have a date to this thing lined up. You could always pick one up on the way down there I'm sure." He knew Reed was teasing him to make light of everything and he appreciated it. Joining Reed at the island, Kent rolled out his shoulders.

"I have enough of my own problems. I don't need to add in someone else's right now. Besides, you can be my date." He gave his brother a big smile, "remember when you pick me up, I don't like flowers, I prefer beer and I don't put out on the first date." His brother went to laugh as he was drinking and started hacking. Kent slapped him on the back a few times till he caught his breath. They both stood there for a few minutes just chuckling. When they caught their breath Reed spoke, "and I always thought you were easy." Reed moved to place his cup in the dishwasher and he turned to go to his room to grab his bags. Kent yelled over his shoulder, "I'm playing hard to get." He heard Reed's laugh follow him down the hall.

Packing wasn't hard since he just got to Reed's four days ago and hadn't even unpacked. He left all his military gear in his locker on base and only brought two duffle bags and a large camping style backpack. He didn't want to mention it to his brother but he really wanted the drive just to think and get his mind straight before he was around everyone. Reed usually stayed to himself and didn't ask too many questions which he was grateful for since he didn't want to talk about anything yet. Kent knew he wouldn't know where to start even if Reed did ask. Thankfully his brother wasn't the nosey or inquisitive type.

"When I get there after my meetings we will have to go get you a proper suit. I can't have my date looking like a hobo." Reed slapped him on the back as he placed his things in front of the door. He would have fallen headfirst into the door if he hadn't put his hand up to catch himself.

"I owe you for that later," Kent brushed his jeans when he got up. His hand ran over his freshly cut military crop. Stubble was already growing on his chin again and he knew he would need another shave again by tomorrow. Usually, he had to do it once a day it grew so fast.

He met Reed's eyes, which wasn't hard to do since they were maybe two inches or so difference in height, Kent being the taller of the two. "When don't you owe me, man," Reed replied with a shit-eating grin. "Don't forget Beauty when you leave," his brother tossed him his car keys. "I just had the oil changed again last week. She should be good for a while." Kent fingered the keys in his palms.

The keys felt so odd in his hands. "Thanks for watching her man."

"Anytime man. Hopefully, you get to play with her for a while." Reed slapped him on the back one last time and pulled him in for a brief hug before letting him go. Walking around him he held the door open. Kent slung the backpack over his shoulder, picked up the other two bags and patted his pocket, making sure his wallet was in there. "See ya in a few days, man." He said before walking to the elevator. He got in when the door clicked open and pressed the button for the garage. Excited about seeing Beauty again, he all but hopped out of the elevator when it slid open. A horn honked and lights flashed as he hit the locator button on the keychain.

Beauty was a black Dodge Charger with black rims and matching black interior. He had red undercarriage lights installed and a new exhaust the last time he was home two years ago. He had Reed install a new Hemi engine into her while he was away in preparation for his return. Seeing her now in all her glory he could not lie, he had a semi hardon just from the sight of her. He pushed the button to open the trunk and stored his bags in it. He let out a grunt as the weight of the backpack eased off his sore shoulder and into the trunk before closing it. Slowly Kent slid his hand over the exterior. Beauty felt smooth as he made his way to the driver's side door.

Once inside he grabbed the steering wheel and eased back in the seat. Breathing in the smell of leather, gas, and metal had his body relaxing. He missed this. Adjusting his rearview mirror and side mirrors before he put the stick in reverse, pulling out of the garage. The sun was already set high in the sky but it didn't stop the crisp of the air making fog on the windshield. The dark black tint on the windows and windshield helped with the brightness but he was still putting on his sunglass anyway. The sound of the engine had his heart rate picking up and his mood felt lighter with every mile closer that he got to home.

Chapter 1

More than four hours later he had taken a pit stop in Baltimore, Maryland to grab some lunch and take a stroll around the harbor. The only other time he had been there was back in basic when he did AT training down at Fort Meade and he wanted to do some tourist stuff before his unit went back home. Back then it was late and they barely got to see anything with all the attractions closed. The area looked completely different in the bright daylight though. The shops all open and bustling with people. Parking in a parking garage close to the water, he adjusted his sunglasses. After holstering his .22 to his hip under his shirt and making sure his car was alarmed under a security camera, he went to go across the busy road to the water.

At night, the water glimmered with lights from the surrounding buildings. They flickered off it like candles flames. The hush of the night had given it a calming effect. That was a complete contrast to the daytime. With the sun shining down on the water Kent thought he should be able to see to the bottom, but that was not the case. The water was a brownish-green and so murky that he bet he couldn't see his toes if he dared to stick his foot in it, which he didn't. that didn't stop people from spending time on the water though. There were paddle boats, tour boats, toys, and even a pirate ship being paraded around. The clutter of people everywhere could have made anyone feel claustrophobic but he was used to confining spaces with groups of people. The only difference was the people he normally got stuck with were people he would stick his life on the line for. They weren't strangers.

He heard a scream and a little girl shout, "My balloon! No! No! No!" He saw a woman chasing after a little girl, who in return was chasing after a small pink balloon on a yellow string. The air in the balloon must have been slowly fading because it didn't float away. Instead, it floated to about his height along with the wind. He watched as the balloon floated past a few people but none of them did nothing. They either were ignoring the situation because of headphones, on their phone or just ignoring the situation in its entirety. He quickly stepped around a gentleman and a little boy to catch the balloon before it glided over the pier to the water.

"My balloon!" The little girl, who he guessed was around seven, squeaked as she got to him. Her hands reaching out to take it from his hands. The woman chasing after her came up to his chin and was very petit. She was trying to catch her breath when she started to speak, "Th... thank you. Tha… That was nice of you." He held up a hand and she looked at him, a hand fluttering to her chest. "She looked as if she would have jumped in the water otherwise," he smiled at her. She smiled in returned. "It was no trouble ma'am. I hope she keeps hold of it this time around though." He bent down to the little girl. She was clutching the yellow string to her chest.

"Sasha, tell the nice man thank you."

He was just about to get up when a small hand shot out to his, "My mom says I should say thank you," he took her hand, "Thank you." She shook it and then took her balloon and went to stand close to her mother.

"You're welcome." He replied getting up. "Have a nice day ma'am." He dipped his chin in response and turned to walk away.

He walked in and out of shops after that encounter. Looking at the sites and taking in the atmosphere. It was chilly outside and he could almost see his breath. The weather kept changing from warm to frost without any notice. It was as if Mother Nature was going through hot flashes. His thoughts of the weather were put on hold when he got a whiff of something that made his stomach grumble. His stomach reminding him he was hungry by protesting to be fed. Kent followed his nose to a small dive bar on a corner. This area didn't look like a tourist spot with its rundown buildings with boarded-up windows down the block and an empty lot on the other side. He would have turned around from the eerie feeling the area gave him but because it was daylight out and the demand his stomach was giving him he decided to take a shot and walk-in.

The interior was dark but the delightful smell that brought him in was stronger. His stomach felt like it was eating itself at this point. The few windows along two of the walls were small and had frosted yellow glass. The walls painted a deep dark burgundy and the room was split into two tiers. The bottom tier had tables and booths along the wall with a bar along the back wall. The second tier had fewer tables, a dance floor and a stage for a band. If it was this dark during the day he wondered how anyone saw in here at night. As it was they had lights on but they were all so dim it was difficult to properly see the whole place.

A woman dressed in black slacks and a white tank top walked up to him and introduced herself as the waitress. Her top was cut so low he wondered if she did that to try to get more tips. She motioned for him to follow her and she sat him down at a booth along the wall. Having a hard time looking at her face due to the amount of eyeliner covering both eyes. It reminded him of a pirate. The top of her breasts almost spilled out of her bra when she leaned over to place the menu on the table.

Before she could even start her spiel and attempt flirting with him Kent ordered a Coke and asked to have a few minutes to look over the menu. She nodded and walked away. Her hips swaying with the extra emphasis he was sure she did on purpose to get attention. He took a moment to look over the menu and had decided on a deluxe burger by the time the waitress came back with his Coke.

She placed the drink down, making sure when she leaned over her breast was inches from his face. "Do you know what you want," she said sweetly as she straightened. He clipped out his order to her not wanting to chat any longer than was necessary. Kent never liked it when women used their sex appeal to smother men with. It was a turnoff. She took the hint and wrote down his order before nodding and walking away again.

His eyes surveyed the room, taking it all in, as he sipped his Coke. There were a bartender, two bouncers, and two other waitresses walking around. The room had less than a dozen people were mingling or sitting about. He was about to pull his phone out of his pocket and check it when he heard a muffled commotion coming from the upper level. Shifting in his seat, Kent squinted his eyes to try to see better in the dim light. He saw what looked like a waitress arguing with a table of men.

As she spoke her body seemed to get increasingly tense. The longer the conversation, the more wound her body got. The white blouse and black slacks hugged her body that had him taking in her plump curves. His eyes traveled to appreciate the thick thighs and nice rounded ass. The woman's stomach wasn't supermodel thin but she wasn't fat either. The outfit hugged her just right, molding out her breast behind the material. Every time she spoke they jiggled and his cock twitched in his pants in response. He scolded his thoughts and used his hand to adjust himself in his jeans. Kent tried to focus on their words when he noticed one of the men stand up from the table and take a step towards her.

"I don't know what to tell you, Billy. I don't know where she is and I don't care to know." He heard her over the hum of the jukebox another customer put on. The song was blaring across the room making it near impossible for him to hear anything. He stood up instinctively and started moving closer before he knew what he was doing.

"Lynn, baby. It doesn't matter where she is. She told us you could cover her." The man sitting in a grey suit on the opposite side of the table facing her said.

The man was so calm leaning back in the chair that anyone looking at them would assume the woman was the only one having a mental breakdown. Kent's gut was telling him differently though. Something about the way the man to her right loomed over her and the man sitting to her left looked like he was poised to jump out of his seat, kept him on edge.

"I don't have anything to give you!" the beautiful creature yelled. Emphasizing her frustration with her hands waving out at her sides. "Besides I told her that last time, was the last time. You will have to find her if you want to get paid." She folded her arms across her chest but all that effectively did was push her breast up even further.

Silently he cursed himself when his mouth began to water and his dick twitched in his pants again. He didn't know why this situation should bother him. He shouldn't care about it at all since this wasn't his business, but it seemed like everyone else in the room was ignoring the scene on purpose too. That also had his senses on high alert. Something wasn't right and everyone else seemed to know to stay out of it.

The woman just stood there, arms folded and staring back. Kent paused behind a pillar in the room. He was only a few feet away from where they were. None of them took notice of him and he preferred it that way. Her hair swished as she moved to turn away but the burly man standing to grab a hold of her arm, effectively stopping her to swing her back around.

"Get off me you jackass." She sneered at him.

The man was dressed in a black suit with a red shirt underneath. It made him look like a modern-day Mafia hitman. Without acknowledging her words, he kept ahold of her arm. Kent clenched and unclenched his fists as anger rose in his chest. He never liked it when a woman was being manhandled inappropriately. She turned her eyes back to the man across the table. He was sitting up straighter now, with a slight smirk to his lips that stated he always got what he wanted. Kent just knew he wanted to punch him in the jaw.

"Tell your goon to let go of me before I really get mad." She spat out while unsuccessfully trying to pull her arm free.

The man in the grey suit who she referred to as Billy just smiled at her words and casually rested his hands on the table. "I can't do that sweet cheeks. You see if you can't cover the cost with cash," he paused dramatically. "She offered you up to cover the cost with your body. I expect to get paid one way or the other. This way is way more fun." His smile had Kent's gut-clenching and his anger rising in his chest. *Who the fuck was this man?*

Before he could say anything else the woman stomped on the guy's foot who held her and she flung her head back connecting with his face. Kent heard him cry out as he hopped on one foot and covered his bloody nose with his hands. He bent over just as the man to her left stood up. Kent rushed from behind the pillar toward them just as the other man had taken a swing at the woman's face.

****

Aaralynn was expecting to feel pain spread across her jaw when her head snapped back to see Jerry's fist coming at her. Instead, she felt heat rush her backside. Her eyes snapped open when a deep voice boomed from behind her, "I would think again before doing that." Her eyes focused on the hand palming Jerry's fist which was inches away from her face before flashing up to meet Jerry's. Jerry's eyes locked on whoever was behind her and his features turned menacing.

She couldn't stop the words before they came out her mouth, "What the fuck." That earned her nothing but a hard body pressing against her back. The contact had her body tingling in response. *Was it getting hot in here*? Jerry's face turned from menacing to something she hadn't seen on him before. Pain. The man behind her must be crushing Jerry's hand in his fist because she could hear cracking and popping.

Inwardly she cringed at the noise. Surprisingly she didn't flinch like any normal person would, instead she stood stock still as the man behind her moved Jerry's hand to the side, still clutching it to his chest. His hot breath fanned against her ear as the man behind her leaned in. He smelled of spicy cologne and sweat. It would have her swooning any other time but her heart was racing with what was going on around her right now. "Play along and stick right by me darling," he whispered low enough so only she could hear it.

The deep baritone of his voice had Aaralynn squeezing her thighs together. Shaming herself for reacting to a man this way she didn't even know, in a hostile situation no less. He didn't wait for a reply before he stood tall, squaring his shoulders and spoke to Billy, completely ignoring Jerry who had started to squirm in the man's grasp. "Is there a problem here?"

"This woman was just settling up a debt. No problem here at all Mr....?" Billy trailed off waiting for the man behind her to give his name. He never did so Billy just went on. "Can you let my man's hand go? He might need to use that hand someday when his old lady doesn't want to get the job done for him." He spoke so matter-of-factly that he could have been discussing the weather. She felt the man behind her nod his head and watched as he squeezed Jerry's hand one last time before letting go. Jerry jerked his hand back to his chest and cradled it while his other hand flew to his gun holstered on his belt.

Billy waved his hand at Jerry to stop. "Now Jerry no need to do that. We wouldn't want to cause an unnecessary scene, now would we?"

"No boss,' he replied. He sounded like he was sulking.

It was so unlike Jerry that it had her doing a double-take. She knew the expression on her face had to be comical but she couldn't help herself. A noise to her right had her realizing she forgot the other man, who was now starting to straighten himself. Never having met him before, he was someone new to Billy's gang, she knew he wouldn't hesitate to do whatever Billy told him too. And that had her mad all over again. Not sure where the sudden burst of courage came from, she turned and punched him in the chest. He grunted but didn't budge.

Silence filled the room like a bad smell and she looked around the room to see everyone was staring at her. "What? He's an asshole." She shrugged. The shaking vibrations coming from the body behind her had her tilting the side of her mouth in a smile. His silent laughter had her body relaxing against him.

Billy cleared his throat. "Now, I would like to get on with my day. Lynn, you're coming with us." Billy ordered as he began to stand and his words had her whole-body tensing again. The man behind her must have noticed because he possessively slid his arm around her waist and pulled her flush to his front. The warmth of him had her blood heating up and she was glad it was dark in the room or else she would be embarrassed from the blush that was creeping up her skin. *What is wrong with her?* She never got all swoony around a guy anymore. It had happened once and she vowed to never let her emotions go there ever again. The rumbling voice behind her pulled her out of her thoughts.

"No, she isn't." He stated. His grip firmed on her and she felt the ripple of his arm muscles through her shirt. Something hard pressed into her backside and it had her flinching, "Ouch." The men didn't take their eyes off of each other, the tension in the room so thick you could drink it like soup. The man behind her must have thought her flinching was because he gripped her. His hold loosened slightly. She wished he hadn't.

Billy nodded his head towards her. His men began moving closer in around both of them. One instant she was standing in front of the man, his hard body behind her, and the next she was behind him. He had swung her around and used his arm to press her up against his back, shielding her. She could hear the gasp of all the patrons in the building. Knew their eyes would only be glued for a few moments before they tried to mind their business and cleared out of the place to safety.

This wasn't the first time something like this had happened. Just like the switch of a button she could hear chairs scraping and feet shuffling. The click of a gun could be heard and she assumed it was one of Billy's men. "No Billy! Don't shoot us!" She yelled from behind him. Aaralynn's fingers twisted into the fabric of his shirt as she pressed herself tighter into him.

"If you don't want anyone shot Lynn, you might want to tell your man with the gun to drop it then," Billy's gruff voice settling in her brain.

Her head rested against the man's back as she blew out a breath she didn't realize she was holding. "Well, assuming really did make an ass out of me," she hadn't realized she said it out loud till Billy started chuckling. It was a sound that sent chills running down her spine and not in a good way.

If the man in front of her had a gun and was protecting her she wasn't going to tell him to put it away. Hell, he could have shot them and she would be grateful. What they had planned for her would be worse than anything he was going to do to them. She couldn't see anything but she sensed the moment the two henchmen started moving towards them. The arm around her flexed as he nudged them back towards the bar.

"You three need to get out," Ray, her boss's voice exploded beside her. *When did he get there,* she questioned herself? She hadn't even noticed him come up but he was there now with a shotgun in his hand. "I already phoned the police. If you don't want tons of questions you will want to leave now." He cocked the gun for emphasis.

Tony, who sometimes served as bartender/ bouncer flanked their other side. He had a baseball bat in his hand and he looked mad as hell. Aaralynn had a sudden sense of calm rush over her. The kind of calm that happens when you see something happening in front of you and you know there is nothing you can do about any of it.

Someone grunted and something smashes to the ground as footsteps receded away. "This day or another, we will be collecting Lynn." Billy's voice faded as he moved towards the exit. "Your tab is due." Billy's last words rang in her ears, sending shivers through her as the clink of the door shutting echoed the now nearly empty space. She heard the men talking around her but said nothing. She didn't think she could even if she wanted to.

"Did you really call the cops?" Her protector inquired.

"No. I just said that to get them out of here. Those thugs are good for nothing criminals but they are still running around like they own everything and everyone." The click of Ray uncocking the gun had her fingers unfolding from the man's shirt. His strong arm didn't move from around her and she was grateful. She didn't trust she could have stood on her own just yet.

She saw the man's black gun in his hand at his side. He really did have one. For some reason, she had hoped it was a joke but it wasn't. "I am going to go make sure they left," Tony replied. He loosely held the bat and walked towards the door, giving her a grim smile as he passed them.

"Thanks for the help," the man she still stood behind said to Ray.

"Thank you for helping our girl here." Ray gestured towards her. Ray held out his hand and the man took the arm from around her to shake his. She missed the warmth of it almost instantly. OK, she must have been losing her mind. That had to be what this was because she didn't act this way, ever.

The man still in front of her lifted his shirt to holster his gun. *So that was what I felt*, she thought to herself. *Dang, that hurt*. She absently rubbed her back where it had pressed into her skin. "Name's Ray. This is my place." Ray's head rolled to gesture the place around them. "And this here is Aaralynn." Ray lifted his chin in her direction before locking eyes with the gentleman's, "and you are?"

Shifting slightly, he took in her face before peering back at Ray. "Kent," he said. His eyes moved back and forth between her and Ray. Those hard eyes softened when they looked down at her and it gave her tummy little butterflies. *Stop it. Stop it right now*, she chided herself. It was useless though, his grey-blue eyes had done something to her and she knew her thoughts would only turn dirtier the longer she looked at him. So, she averted her gaze back to Ray. Ray looked her up and down. His chocolate-colored eyes assessing for damage. She saw them fill with concern before her eyes trailed back to Kent.

Kent was still looking at her but where she saw sweetness before it now mirrored Ray's features. She still hadn't said one word and she figured that was why. Right now, all she wanted to do was grab onto Kent's shirt again and feel his body pressed against hers. Her legs started to feel wobbly as Ray spoke, "Lynn, are you ok? You need to sit down?"

The air felt heavy around her suddenly and it became hard to breathe. She pressed her hand to her chest focusing on her breathing, trying to center herself. She was not sure what was coming over her but whatever it was she couldn't control it, and that terrified her. "No. I am ffff…," was all she got out before the color drained from her face and she collapsed.

****

Chapter 2

Kent grabbed for her as she was going down. His arm wrapped around her neck but he didn't cup her head fast enough. It hit the wood floor with a loud smack and he knew she would be feeling it when she woke up.

"Shit," Ray stated from behind him.

"What the hell happened," Tony bellowed as he rushed to Aaralynn, bending to pick her up. Kent wasn't having any of it. Something inside of him had him feeling protective and no one would be touching her but him. He made a mental note to ponder on these feelings later.

"I've got her," Kent ground out as he slipped his other arm under her legs and lifted her. He pulled her tightly against his chest and looked around the room for a place to lay her down.

"Take her in the office. There is a couch to lay her down on." Ray barked out in a rush.

Nodding his head instead of turning around, Kent headed toward the door along the back wall he assumed led to the office. No one protested as he opened the door and walked thru, careful not to hit any of her body parts on the door jam.

"The end of the hall," Ray said from behind him. Tony cursed under his breath and Kent smiled to himself. The man must have some feelings for her from the look in his eyes when Kent scooped her up, but he didn't care. *What was it about this woman*? He shouldn't be in here at all but here he was. He didn't know this woman or have any obligation to what happens to her but for some reason, he needed to. His thoughts still reeling as he walked into the small office. It housed a large desk on one side and a long black leather couch on the other. Bookcases lined the walls and two chairs sat in the center with a small table between them. The furniture made the already small space feel even smaller. *How did someone not get claustrophobic in here?*

Her body was still limp in his arms. She couldn't weight any more than 150lbs but now she was nothing but dead weight. "You can lay her down there," Ray instructed, pointing to the couch. Kent strode over but instead of laying her down, he sat down with her still curled in his arms. He pulled down a blanket that was draped over the back of it and wrapped her in it as best he could. He took his hand out from under her legs and felt her face. She was cool to the touch, which was good. It meant she didn't have a fever.

"So, is anyone going to tell me what happened when I left him alone with Lynn?" Tony's voice got so low and accusing it had Kent gritting his teeth. Tony stared from him to the girl in his lap and back again.

Ray slapped the back of his head with a loud 'smack', "she fainted you jackass. He didn't do anything." He let out a breath of air and gave Kent an apologetic look before rolling his eyes. It made Kent grin in response. Without another word, Ray herded Tony out the door and closed it behind him, leaving him alone with Aaralynn.

The bright light of the office was a big contrast to the dim light of the dining room and bar. He could clearly see the woman lying in his lap. She had her fiery red hair up in a bun away from her face. Its mess trapped there. Her white skin had touches of pink that let him know she still had blood coursing through her veins. Right in his assessment earlier, she had curves and she wasn't a thin girl by any means. That didn't bother him though. He liked girls that were confident in their skin. Her breast rose and fell with every breath her sleeping form took. His heart squeezed in his chest at the tiny bump under her hair where she had hit her head. His fingers traced the area lightly, to examine it. It was about the size of a dime and didn't seem to be bothering her when he touched it.

She never flinched or made a noise. Leaning back against the couch he focused on her breathing. Every soft movement she made was comforting him. She was still alive. He had dealt with a lot of violence and sticky situations overseas and couldn't believe he had come home just to deal with some more. What had she done to owe those men anything? Unless she woke up Kent would never know. Watching her in silence had his eyes getting heavy too. Still not used to the time difference and his sleep pattern all off. His head leaned back against the couch and he soon fell deep asleep.

****

The rushing in her ears and pounding in her head had Aaralynn not wanting to open her eyes. She wanted it all to go away. She fluttered one eye open, then the other. Slowly she blinked a few times till she realized where she was. Taking in the familiarity of Ray's office while trying to sit up. An arm around her stomach had her freezing, as something moved behind her.

Cautiously, Aaralynn tilted her head to the side. The man, she believed he said his name was Kent, was sprawled out behind her. His head was back, one arm resting on the back of the couch and the other around her middle. He was sleeping. She was wrapped in a blanket and curled up against him. Resting her head back down on his chest, while listening to the slow drum of his heartbeat, she tried to recall what had happened. No recollection of being brought back to the office or being wrapped in a blanket.

The last thing she remembered was Billy coming in the restaurant looking for her mother. He had argued with her and Kent had gotten involved. The sounds of patrons gasping and leaving. Ray and Tony defending them. She remembered her heart pounding as she waited for the other men to leave and the look on Ray's and Kent's face. After that, her memory is blank. Could she had blacked out? *No*, she contorted, she didn't do that sort of thing. But then again, there was no other explanation. She wasn't weak by any means, she had to deal with a lot growing up, mostly about her mother. She couldn't believe she had passed out, that she had been that feeble.

She sat up, the hand around her waist falling to her hip. Her eyes flung to his face watching to see if he woke up. His breathing remained the same, soft and steady. Taking in his relaxed face and gorgeous jaw line. He looked so peaceful in sleep. He was thicker but not in a bad way. The bulky muscles were evident under his clothes and she guessed he must work out a lot or do some type of physical labor. His biceps were the size of her head. The thighs pressed against her ass were hard and thick too. Aaralynn couldn't see his beautiful eyes as he slept and she missed them. Kent has stubble on his chin indicating the beginning of a beard and she could see a light sprinkle of hair from the lower cut of his tee-shirt. His dark chestnut colored hair was cut short and the sides faded. Reminding her of a cop or a solider.

The blunt inspection of him had her feeling a little dizzy and her cheeks flushing. Shifting to sit up had her on his lap with the blanket slipping. Shivering from the cold she felt, she prayed she didn't wake him. She palmed her head in her hands when the dizziness came back, feeling a slight bump on the top of her scalp. When did she get that?

Her finger ran over it again, "Damn it," she winced.

Her heart jumped up her throat when Kent moved under her to snap up with a start, "What?! What's wrong?" His arm pulled her close against him as if he was afraid someone was going to harm her. The air rushed out of her lungs and that had her dizziness coming back in waves and spots dotting her vision. Her eyes slammed shut and her head leaned back, resting on his shoulder.

She sensed the moment his mind came back to him. Kent's muscles relaxed, including his arm that was around her and his other hand ran through her hair. "Sorry about that," he cooed in her ear, "you startled me." The repetitive motion of his fingers had the pounding in her head easing.

"Mmmm," she hummed. She loved her hair being played with. The only other person to ever do it was her mother when she was a toddler. It hasn't been done since. She felt his fingers from the hand on her stomach move to rub up and down her side, under her shirt. The contact of his hands on her bare skin had goosebumps rising and she started getting a warm sensation deep in her belly. She had to squeezed her legs together to stifle the ache beginning to form.

"You had me worried when you collapsed."

His voice was husky against her ear. It only served to make her involuntarily rub against his crotch when she squeezed her thighs even tighter together. Trying to push back the wetness she was already beginning to feel. He grunted behind her and placed both his hands on her hips, effectively stopping the movement. That is when she felt it. His hardened length pressing against her bottom. Her eyes snapped to his but his gaze was on her mouth. He seemed to be fixated on her lips and it had her darting her tongue out to wet them. His hands tightened on her hips and he let out a low rumble in his chest. The urge to kiss him was so strong that she unconsciously leaned forward.

She had jumped into situations and relationships before based on her attractions, it never ended well. In fact, it had ended so bad the last time that she hadn't dated for over 3 years. Sure, being alone got to her sometimes but it was better than putting herself in horrible circumstances. He went to lean in towards her but before their mouths touched she flattened her hand against his chest. The sound of footsteps came from beyond the door.

Breathing out a sigh she lifted to move off him but his hands had her sitting right back down on his lap. "I wouldn't move just yet," he said briskly. "I need a few seconds before you get up." Understanding dawned. He wanted her to wait for his erection to go down. She nodded just as the door opened, pulling both their eyes to the three men walking into the room.

Tony rushed over to her and cupped her face in his hands. "You feeling better girl?" Ray asked as he moved behind his desk. Stan, the other bouncer, followed Ray. She nodded and removed Tony's hands from her face.

Tony's face was a mix of emotions. Aaralynn knew Tony liked her, maybe even more then she thought, but she never did anything about it. Mainly because she didn't like him as anything more than a friend or brother figure. His tall frame matched Kent's but where Kent was thick with muscles Tony was lean. "I'm fine," she patted Tony's hand, "just a bit dizzy." Tony nodded and squeezed her hand. The thin line of his lips showed her he still wasn't reassured.

"I'll go grab you some water." Tony looked at Kent, giving him a hard-disapproving look before getting up. Tony's eyes softened when they came back to her face, "you want anything else?" With a shake of her head Tony turned and walked out of the room. She knew he wasn't happy with her but there was nothing to be done about it now. Tony's feelings were the last thing on her mind at the moment. She had to figure out what to do about the predicament she was now in because of her mother. Why did she have to be her mother's daughter?

Kent shifted her off his lap and onto the couch before he stood. She watched as he stretched out his legs not realizing Ray said something to her until the object of her admiring turned to stare at her too. "I'm sorry?" she said as sweetly as she could. She wasn't fooling anyone because all the men gave her knowing looks. She blushed but could care less right then. Her annoyance growing when no one spoke. "Well are you going to repeat what you said or do I need to start throwing things?" Kent's eyes narrowed but Ray and Stan looked at her with laughter.

Stan chuckled, "the boss man told you to take time off."

Her mind didn't register what he said for a few minutes. She blinked a few times before speaking, "I need to work. Ray you know that," she turned her head in his direction but he was already shaking his head.

"I think it is best if you take some time off." Tony came back in the room and looked almost relieved when he realized she was alone on the couch. Tony ignored the look Kent shot him when he sat on the couch, their legs touching, and handed her a glass of water. Tony's leg rubbed up to hers and his arm rested behind her on the couch. "I can't take time off. You know I need the money," she gave the cup back to Tony after taking a gulp. Her head started clearing more for her to focus.

"Those guys are nothing but trouble and you know they will come back. I think it is best if you weren't here."

"I agree," Kent said. "Those men didn't look like they give up easily." Kent's eyes never moved from Tony. He was staring into the man but Tony didn't notice one bit because he was fixed on Aaralynn. She would have laughed if she wasn't mad at the situation playing out in front of her.

"Do I have any say in this?" Tony reached for her hand but she moved it before he could touch her. He didn't take the hint and placed his hand on her leg, his thumb rubbing back and forth. If looks could kill Tony would be dead right now from the hard look on Kent's face.

"Not on this you don't." Ray said without room to argue. But Aaralynn wasn't the kind of woman to stand down. If she could argue through it she would and her livelihood was something to argue about. "Ray you know if they want to they can find me anywhere. Who's to say they don't already know where I live? You know they probably already do."

Ray sighed and used his hand to rub the back of his neck. "I can take her home," Tony said next to her. His hand gave a light squeeze on her thigh. She felt like she was going to get sick.

"I don't think that will solve your problem," Kent started, "if they know where she lives they will bring more men to get her." Tony stood at his words. Facing him he barked, "are you saying I can't protect her?"

Kent fisted his hands at his sides, measuring up the man in front of him before rolling his shoulders back. "I am saying she may need more than one man to be safe." Kent clenched his jaw, "look I don't know what all is going on here."

"That's right you don't. So why don't you stay out of it." Tony snapped. The two men got nose to nose. She knew it would only be a matter of time before it came to blows. She was about to stand up and get in-between them but Stan beat her to it. Pushing them apart.

"Put your dicks back in your pants. We have enough to deal with right now." Stan said loud enough to get the men to look at him.

Ray came from around his desk, "Tony back off. Kent helped earlier. He isn't the problem here." Tony looked at Ray and took a few steps back, crossing his arms over his chest and waiting. "Now Kent, what were you getting at?"

Kent flexed his hands and took a breath. When he spoke, it was surprisingly calm and even, "If they can find her at home she won't be safe. You can't watch her all the time and even he," he said pointing at Tony, "won't be able to stop a handful of men alone." She wasn't liking where this conversation was going. It gave her a bad feeling in the pit of her stomach. Her hands cupped her head as she leaned her arms on her knees.

"So, what do you think should happen?"

She could hear Tony's grunt before Kent spoke. She knew he wasn't happy about this either but for a whole other reason. "look, I am not from around here. In fact, this was just a pit stop for me. I am on my way to my brother's wedding in another state. Maybe the best thing for her is to come with me where they won't think to look for her. I will be there for a little less than a month. It will give them time to give up or at the very least her time to think about what to do. You might even have a plan in place by then." She looked up at him. *He couldn't be serious*? She didn't even know him. He was looking at her with a hopeful gleam to his eyes. Kent wanted her to go. She could see it.

Behind him the other two men were nodding in agreement. Their soft mumbles told her they were considering this plan. Tony stood off to the side looking mad and defeated all at the same time. Aaralynn felt pity for him. Tony wanted to be the one to help her but he knew he had to concede he couldn't. She wished she was attracted to him like he wanted her to be at that moment in time. She was sad that she wasn't but it was sadness for Tony, not for her. When he found the one he was meant to be with, Aaralynn would be nothing but happy for him.

"How do I know you're not worse than Billy and his men? I don't even know you." Ray replied. *He had a point*, she thought. None of them had ever met him before. He showed up out of nowhere and could be bringing her into a worse situation then what she was already in. Although she didn't know how her situation could get any worse.

"Here," he pulled out his wallet and tossed his license on Ray's desk. You can check me out. I have nothing to hide and I can guarantee I am a lot safer to be with then going home and waiting for whatever to come." Ray took the license and pulled his phone out. He must have typed Kent's name in and searched because Aaralynn saw him move his finger on the screen like he was scrolling. After a few moments, he put his phone away and handed Kent back the license.

"Okay," Ray said. He leaned on the desk behind him and crossed his arms. "but I want frequent updates and if anything happens you call me right away."

Kent squared his shoulders and shook his hand. Both men sizing up the other. "Agreed."

****

Chapter 3

Kent knew the woman in his car next to him was not happy. She hadn't said more than three words since they left the restaurant. Right now, she was slumped down in the passenger's seat, pouting with her legs pushed to her chest. He thought she looked adorable but he wouldn't tell her that. He witnessed a hint of her temper earlier and knew she had a mouth on her. That was one of the reasons he was worried. He figured she would have given more of a fight before they left but after Ray said something in her ear she clamped her mouth shut and just followed him out.

The other man, Tony gave him a bad feeling. It coiled in his gut. Kent knew the other man had feelings for Aaralynn and from what he could tell she didn't feel the same way. The moment the other man got near her Kent's first instinct was to wrap his arms around her and pull her away. When Tony had placed his hand on her leg in the office, Kent had to hold himself back from punching him in the face. The urge was so powerful he could have sworn he saw red. As Aaralynn was leaving Tony looked like he was going to say something but Ray had placed a hand on his shoulder, halting him. For that Kent was grateful. He didn't want to get into a fight being back only a couple of days.

The monotone voice of the GPS informed them that they would be at her building after this turn ahead. It had gotten dark out while he was inside. Kent had been surprised to see the clock on the dash read 7:11PM. He didn't realize they had been asleep that long. He must have needed it as much as she did. Kent almost wished they were still sleeping. He hadn't fallen asleep so easily in months. The memory of her body laying against his, the smell of her skin eloping his sense, had him twitching in his pants again.

Pulled back to the present when he heard her pouty voice tell him he could park up ahead. Doing as she instructed, he pulled over to park in front of a brick rowhome. The homes all looked the same and he wondered how anyone knew where they lived when you couldn't decipher one home from the next. Even the doors all resembled each other. He opened his door and got out to go open her door but she was already out and closing it by the time he got to her. "Don't worry about it," she replied to his outstretched hand. He dropped his hand to his side and gave her an awkward smile attempting to show no hard feelings. Her eyebrow arched skeptically. *Who had she been dating to act this way*, he wondered to himself.

Locking his car and setting the alarm, he followed her up a set of steps. She fiddled with the keys in her hand before putting one in the lock. The shaking of the keys giving away the nervousness that she must be feeling. When they got into the building they were in a hallway. There was a door at the end and a set of stairs that went up to another door off a landing. That is when he realized that this is an apartment complex.

She turned to face him so abruptly that he bumped right into her with an 'Oomph' and she put her hands up to grab his arms. He knew the motion was to steady herself but he still felt his skin prickle at her touch. Kent was unsure if she felt it though because she dropped her hands and backed up. "Sorry about that," she wiped her hands on her pants and readjusted her bag on her arm.

"Hey," he used his finger to lift her chin to look at her eyes. He could see tears forming and a part of his insides melted. "It's ok. It will be ok." Trying to sound soothing.

She pulled back like he had hit her and swiped at her face. He was confused but said nothing. She dropped her eyes again. If she didn't want to look at him he wouldn't push it. This had to be hard.

"If I am going with you," she began, "I am taking Ash." He cocked his head to the side. *What*? He didn't understand what she said.

"Who is Ash?" Did she have a kid he didn't know about? He wouldn't have a problem with it but it brought back the recognition that he really didn't know this woman. He didn't want to question that too long because he knew he would second guess himself and he never wanted to do that. His life and many others have depended on him being sure of his decisions. She looked way too young to be a mother but in today's society he couldn't be sure.

Her chin lifted, her eyes boring into his. Her voice was steady as she said defiantly, "she is my dog." She pushed a finger to his chest, "and do not even dare say no. You want me to go with you then she comes to." He put his hands up in defeat. "Ok. Ok." She backed up and put her hand back down. When he noticed she wasn't moving or talking he prompted, "so are we going to get your things and your dog or not?"

She blinked twice and then turned without saying a word. He guessed she was expecting him to argue with that but he didn't need to. If she had a dog then she had a dog. She walked up the stairs without any noise. How she did that when every step he took the floor creaked was a mystery to him. His feet have always been heard on steps even when he was little and tried to sneak down to see Santa in his pajamas. It never worked then and it sure isn't working now.

Kent's senses were on alert the closer they got to the top landing. Something didn't feel right and he didn't like it. Aaralynn let out a small cry when they reached the top. Looking over her head he saw what must have been her door. It was open and the lock was completely removed from the door. What he could make out inside the apartment wasn't good. It looked like whomever had broken in tossed the place.

He walked around her and pulled out his .22 before inching his way forward. He heard a curse behind him and looked over his shoulder to see Aaralynn mumbling and punching the wall. She hit it with such force it cracked, leaving a fist print. He would have been impressed if he wasn't trying to focus on the problem inside. He wasn't sure if whomever broke in was still in there and he didn't want her in danger. Taking notice of the glare she gave him when he softly shushed her.

Kent pointed behind him for her to stay close and he didn't start moving forward till he felt her holding onto his shirt like she did earlier. His initial response would be to charge in after clearing the door but he couldn't do that with her behind him. So, he moved slowly, sweeping every room. It was as he thought. Every room had been trashed. Furniture was broken, drawers were thrown around everywhere, clothes and items littered the floor, mirrors were broken, and even her kitchen appliances were moved.

There was only one reason someone did this. They were searching for something. They got to the hallway that had three doors. He opened the first one and it was the bathroom. The inside resembling the other rooms. Leaving the door open he moved further down the hall. Kent felt his shirt get pulled back hard, stopping him in his tracks.

Scanning around he didn't see anything life threatening. Kent peaked over his shoulder to see Aaralynn looking like she was going to faint again. Her eyes were shut and her skin looked pale. The trembling of her body and tears streaming down her face gave him a s our feeling in the pit of his stomach. "Darling, breath." He tried to keep his voice soft but he wasn't sure he accomplished it. If he wasn't worried he might need his hands, he would turn around and take her in his arms but someone could still be in the apartment. "Look at me," he urged, "That's it sweetheart. You are safe with me." He wrapped his arm backwards to pull her close as they stared at each other. "Just stay close and hold on." She nodded and he felt so proud of her for working with him on this. She wasn't fighting with him like he figured she would have. Instead she was listening.

They started to move down the hall again but then a noise had Kent stopping abruptly. He wasn't sure what it was but then he heard it again. It sounded like growling and something tearing. A very loud bark boomed through the walls. It came again and felt like it vibrated the apartment. Suddenly Aaralynn shot around him and burst through the door at the end of the hall. He ran after her. When he got into what must have been her bedroom he saw her trying to move a very tall dresser from in front of a door. She was grunting and breathing hard while trying to push it. Sounds of scratching from the other side.

Nudging her aside, Kent lifted one corner of the dresser. It must have been solid wood because it was heavy. He didn't realize how heavy until he went to pick it up and his shoulder cracked but he ignored it. As soon as the dresser cleared the door a black mass broke through it and barreled into the room. Aaralynn shrieked and flew at the mass of fur. He dropped the dresser with a thud and leaned it. She had wrapped her hands around the animal and was hugging it tight to her. A sob escaped her lips as she kissed its fur. The mass of fur turned toward him and growled as he stood. Kent cautiously took a step back.

"That's not a dog." Kent's voice cracked as he stared into the eyes of a wolf. A very big, black, pissed off wolf that looked like he wanted to tear his head off. The wolf hunched back on its hind legs about ready to strike just as Aaralynn stepped between them.

"No," she said sternly, staring into the wolf's eyes and pointing to the floor. "Ash, sit." To his amazement the beast let out a whimper but sat down with a thud. He would have laughed at the animal's pouty protest but he decided it would not be wise to antagonize the beast.

Aaralynn turned and looked at him. He watched her eyes as they trailed down from his face to his hip and then looked back up at his face with a frown. His brows furrowed and he looked down to see what she was upset about. The hand with his gun was pointed down at the wolf and he hadn't even realized it. "Reflex," he shrugged. He was not going to apologize for being wary of a freaking wolf. He lowered his gun so it pointed to the ground, Ash's eyes followed the movement. The woman standing between them let out a loud breath of air.

His tone hard and left no room for argument, "you stay here while I finish searching the place." The worried look in her eyes had him pausing for a moment but she nodded and sat down next to Ash. The wolf licked her face and leaned into her. Knowing the animal's fur was still spiked, indicating she was on protection mode gave him a bit of comfort. If he wasn't around, Kent had no doubt that animal would protect her to.

The apartment had an eerie glow with half the lights either broke or sprawled on the ground. Faint sounds of glass being crushed under his boots had him inwardly cursing as he moved. The other room he checked was completely empty, of anything. He was surprised but didn't think twice about it. When he was sure no one else was there he pulled out his phone and called Ray.

"That was fast. You couldn't have made it very far. I thought you said you were going out of state." The gruff voice from the other end said.

Kent all but growled into the phone, "someone broke into her place. It's trashed."

He heard scrapping which he assumed was a chair and then Ray's voice, "she ok?" He could hear the urgent tone. Kent ignored the pang of jealousy he felt. Aaralynn had some people in her corner and for that he was grateful.

"She's fine. I am surprised I still have my limbs though."

A small chuckle from the other end rang in his ear, "I see you met Ash. Fierce looking thing, isn't she?"

"You could say that." He grumbled. "How come no one told me about her?"

His question was pushed aside or completely ignored, "did you get anyone? Call the police?" Now he heard another voice in the background.

"No one was here. I scanned the whole place." The voice in the background was getting louder and he heard Ray to tell someone to "shut up" before Kent went on. "I haven't called the police yet. I am going to do that now and she will get her things. You asked to be informed so I am informing you," he heard a bang come across the other line. "What was that?"

"Just Tony getting mad. I got it." Soft whispers on the other end again, "call the police and have Lynn call me when she gets where you're going. And Kent," the other man paused, "you promised to take care of our girl. I expect someone with your background to do just that."

"I will." With that he hung up.

On his way, back to the bedroom he dialed 911 to report the break in. He found Aaralynn and Ash still huddled where he had left them on the floor. She was straddled around the animal and it looked like they were giving each other a hug. They both turned toward him as he spoke into the phone from the doorway. Relating to the dispatcher on the other end everything he knew was time consuming. They were instructed to go wait outside while she sends officers to the address. They were not to touch anything and remain together. Kent agreed then ended the call. Before he put the phone in his pocket, Kent shot his brother a text letting him know he was running behind schedule and that he would now be bringing a plus one. He asked if he wouldn't mind informing Gran of it. Not that he figured anyone would care but he didn't want to just show up with someone unannounced. It would be rude. His phone vibrated in his pocket notifying him he received a text but he would look at it later.

"We need to wait outside for the police to get here. Here," he moved closer to give her a hand but as he got within touching distance, Ash started growling again. Kent's mouth formed a thin line and she saw the muscle in his jaw tick. Aaralynn gave him a roll of the eyes indicating, "what are you gonna do" and brushed her pants off when she got up. Ash stood as well, leaning against Aaralynn's leg.

She was shaking her head from side to side. "The police can't come here. They will see Ash." She looked very nervous now, her voice a bit higher now. The strong, confident girl he had seen earlier was gone and this worried one took her place. Kent watched as she looked down at the animal and chewed on her bottom lip. He wrung his hands together and wiped one palm over his face. The nap from earlier wasn't long enough but he knew it would have to last him a while.

"You can put her in my car before they get here." The words practically falling out of his mouth before he could take a moment and thought about it. He didn't know this animal, what if it ripped up his car. Images of his car in shreds had him second guessing his response. As he opened his mouth to retract the offer, she responded. "Thank you," her words were murmured so softly he almost missed it.

Her slumping shoulders rolled back and she looked at him. He knew at that moment he did the right thing. Her eyes rimmed with unshed tears as she gave him the smallest smile. Kent wanted to take her in his arms but he was afraid Ash would protest and He wasn't about to test that theory. "let's go do that before they get here," not able to handle the look of need in her eyes, he turned without waiting for an answer.

Footsteps followed swiftly behind him. After getting Ash in his car, they walked back towards her building. His expression must have had her thinking because Aaralynn kept reassuring him nothing would happen while they were gone. Kent just smiled in response. They could hear the sounds of sirens when they reached the steps, so they stood and waited.

****

All the people walking in and out had her getting dizzy with a headache. She was starting to feel more and more tired. After an hour and a half of questions, photos, and whatever else the parade of people had done in her apartment, Kent had all but pushed all of them out. She could tell he was frustrated and just wanted to get a move on. The longer they were there the more danger they were in. At this point, she could only guess who could have done this.

Kent walked up to her and rubbed her shoulder when everyone had left. They were still standing outside her apartment on the landing. The tears she had shed were dry now and had her feeling more and more tired with every passing minute. Closing her eyes when Kent's hand rubbed her shoulder before moving down to knead the muscles at her back. Involuntarily she released a soft moan as she fell back against his body, his arms wrapping around her middle. His hot breath feathered her neck. Wetness began between her thighs that she tried to ignore. A gentle kiss to her collar bone made her shiver and she felt his arms squeezed her tighter against his solid frame.

"Sweetheart, we need to move." She didn't want to move anywhere. She was so tired and he was so warm. His masculine scent undeniably inviting, making her want to stay in that spot forever. "I could hold you like this all night," he mimicked her thoughts, "but it's not safe. We need to get going." The feeling of loss settled over her as his hands unraveled from her waist and he lightly nudged her towards the door.

"But," she started and didn't get to finish.

Kent's voice cut her off, "you are going to grab whatever you need or is important and we are going to head out." When she was inside his hand fell away and she blinked a few times trying to come back to herself. 'I'll try and fix your door as best I can before we go. Ray said he would be over in the morning to put a new one on and you can pick up the key form him when you get back in town." Aaralynn didn't know when he talked to Ray but she was grateful.

She moved quickly. Taking note that Kent followed her around as she filled two suitcases and a duffle. She stopped halfway down the hallway and he almost ran into her. She turned to give him a sly smile before lifting her hand to feel the molding for the familiar notch. When she found it, she pressed and a part of the wall opened revealing a safe. The surprise on his face had her bursting out in giggles. He looked adorable when he was taken aback.

Opening the safe, Aaralynn pulled out the large lockbox before closing and snapping the wall back in place. "I'm ready." She said hauling the duffle bag and lockbox down the hall. Kent followed carrying her suitcases. She saw him fiddle with the door, using screws and a hammer to lock her door in place.

Putting her things in the car proved to be a bit challenging since he already had somethings stored in the trunk but with some maneuvering and shifting the rest they got in the back seat with a sleeping Ash. Ash woke up when the car door opened. Aaralynn knew she wasn't happy about being in a cramped back seat but was too elated to see her to care. Her baby sniffed her a few times, then licked her face. It had her giggling, "I'm ok girl. It's all ok." After a few more licks she was able to get her to sit back down.

Kent held the passenger side door open for her and she momentarily paused. Not used to the kind act, she felt she for a split second before shrugging it off. Kent closed it after she slid into the seat. He walked around and opened his door. A growl came from the back seat as he went to get in. Aaralynn watched as Kent froze and looked at Ash. "Cut it out right now," he said sternly. Leaving no room for fuss, "I won't deal with your bullshit. Calm down and sit down."

That had Aaralynn bristling but she understood where he was coming from. Still, no one talked to her girl like that. When Ash didn't respond to him Aaralynn turned her head. Motioning with her finger, "Ash lay." When her girl laid down she cooed, "good girl," and patted her head. She received a nudge on her hand as gratitude.

Kent didn't relax any but he got into his seat and moved over to put her seatbelt on. The scent of spice and sweat made her mouth water. The movement had Ash getting up and squeezing her head between them, "Damn," he bellowed. "She needs to always be in the middle of everything?" His words more of a statement than a question.

"Yes. She is very protective." Aaralynn rubbed her chin, "I am her mom after all." She hugged the animal's head and he rolled his eyes. "Now Ash, be nice. Kent is good." For emphasis, Aaralynn took her hand and ran it along his face. Ash turned her head and sniffed his face where her hand had been. When Aaralynn removed her hand, Ash rubbed her fur where her hand had been on him. The half-smile Kent gave sent a tiny flutter in her chest. He was gorgeous. His tan skin and scruff suited him. *I wonder if he is tan all over.*

Kent's hand rose to try and pet Ash but she gave a low growl, "we will work on that," he said turning and placing his hands on the steering wheel. The car revved to life and Aaralynn pointed for Ash to lay down. The wolf turned around a few times before finally laying down on the open seat.

After pulling away from the curb she took note of Kent looking through all the mirrors and searching around. The look of seriousness on his face had worry creeping up her spine. *Had he seen something? Is something wrong?* She couldn't be sure but maybe he was just a very cautious driver. After checking the mirror once again he looked over at her. They had just made it out of the city and the lights on the highway were becoming fewer in-between exits, making it hard to see his face. What she did see she couldn't figure out. His jaw ticked and he seemed very focused on their surroundings.

"I was making sure no one was following us." His voice level and calm. The complete opposite then what she felt. He was worried they were being followed. He must have seen the concern she was feeling on her face because he tried reassuring her, "No one is following us. We are safe. Now if you can try and get some rest. We still have hours before we make it where we are going." He shifted gears as his eyes looked her up and down, coming to rest on her eyes. Aaralynn felt awkward under his gaze and bit her bottom lip. His eyes locked on the movement and his mouth slightly parted.

They passed another street light and the car was bathed in darkness again. The glitter of his eyes moved back up to hers and when they came to pass under another light, she could have sworn saw a hint of lust in his eyes just before he jerked his eyes back on the road. Unconsciously Aaralynn rubbed a finger over her lips where she wished his mouth would have been. A small gasp escaped at her own thoughts. She was glad he couldn't see her or else she would be embarrassed even more for the redness she was sure was on her cheeks. Suddenly his hands gripped the steering wheel hard. Rubbing into the leather fabric with a fast motion that it made the familiar squeaking sounds. She wished she knew what he was thinking about.

When they reached the highway the street lights ended. The only thing lighting the inside of the car was from the dashboard. It made his face glow and she could see faint lines of his skin. Smooth in some places and scruffy in others. She yawned and rubbed her eyes with the back of one hand. His words came out gruff and low, "lay back and try to catch some sleep." She knew her eyes were getting heavy but she didn't want to sleep yet.

"I don't think I can," was her reply. Contradicting her own words when she leaned her head back and propped her body up on the seat to try to get comfortable. Her body relaxing and her eyes getting heavy.

Without saying a word his hand rested on her thigh. Slowly, his fingers rubbed back and forth on her leg and the effect was making her yawn again. "Shhhh," he said soothingly. His voice like a warm glass of milk to her senses. Not being able to stand it much longer she shifted in her seat again. Her head laid down to rest on his arm, effectively pinning his arm in place. The hand on her leg gave a light squeeze but didn't try to pull away.

"Thank you," she mumbled sleepily. She rubbed her chin on his arm feeling the tough muscle beneath her head. "I love your arms," she said without realizing she voiced her thoughts aloud.

She missed the light chuckle he gave as she drifted off. She missed him leaning over and brushing the tiniest kiss to her hair. She missed it when he said, "no need to thank me," as he gave her leg one final squeeze before focusing on the road once again. She fell into a deep sleep for the first time in months knowing she was safe and protected.

****

Chapter 4

Hands grabbed and shook her. They were snaking around her neck and she could feel the tears streaking down her cheeks. The cold wetness leaving trails as a hand grabbed her throat. She tried to scream but could only get out a scratchy cry. She clawed at the hand, tried pushing whoever was there but she hit nothing. Only air. Out of nowhere, a slap ran out across her face and for a moment she saw white stars glitter her vision. In that instant, a calming resilience came across her. She knew she was going to die. This suffocating feeling that no matter how much she fought it, it was the end. The sound of her arm snapping and the pain that accompanied it filled her ears and head. It had her body wracking and the need to vomit rising in her throat. Her scream came out a garbled mess from the hand squeezing down on her throat. It had her wishing for death so she could escape the torcher. One last effort to get out of this grasp...

Waking with a scream and her hands out. Her mind still reeling from the dream. She was pushing back against something hard. It was the door. She was... she was... in a car? Yes, in a car. "Whoa, sweetheart. You are ok." The voice floated into her haze. It was familiar but she was still having trouble placing it. "You had a dream. You're ok." A dream? Was it a dream? A wet tongue unexpectantly started licking her face. Fur rubbed against her and then she was aware of a weight on top of her. Ash. She started to remember where she was. Slowly her mind was returning. Pulling her back out of the stupor she was in.

Aaralynn pushed Ash back and told her to sit. Ash complied while Aaralynn adjusted herself in her seat. Sitting up straight and stretching out her sore muscles. They were pulled over on the side of the road and Kent was staring at her. His face awash with worry and concern. "Sorry," she said and she was. She hadn't had a nightmare in over a month but she knew that when they happened, they could be bad.

"Geeze, you scared the crap outta me. You need to forewarn people about that unless you're fond of car accidents." Laying his head back against the headrest, Kent rubbed his temples. His eyes closed and his nostrils flared. He was breathing heavily like she had really scared him and she felt bad about it. He was right she admitted to herself. She should have mentioned something but she wasn't expecting to have one. "You were screaming and moving your arms around. I had to pull over before something happened." The sun had started shinning and she looked around out the window. How long had she been sleeping? Not wanting to talk about her nightmares she sidestepped his statement.

Taking in a big gulp of air and letting it go, "What time is it?" She turned to look at him. He didn't even open his eyes or turn his head. Still laying back on the seat the only thing that moved was his mouth.

"It's just after six in the morning." He still didn't move. Waiting for him to go on she kept looking at him. The rising sun shined in the car, allowing her to get a good look at him. The line of his jaw and the curve of his neck was sexy. She could see the slight rise and fall of his chest and his Adam's apple moved when he swallowed. He looked tired and he needed a shave, but she didn't mind that. A little scruff never hurt anyone. She just wasn't a full-on beard girl. When it was clear he wasn't going to say anything else she broke the silence with another question.

"So, you never said where we were going. Are you going to tell me?" He didn't move his head but his eyelid opened, looking at her out of the corner of his eye.

"I have a family event to go to and you're coming with me." He took in her expression of annoyance. He was evading the answer and she hated when people did that. She likes things straight forward. That answer got under her skin some and she had no problem voicing her annoyance.

"I am obviously coming with you. I am in the car ain't I?" She crossed her arms under her chest and moved so she could fully face him. "Where is this family event? Like, the actual area or address or place."

Not missing when his eye looked down where she had rested her arms and then looked away to close his eyes again. He made a gruff noise that sounded like a groan and sat up straight before opening his eyes again. She averted her gaze when he turned to face her. Her eyes landed on his crotch but quickly moved when she noticed he had a bulge in his pants.

She looked in the back seat and saw Ash just sitting there staring at the two of them. "it's in Montana at my family ranch. That is where we are going." Her eyes snapped to his. He had a lazy smile on his face like he expected her to be happy about this.

"That is really far to drive." Her statement not bothering him in the least. From the looks of it, he got more relaxed at the thought. He just nodded his head at her. Then he pointed his thumb in the back and it made him look like he was a hitchhiker. "She need to go to the bathroom while I'm pulled over?"

Aaralynn looked in the back and nodded her head. With a sigh, she unlocked the car door and got out. Opening the back-door Kent spoke up again, "don't you need a leash or something?" He had turned to lean in the back seat some to look at her. She gave him a proud smile and a shake of her head.

"Nope. Ash never goes far unless I tell her to H-U-N-T." Aaralynn slowly spelled out the word. "Even then she stays within earshot. If you haven't noticed she is protective of me. I am her pack." A flicker of amazement and what she thought was pride went across his face. It had her smiling again, the urge to puff out her chest coming over her but she refrained. Ash bounced out of the backseat and sniffed the ground. It was early and a Friday so the traffic on the road was light. However, she took her into the wooded area so no one freaked out about a wolf being on the side of the road.

After Ash finished her business they returned to the car and Aaralynn got her back in the backseat. Stretching her legs out had felt good and settled her stomach. The bile had felt like it was going to come up a few times and she had to keep urging it back down. She knew if she threw up she might not stop since her stomach was empty and she hadn't eaten at all. Dry heaving was not only unattractive but felt like a bitch. She stretched out a few more seconds before climbing back in the car.

Kent was on the phone when she got back in so she remained silent. One finger lifted signaling to be quiet and a wave of irritation coiled in her chest. Taking a deep breath she squashed it down though and just listened.

"Yea, I ran into complications." Mumbling on the other side, "I'll tell you about it when I see you." A pause, "no, I am going to stop for a bit and get some rest. We should be there either late tonight or early tomorrow." Another pause and then some mumbling on the phone. "I know. You told them I was bringing a plus one, right?"

Aaralynn bit the inside of her cheek. She didn't want to be an inconvenience and it sounded like she might be. "Good. Now I need to get moving." He blew out a breath, "Have fun at your meeting brother. I will see you at the ranch." She waited as he hung up the phone and placed it in the cupholder.

She buckled her seat as he did him, then sat drumming her fingers on her legs. Knowing she looked as impatient as she felt, she tried to hold in all her questions. She was about to speak when he beat her to it, "sorry about that. My brother likes to talk and I have to get him off the phone sometimes." *Like that explained everything* but she didn't say that. Instead, she sat there quietly.

"Look, I am hungry, dirty, and in need of some sleep. I need to find a place to do those things and having the 'dog' with us might become a problem." She didn't like the way he said dog but she let it go. He did look tired and the slow movement of his hand kneading his neck had her softening to him. She inched closer to him, at least as far as she could with the middle console in her way.

Ash perked up but didn't get in the way this time. Stoic and just watching as Aaralynn picked up Kent's hand to rub the back of it with her thumb. She didn't even know why she did it. She just had this overwhelming urge to touch him. The muscles in his arm had tensed at first but the more she rubbed, the more he relaxed. He watched their hands. Then look on his face told her he was unsure of her actions. But he never once pulled back or complained. After what felt like an hour but was probably closer to five minutes, he cleared his throat and entwined their fingers.

Dropping her gaze to their hands, "It doesn't have to be a five-star place. We can find a place where we sneak her in or I don't mind staying in the car while you go get some shut-eye." It wouldn't be the first time she slept in a car or even the worst place she had slept. Her life hadn't always been roses but she tried to never let that get her down. Her surprise gasp filled the quiet space when he tugged at her hand. Pulling it towards his mouth, he brushed his lips over her knuckles, giving them a light kiss before placing her hand back into her lap. Untangling their fingers Kent put the car in gear before starting the engine.

Kent punched something in his phone as they pulled onto the highway again. "You are not sleeping in the car." His words stern as he sat the phone back in the cupholder. "I can find a motel we can sneak Ash into. I am not leaving you alone in case something happens. Even if you have her," he pointed to Ash, "I would feel more comfortable being around for you." His phone chirped out a direction and that is when she realized he had put the GPS on. A rush of happiness and relief that he wasn't going to make her stay in the car settled over her. She might not want to ask for help or admit that she felt better with him around but she appreciated it anyway.

Neither of them said a thing the whole way to the cheap motel he found. The outside could have fit in with a B rated horror film in her opinion. When they got there, she was glad for the tinted windows that masked Ash. She sat in the car while he went in, paid, and got the keys. He must have asked for a specific room because it was around the corner in the back. It helped for sneaking Ash inside. As soon as they got Ash inside Kent went back out to grab some of their bags.

Hauling the bags in, "I am going to order food then get in the shower. If the food guy comes before I am out, please try to keep Ash quiet." His words clipped as he grabbed his duffel bag and walked past her into the bathroom without another thought. She heard him talking behind the closed door and assumed he was on the phone. The shower coming on drowned out whatever he had been saying. Sighing to herself, the shower noise making it impossible to eavesdrop, she gave up.

There was only one bed in the room with a couch. Along the wall of the door was a dresser with a TV, a small fridge, and a table with two chairs. It wasn't a big room and she doubted it was very clean but it would serve for what they needed. She pointed to the small couch and Ash jumped up, circled a few times, and laid down. Aaralynn jumped onto the bed and bounced a few times testing out the mattress. It wasn't soft but it wasn't like a cement block either. The bed was bouncy and it gave her an idea.

Ash's head popped up when she took her shoes off and climbed on the bed. Wanting to get out some frustration, she jumped on the bed like she was a five-year-old girl instead of the twenty-four years she was. She loved every minute of it. Finally starting to tire out she plopped down. Her hair and limbs spread out across the mattress. The sound of the shower still running was the only sound filling the room and it was calming to her. She knew she wasn't alone.

She picked up the TV remote and flicked through some basic channels. When she found a channel showcasing food she placed the remote down and just waited. The delivery guy still hadn't come by the time Kent came out of the bathroom. His hair was damp and he had on unbuttoned jeans that hung low on his waist. The V starting from his hips and dipping below his jeans taunted her. The sight making her mouth water for a whole other reason. His chest was bare and the thick muscles glistened with droplets of water. His bulging arms had her mouth going dry and all thought left her head. She couldn't help but blatantly stared at him.

****

The shower relaxed his stressed-out body. His muscle had hurt from sitting for so long and his mind hurt from running over everything that had happened. All the things that could go wrong plagued the back of his mind.

It also didn't help that he kept getting a hard-on being around Aaralynn. Having to rub one out in the shower didn't calm down his need for her. He was still hard but at least now he was clean and shaved. After being overseas and on missions he appreciated being able to wash off daily. Thankful the body wash he had with him overpowered the moldy smell of the room as he opened the bathroom door and stepped out to see Aaralynn. Her mouth slightly parted as she openly appraised at him.

Damn if he wasn't getting hard again. Kent's tone came out gruff as he spoke through gritted teeth. "Did the food come yet?" He inquired as his tone came off hard but unable to help it. The room seemed to get muggy as his body tensed.

He was getting frustrated by being so close to her and not reacting to his attraction for her. The compact quarters of the car when she laid on his arm was torment. Now he was in a room with her. It may be a bit more space than the car but this time they were in a confined area with a bed and his body knew it. His sweet and sour part of life right now.

"No, it hasn't," her voice trailed, so feminine and light it had him adjusting himself as he walked over towards the bed where his bag sat.

"I'll wait for it while you go grab a shower." He offered. "I left my toiletry bag in there if you need something." She jumped off the bed like she suddenly couldn't wait to get in the bathroom. Without another word, he watched her dart inside, closing the door behind her. Frowning at the closed door, Kent wondered out loud to Ash, "What was that all about?" Kent tilted his head towards the bathroom. The dog, as she liked to refer to the animal, just stared at him blankly and he could have rolled his eyes in response. Why ask when the dog wouldn't give an answer?

Kent was not about to sleep on the bed sheets that looked like they should have been thrown out two decades ago. Instead, Kent pulled out the sleeping bag he kept in his duffle and laid it out on the bed. His dirty clothes got shoved into the duffle bag making a mental note to wash them when he could. Placing his duffle on the chair by the table, he grabbed the remote. Noticing the food channel that was already on he decided to just leave it be.

Pulling out his phone, he shot Ray a quick text to make sure the door got fixed. A few seconds went by before he received a reply confirming the door was changed out and Aaralynn could grab the key from him when she got back into town. Ray also mentioned the police had been by the bar to check out her place of work. Kent scratched his head, thinking it was a bit odd but didn't comment on it.

A noise came from the bathroom. Moving closer to the door Kent could hear Aaralynn was signing to herself. The tune "Baby it's cold outside" floated to his ears and he smiled. She was good at it. Her voice did something to him. His heartbeat so hard in his ribs and he felt his breathing speed up. Vibration in his hand stole his attention. He received another text but didn't recognize the number. Frowning he opened the message.

Unknown: It's Tony. Have her call me.

Kent: She is in the shower. I'll tell her you want to talk.

Kent smiled at himself for that response. He was madded that the asshole got his number but he knew that response would have him upset and he was glad. He didn't like the thought of Aaralynn talking to another man, one who obviously was interested in her. He saved the number to his contacts before shoving it back in his pocket and putting the remote back by the TV. His phone vibrated again after a few seconds,

Tony: Have my girl call me.

Five little words, only five and they had him clenching his fist. She might not be his, he may have no claim over her but neither did this guy. Shaking his head, he didn't respond to that message. No point in it. He shouldn't even be doing this but his spur of the moment help got him in this mess and he wasn't even sure what this mess was. Kent never asked her what the whole situation at the bar was about. He had been too wrapped up in the emotions swirling in her eyes and obvious bad men hanging around. Deciding to ask when she was out of the bathroom so he would fully understand the circumstances and what they were now up against. The shower shut off at the same time someone knocked do the door.

Picking up the gun, Kent slid it in his back pocket before going to check the door. He looked out the peephole and saw it was the Chinese delivery man with their food. The sound of his stomach growling filled the room as he opened the door.

"Hi. Asian Gourmet order." The young boy looked at the receipt he had in his hand, then flicked his eyes up to meet Kent's.

Kent pulled his wallet out of his other back pocket. "Yes, how much do I owe you?' He started to pull out some bills.

"Thirty-six dollars and seventeen cents." Kent took the bags from him as he handed the boy a fifty-dollar bill. "Keep the change," He said. The boy looked at him and gave a wide smile. Nodding his head in thanks, the kid turned and walked away as Kent closed the door. The smell of food swirled around him making his stomach rumble even harder.

He heard the bathroom door open behind him as he was placing the food on the table. "Foods here. I hope you're," his words stopped in his throat as he faced her. Her long wavy red hair trickled down over her shoulders, dripping wet. Tendrils laid overtop the towel she had wrapped around herself. If the towel was any shorter she would have to choose which body part to cover. As it was now, her breast almost spilled over the top and he could just imagine the sweet spot between her legs. Aaralynn's skin was so creamy looking that he wanted to lap it up like milk.

A light cough pulled his attention from assessing her body back to her eyes. "I forgot my clothes," gesturing towards the bed where her bag sat. Slowly, her feet moved towards the bed but stopped short. Kent watched her tongue dart out and lick her bottom lip. Her gaze was stuck on his pants. Kent followed her gaze and noticed they were still open and showed an outline of his obvious arousal. He palmed himself through his jeans and her green eyes snapped up to his. A beautiful pink crept up her neck. "Sorry," she began to move again. Rubbing against his arm as she eased past had her towel coming undone.

"Don't be," his voice deep and sensual. Kent's hand shot out and grabbed her arm at the elbow, lifting the corner of the towel that started falling, before it was too late.

"Oh," was all that came out of her mouth.

Not realizing that Kent held the corner of her towel, Aaralynn pulled back out of his grasp and the towel slid off her. He clutched it in his hand as she used her hands to cover herself, which wasn't working. "What the he…" she didn't get the last of the words out before his mouth came down on hers. A hard-searing kiss that had his blood boiling and his hands snaking around to cup her bottom. Kent hauled her against his hard length and moaned in her mouth when he felt the V of her thighs rub against his pants.

Her hands slid up to his chest, rubbing him as his tongue lapped at her lips. Swiftly, he urged for her to open her mouth so he could taste her. Finally, she let out a small moan and he guided his tongue inside. His efforts were rewarded when her hands wrapped around his neck to deepen the kiss. Every breath had her breast rubbing into his skin, leaving a searing heat.

She was so soft and warm. The needy side of him ached to lay her down and taste her everywhere. His body wanted to so bad and he would have too if she hadn't slid her hands back down and pushed on him to move back. They were both standing there panting hard when he released her and she took a few steps away. Her hands slid down and his erection throbbed in his pants as she bent down to the floor. Disappointed when she came back up wrapping the discarded towel back around her.

He was not expecting her hard stare and angry eyes. "What the hell was that for?" Her demanding tone was emphasized with her crossing her arms under her chest. It didn't have the effect it should have since all it did was push her breast up higher. Once his eyes focused back on her eyes he remembered she was waiting for an answer. Her eyes narrowed as her patience waned and she stomped her foot with an "Umph" sound as he briskly stomped towards her bag.

Standing to turn around, Aaralynn almost plowed into Kent. She would have if he hadn't placed both hands on her shoulders to stop her. "Do you mind?" she snapped.

Kent wasn't mad and he didn't understand why she would be either. That kiss had every virile part of him singing to life. Maybe she didn't feel the same way, but that couldn't be true. He had felt her respond to it too. So, then what had her so riled up?

Kent blinked a few times as he realized he was still holding her shoulders. Letting out what he hoped sounded like a cough, his hands fell to his sides. "Why are you mad at me?" Figuring if she was already mad that just plainly asking her couldn't make her madder, could it? She surprised him even more though.

"Get the hell out of my way." Her words like ice as she shoved around him, her clothes still clutched in her hand.

He sidestepped to get back in her way, "No." One simple word with so much force. Mentally preparing himself for an argument. He wasn't going to let her act like it never happened. The words were right on the tip of his tongue but died there when he hears a sniffle. His heart dropping into his stomach.

She was crying and he didn't understand why. He grabbed for her, to pull her against him when she shot a hand out, "Don't. I can't," wiping her nose with the back of her hand. Her voice cracked slightly, "I just can't." His arm fell to his side and she walked around him. Without taking one look in his direction she closed the bathroom door lightly and small muffled sounds came from behind the door.

Heart pounding and his mind reeling, Kent just stood there staring at the closed door wondering what had just happened. This woman had him so confused. She was hot one minute, mad another, and now a cowering broken mess. What had happened to her to have her react that way? Getting answers out of her felt almost as dangerous as a minefield.

　　With that insight, he knew he had to take his time or she might just run. A flicker of the need to flashed in her eyes just before she broke down. The need to getaway. That is why she fled to the bathroom Kent thought to himself. Now with her tiny sobs coming from behind the door, it filled him with sadness and a need to make it all better. But how?

****

Chapter 5

The bathroom floor was cold and her small towel did nothing to help get her warm. The tiny green tiles almost matched the vomit color green of the walls. If anything, it made her want to do just that. Her stomach lurched as her anxiety spiked. Replaying what just happened in her mind had her body screaming so many emotions. Sure, she had gotten swept away by the kiss they shared. The feel of him pressed against her and the tangling of their tongues. Inwardly Aaralynn moaned at the memory.

Her body had wanted more but her mind yelled she couldn't act on it. The last time she had reacted in the moment she had been put in a bad situation and couldn't go through that again. If she learned anything from her mother it was you need to be on your own. You can only trust yourself to love you, no one else would ever truly accept you for who you are. People always wanted something out of a relationship and time always revealed what it was. She didn't know what Kent could want but she couldn't trust herself when it came to men or women. This thought had her trembling with sobs once again.

Why is it so hard to find happily ever after? *Because you are not worth it*, her ex's voice rang in her head. *You were only good for one thing and even that was shotty*. Remembering the look Cory, her ex gave her after being with him for 3 years still gave her shutters. Remembering how he always looked around a room they were in, at first, she thought it was a gesture of predatory observance but now she knew he liked to take in all the tail in the room. Surveying his odds at which numbers he could get and act on later.

Silently she chided her past self. She had been so stupid.

Now she was enclosed in a tiny hotel room with a man she barely knew and stuck in a situation, that wasn't great. The feelings she got while she was around him were not like the ones she had for Cory. With Cory, it was all about excitement, naive excitement. She didn't know what it felt like to be on someone's attention radar. When Cory gave her the time of day she thought it was because he genuinely liked her. Spending money on her and giving her gifts. She took all of it in because growing up as she had, it made her feel special and good. She hadn't wanted it to end but end it did and with a big splash.

The flutters and tingles she got from thinking of Kent were tiny compared to the ones she got when they kissed just now. Her skin got so hot she could have burst into flames and pooled into a puddle at his feet. It was nothing like Cory. He was nothing like Cory, at least from what she could tell. A light rap on the door jarred her back to herself. "Yes," she said loud enough she was sure he could hear.

"Food is ready. When you come out we can sit and talk." A small rustling noise came from the other side of the door. What would they talk about? She wasn't sure she could handle more embarrassment. He must think so many different things about her right now after running off to the bathroom like a scared rabbit. "Hurry up before it gets cold." More rustling before his shadow disappeared from under the door. A resolute feeling crept up her. She would need to talk to him eventually. Blowing out a breath, Aaralynn wiped her face with the towel that was around her and blew her nose.

Standing, she wiped at the foggy mirror, taking stock of her appearance. She looked a frightful mess. Her eyes were blotchy and her cheeks were all pink. Her fingers ran over her slightly swollen lips where she had just been kissed. Reveling in the feeling and the memory it gave her. With a huff Aaralynn quickly got dressed, throwing on her sweat pants and a tight tank top. Brushing out her hair as best she could she twisted it up and clipped it with her butterfly clip. How could she ever get out of this mess her mother had gotten her in? Somehow, she didn't think there was an easy answer to that question.

The bathroom door swung open with more force than she expected it too and it went slamming into the wall with a bang. The sound had Kent and her jumping. Her hand flew to her chest as she let out a squeal and he stood up so fast that the chair he had been sitting in knocked over. He was in front of her in a split second. His hands grasping her upper arms in concern. "What's going on?" the words clipped as they rushed out of him.

Placing the hand that flung to her chest on one of his outstretched arms she shook her head at him. "Nothing. I didn't expect the door to do that." Seeing his eyes shift over her face, questioning if she was ok, she averted her gaze around him. Opting for easy sarcasm she inquired, "Is there food left for me?" With a nudge of her head, Aaralynn motioned towards the table where white boxes and plates had been placed. From the looks of it, she could tell he had already dug into some of the food.

He backed up, his shoulders relaxing and his arms falling to his sides. "Did you think I ate it all within the ten minutes you were in the bathroom?"

The slight tilt of the corner of his mouth had her mouthwatering for a whole other reason now. The man at least had a shirt on now, a dark blue one and his pants were closed. Aaralynn took in a breath to try and relax her body from the need to undress him but Kent's cologne assaulted her senses and had her wanting to do it even more.

"You seem really hungry," she replied jokingly. The look in his eyes bluntly expressed just that and he had said it to her a few times already. She heard his stomach rumbling earlier along with hers so she knew he was hungry too. It could have just been her but Aaralynn swore his eyes visibly darkened. As those dreamy hazel eyes of his deepened, his chin tilted down towards her lips.

The gruffness of his voice betrayed his true emotions even if his words implied it, "Oh, I am hungry alright." He took in a few short breaths, "and not just for Chinese." His hand came up and began stroking the side of her bare arm. Was he was seducing her? She wasn't sure but she knew she couldn't handle it right now. Aaralynn swallowed, hard. "Damn, you're gorgeous." Kent's voice lowered an octave. Trying to contain the shiver that wanted to break free was difficult but she held it at bay. *Shit, why did he have to say things like that?* It wasn't fair that his words had her insides melting and her body swaying towards him. *He hadn't even earned that right yet.*

Sidestepping him she made her way to the table. Kent had already laid out the plates, with his already full of food. She heard him shuffle behind her and a chair being pulled out. Their eyes locked for a brief moment and he gestured for her to have a seat.

Instead of taking the offered seat, Aaralynn pushed her own chair up to the table. Bringing her legs up to crisscross in her seat had her sitting up straighter and took some pressure off her other muscles.

The tightness in her muscles was not just from the strain of the day but from the ache of what her body craved to do with the man across from her. Internally she wondered why she was denying herself. Her hand came up unconsciously to rub at her neck, at the same time she heard a faint grunt. Her eyes found his and took note of the way he was staring at her. There was no amusement on his face. Void of all emotion as he watched her with prodding eyes. Her heart beating hard in her chest.

****

What was wrong with him? Seriously, he never acted like this towards a female, especially a female he didn't know. It had been so long since another girl piqued his interest that he factored it down to him being out of the game for so long. Sure, there had been girls within the unit or overseas but he was never interested in any of them more than just a one-time roll in the hay. He had one or two that he would occasionally go back for another round but he hadn't done that in months. Now, he was wondering if this could be accredited to that. Kent watched as Aaralynn poured some Chinese food out of the containers and stopped to take a few bites. Her eyes drifting closed every time the morsels passed her lips. He barely heard her soft moans of pleasure as she savored every bite and he wished he was the one giving her that look of pure rapture right now.

Who was he kidding? The woman in front of him had captured his attention from the start with her full curves, wonderful eyes, and lush mouth. The mouth that also had a wicked tongue when she was feeling up to it. The memory had him wondering what other sinful things her tongue and mouth could do. Clearing his throat, he set his fork down and waited for her to finish what was currently in her sweet mouth.

"So, we need to talk about what is going on." His stare never wavering from her face, even as her cheeks flushed. Assuming she thought he was referring to their earlier encounter he clarified, "I need to know the situation you are in so I know what happens next."

She swallowed while wiping at her mouth with a napkin. Her chest heaved upward as she shifted to bring her right leg up and under her while she pushed her other leg down on the floor. She was so beautiful, he mused. Her tank top dipped so low he saw the top of her bra peeking out. He also couldn't help noticing how her sweat pants hugged the curves of her ass. Shifting in her chair, had her sitting up straighter and her chest heaved outward. Drawing his attention right there.

Unable to stop himself he shameless licked his lips in response. His groin tightening in his jeans at the memory of what she had felt like against his bare skin. Shaking his head, he slowly raised his eyes to hers when her fingers started drumming on the tabletop.

"Did you hear me?" *Nope. Not one word*, but he wasn't about to tell her that. He leaned back in his chair and folded his hands in his lap trying to cover the bulge that was now taking up residence in his pants.

Not sure what she had said he just stated where he wanted her to start, "Tell me about who the men were in the bar and what they wanted." His foot tapped involuntarily on the ground as he waited.

Aaralynn bit into her cheek as her gaze swept around the room for a few seconds. When her eyes came back to his, Kent got the sense that she was worried. Kent could see the uncertainty in the doe look she gave him. That had him very eager to know what she was thinking.

The words came out very monotoned at first but as her words spilled out she got increasingly animated, "Billy and his two cronies were there looking for my mother. Or so I thought that was their intent." Her hands clasped together and she began twiddling her thumbs. "Turns out they were there because my mother told them they could collect her debt from me. I assume it was because they couldn't find her and knew where to find me." Her eyes fell to her pants. Now, she was picking at an invisible piece of lint and breathing in heavy breaths.

"Why would your mother owe them anything?" Without moving from his position in the chair, Kent forced himself to relax his features. Trying to ease her discomfort a little by not shifting around like he normally would love to do in awkward situations like these. The military had taught him how to remain calm even when he felt like a wrecking ball inside. Kent had already come to his own conclusions about what her mother might be wrapped up, but he wanted to hear it from her.

Taking a gulp of stale air Kent eyed her as she shifted her focus from her pants to the plate in front of her. "Who knows what it was from this time." Her voice broke at that and he saw one lone tear sneak down her cheek. He sat up then, ready to wipe it away but she had already done that with the napkin she held. A tiny sniffle escaped her lips, "she usually came around looking for me to help her out of whatever financial situation she was in but the last time I told her I didn't want to see her anymore unless she was clean and there for just me," emphasizing the last two words. "I shouldn't have to take care of my own mother, you know?"

She couldn't see his nod because she was still staring at her plate but he did it none the less. Kent got the sense this couldn't be easy for her so he silently sat there and just waited for her to continue. "She has always had one guy or another since I was little. Some of them boyfriends, some of them sugar daddies, but as I got older she started to do things for more income. After that point, she also started using drugs." The tears were coming down without abandon on her face now and she wasn't even trying to wipe them away.

Something shifted in Kent's chest just looking at her coming undone. Her voice was a matter of fact. It was the voice of someone who was numb and unfeeling because they were broken. The sorrow he felt changed to searing rage and he itched to hit something.

"How old were you?" His tone was low from and menacing. Slowly, her eyes turned to look at him and she blinked. Once, twice, and her mouth formed a thin line. "How old were you," he repeated.

"How old was I what?" She asked, confusion playing over her features. Kent closed his eyes for a moment. Breathing in and out to calm himself. Before opening his eyes, he listened to what he thought was her heartbeat but was actually blood rushing to his ears. His hands were itching to go to her and hold her. It took everything in him to remain in his seat.

"How old were you when this all started?" He questioned for the third time.

Blinking again she wiped at her tears before answering, "The guys started coming around before I could remember, but the first one I really noticed was when I was six." Aaralynn pushed her plate back and lifted her legs in her seat to lay her head across her knees. She looks like she wanted to curl up into herself and maybe she did.

Kent pulled his chair around to hers. His hand brushing a lock of hair that fell out of her clip and had stuck to her wet cheek. Placing it behind her ear, he cupped her cheek in his hand. Aaralynn tilted her face into his palm and rested there. Eyes closed she let out a shaky shallow breath.

"It's ok. You can tell me." He cooed. The beast in him calming some as he felt her skin against his. It wasn't enough though and he knew it but he wanted to give her time to talk first before he did anything else. He could tell she needed this small reprieve.

"My mother dated," she let out a sad laugh, "what she called dated but really who knows what it was," he dropped his hand when she lifted her face to look at him. Those glittering red eyes and flushed tear-stained cheeks had his heart squeezing in his chest. Even in the state she was in she was still gorgeous to him. "Some of the guys came over but I think they came over not just to use her but to try to use me." His hands fisted at his sides and his muscles tensed as a mix of emotions went through him unfiltered. He clenched and unclenched his jaw to stop himself from breaking his teeth.

The look she gave him in return for what must be all over his face was borderline fear. She was afraid of him or maybe what he would do. He blew out a breath. Once, twice, three times but it wasn't helping. Gritting out through clenched teeth, "I would never hurt you." Kent ran a hand through his hair trying to do something, anything with his hands.

He turned her seat towards him and propped his legs on either side of her chair caging her in. "Look at me," he said with both his hands on her armrests. Aaralynn crossed her arms over her drawn-up knees and her chin rested on them to look directly at him. The look of fear she showed before began easing from her.

"I am not mad at you. I would never hurt you. Believe me." He ran his hand over his face before placing it back down on the armrest. The slight nod she gave him had him still wondering if she truly did believe him. Either way, he had faith she would come to trust his word. They would be spending a lot of time together after all. "I am just mad that anything like that happened to you. I am mad for you." He let out another breath. "I am really mad that your mother all but did this to you."

With his last statement, she was rubbing her hands up and down her arms with hands that were so much smaller than his own. Kent knew she wasn't cold but he concluded the movement must be comforting to her. The faint noise of the TV in the background filtered through the silence that stretched as they stared at one another. He heard the heater in the room kick on and a truck that must have driven by outside. His hands came up to gently rub at her shoulders and down her arms. His face moved closer to hers. "I would take care of any of those men if you told me their names," he promised. No doubt in his mind that he would do just that.

Aaralynn's eyes widened at his implication, a ghost of a smile touched her lips just before it was replaced with another sad look. "I don't remember their names. The last one was when I was fifteen. My mother had gotten messed up on some cocktail of drugs and passed out in the other room. The man came into my room," she looked down at her hands, "he said he was looking for the bathroom but I knew better. The way he looked at me told me something entirely different." Tears started to slide silently down her cheeks again and this time he wiped them away for her with the back of his hand in a soft caress. "When I called for my mother he laughed. I will never forget that laugh. It didn't sound normal and it gave me chills back then." A slight cough escaped her, "now it just makes my stomach roll." He scooched closer to her and pulled her to his chest. She turned her head to lay the top of her head against him as he wrapped his arms around her. It was an awkward position with her legs still being pulled up but he didn't care. "Christopher, that was his name, moved towards me when calling my mother didn't work. I had stood to go find her but he pushed me down onto my bed." A soft rumble ran through Kent's chest and he knew she could hear it. Her sliver of a shiver proved she could hear it. He was outraged that the little girl she had been was let down by those who were meant to protect her. "If it wasn't for his distraction of unbuttoning his pants and the fact that my legs were laying off the bed I am not sure what would have happened. I screamed and my knee kicked him in the nuts." Kent felt a sense of pride as she winced at the memory.

"Ouch," he said through a laugh. He stroked a hand through her hair. It was so soft against his fingers and smelled so good. "Then what happened," he prompted. A soft sigh reached his ears before she went on.

"I got up as he was cursing and ran to my mother's room. She was laying there out of it. I was so scared. I couldn't wake her so I grabbed the house phone and called the cops. The guy heard me on the phone and took off. When the police came, they called for an ambulance. They admitted her overnight for observation and detox. It wasn't the first time." Aaralynn had stopped crying and was breathing through the tremors of the tears she had shed. The resignation of her life plain as day. "I stayed with a friend after that. When she came home I was packing up the last of my things. The look of brokenness that was on my mother's face would have torn me to pieces but by then I was already so numb that it didn't matter anymore. I just knew I couldn't live like that." He stopped stroking her hair and lifted her chin from her hands to look at him, "I only saw my mother every once in a while after that. She would find out where I worked or was living and would stop by when she needed something. Funny thing is my friend's house wasn't much better either."

Kent gave her a questionable frown and she shrugged. Seeming to have already let the past be the past but he wanted to know. When she tried to move her face away his grasp on her chin didn't move. "My friend's step-father wouldn't leave me alone either. He never tried anything but he implied a lot and that started tension with my friend and her mother. I outted him before I left when I was seventeen and she hasn't spoken to me since."

Both his hands cupped her face and he lowered his lips to hers. The joining of their lips was softer than before. This kiss wasn't heated and demanding like before but comforting. Soothing down the fire within both of them, while their hearts were not pounding out of their chests, it was no less satisfying.

****

There was nothing else to do but lean into this kiss they shared. Aaralynn needed the comfort Kent offered her. If he wanted to erase or try to erase all her demons, she wouldn't stop him, not when his method was so enjoyable. Her body and mind were so worn down from fighting and reliving the nightmares. The air in the room felt thick and her face felt crusty from the dried tears. Her eyes already feeling the weight of not sleeping well in the car and the lack of food. Her eyes were still closed when he pulled back. A tiny whimper escaped her lips. The absence of him made her feel cold when he had given her warmth just moments before. Her eyes fluttered open as he tenderly kissed her forehead with little effort, he picked up her chair and turned her back to face the table.

"We are not done talking," pausing to give a stern look, "but you need to eat." He kissed the top of her hair and squeezed her hand before moving his chair back to the other side of the table. Unfolding her legs to sit up had her body cracking. She didn't realize she had been that tense. A big yawn came from the corner of the room, reminding them they weren't alone. Aaralynn gave a light chuckle. Smiling at Ash, she placed some food on another plate and laid it on the floor. With that, she snapped her fingers and Ash lifted her head. Sniffing the air, Ash lazily crept off the couch, trotted over to lay on the floor, and began eating her food. Kent laughed, "Either she is the laziest wolf I have ever seen or she has the right idea." The random comment had both of them laughing for a few minutes. The tension she had been feeling around her heart easing.

When she knew she wouldn't throw up anymore, Aaralynn pulled her plate back in front of her to begin picking at her food again. Kent followed suit after putting more food on his plate. "So," he began over a mouthful of food, "what was Billy talking about owing them? I assume it has to do with your mother's habits." He poured some of the bottle of soda that she just noticed was on the table into two cups, handing her one. She took it and vigorously gulped some down.

"I don't know exactly what she did to owe them this time but the only way to pay a debt is to either pay them with money or work it off for them till they decide it's good enough. With Billy though, has been interested in me for years now. I guess he figured I could personally work it off with him. From what he said, my mother told him just that too."

Aaralynn gave a gagging sound and Kent gave a look that told her he would rather break the man's face. Aaralynn inwardly smiled at that. The man across from her wasn't like the guys that normally circled around her. That she knew for sure. Kent made her feel wanted; in a good way.

"Well they are not touching you and you are not paying anyone any favors." The muscle in his jaw jumped, "if they are still looking when we get back I will handle it." Something in his tone assured her he would make good on that. Some of the trepidation she had been harboring seeped away. "You won't have to worry about them anymore," his words reaffirming her thoughts.

They ate in silence for a while. Kent took Ash outside when she finished her food. Granted it took Aaralynn walking with them to the door before Ash would follow Kent outside but she grinned at the stubbornness of her pup. Kent told Aaralynn to sit back down and finish eating while he took the trash out. Instead of fussing, she did just that. When they got back in Ash curled up on the couch again and Kent came to sit back down. Man, she was stuffed and they still had food leftover. Getting up, she cleaned up the containers and place them in the small fridge as Kent started clearing their plates from the table.

"Where is your father?" The question caught her off guard. Not prepared for the inquiry Aaralynn froze. It wasn't a big secret but still, she didn't quite know what to say. "I don't know. My mother never told me and there is no name listed on my birth certificate." After throwing away their trash he pulled the bag out of the trashcan. Nothing was said about her omission regarding her father and Aaralynn figured it was appropriate not to. There was nothing else she could say on it anyway. Kent mentioned taking out the trash and while he did that she used the bathroom.

She was looking at the sleeping bag on the bed when he returned to the room. He looked back and forth from the bed to her before commenting. "I didn't want to sleep on those sheets." Aaralynn had slept on nastier things than those sheets before but she could understand his resistance if he wasn't used to it. She shrugged and started to walk over towards the couch. "Where are you going?" He moved to stand in her way. His arms folded crossed his chest.

"I was going to sleep with Ash if you are sleeping in the sleeping bag." She pointed to the bed. The bag was for a single person and she didn't want to take over his sleeping space. "It's ok, I have slept in worse places." His hand rested on her upper arm as she went to move around him. It had her looking up into his downturn face. The blue and grey of his eyes meeting her pale green ones. Another shadow of a beard and faint tired lines were beginning to show under his eyes. They probably mirrored her own, she thought.

"So handsome," she said breathlessly.

"Not me," he replied and she blushed. She hadn't meant to say that out loud. When his words registered she blinked a few times. *No taking it back now.*

"What do you mean not me? You have to know you are. I mean, girls look at you all the time, or did you not notice that?" She wasn't one who believed in vanity but she couldn't believe this man didn't

know he was handsome, gorgeous, beautiful, sexy…
ok, calm down Aaralynn. You need to keep your cool.

The side of his mouth quirked again making her breath catch. The boyish charm mixed with the manly protectiveness did something to her insides. He didn't reply to her question but rather he surprised her with what he did say. "You are sleeping in the sleeping bag. Go crawl in. I'll be in, in a minute." With that he turned and walked into the bathroom, closing the door behind him. She stood there for a few minutes, her mouth agape as she blinked trying to decide if she should listen to him or just go to the couch. Pushing past her reservations she decided he would probably come out here and move her anyway if she disobeyed him and went to the couch. So, she just did the easier option and curled up in the sleeping bag. Her eyes drifted shut almost immediately after her head hit the pillow. Briefly noting the warm body sliding in behind her. She heard a soft moan when she wiggled back unconsciously cocooning herself within his arms. She missed the kiss to her head and the whisper of a "good night" in her ear before Kent followed her in sleep.

****

Chapter 6

A very wet tongue lapping at her hand woke her from sleep. Her eyes fluttered open to see Ash standing on the side of the bed turning around in circles indicating she wanted to go outside. "Give me a minute girl," she mumbled wiping her eyes. An arm was curled under her head and a warm body was pressed up against her rear. Remembering she was in a sleeping bag with Kent she knew she would not be getting out of this without waking him up. The man was like a furnace in the confined space, but she didn't mind one bit. Normally she would have to have several blankets and clothes on to stay warm and now she was almost sweating. It felt wonderful. Kent was laying on his back, breathing steadily. A turn of her head and she saw he had one hand across his stomach. Kent's other arm was under her head as a pillow. His expression blank.

Just as she was about to turn and wake him, he started mumbling in his sleep. She laid completely still and listened. Unsure what to do, she looked at Ash, who tilted her head to the side not understanding what was going on either. Her black fur still relaxed but her ears perked up and Ash was looking past her at Kent.

"No…taking fire," he mumbled out between small flinches. All his muscles began to tense and she felt his arm lift slightly before laying back down. Something else came from his lips that were incoherent and then he let out a yell just as he jolted upright, pulling the sleeping bag with him. Aaralynn wasn't sure when Ash had moved but she was on Kent's side of the bed and in his face licking him. *Licking him*! Aaralynn had sat up and was looking at

Kent who seemed to take a few minutes to focus before putting his hands-on Ash to get her to stop.

"I didn't know you had a support dog," Kent replied after he collected himself. Kent pet Ash a few times as she sat atop his legs. She was staring at him and waiting. Aaralynn had only seen her act like this when Aaralynn had a breakdown or panic attack. Is that what Kent was having?

"She only does that when I am stressed. She isn't a support dog." replying matter-of-factly.

He rubbed Ash behind her ear one last time before she jumped off the bed and sat near the door. He turned and gave Aaralynn a dazzling smile. "Then she is very in tune." He ran a hand through his hair. She was starting to suspect he did that when he became nervous. The movement bothered Aaralynn for some reason but she was unable to focus on that. The muscles in his arm rippled and flexed. The curve of his neck and the angle of his jaw bone had her staring. Taking notice that he again had no shirt on. He didn't have pants on either. Only a pair of black silk boxers clung to him and from the look of them, the fabric was straining too. Every stitch was pulled taut against his flesh that she could make out every bulge. *Did he just twitch*?

She wrung her hands together and shivered. *Had it gotten cold in the room?* Not sure how long they were sleeping but the light outside the curtains had dimmed. "Come here," he said pulling her back down to the bed, cradling his front to her back. The instant his arms entrap her, she felt a warming sensation spread throughout her body.

"Mmmmm," she said rubbing against him. His hands rested on her hips and tightened in response. The grip stopped her movement.

"I am sorry for waking you but if you don't stop wiggling I might be sorry for a whole other reason." His voice gravely and ruff against her ear causing her to shiver again and sure enough, he was hard. His erection was pressed up against her ass in all its glory. How had she not noticed it earlier? "Damn," he mumbled just before nibbling on her neck.

"Oh," her hands flew to wrap around his neck from behind her and it instantly had her rubbing her back against him again. He growled, low and deep in his throat. The sound rippled through her and she knew she was damp between her thighs. Why did he have to kiss her there? *Those lips*. It was the one spot that was so sensitive it always had her responding.

Her eyes closed, her head lulling further to the side. She knew by how much he was suckling on her neck and up her throat, she was going to have marks. At this point, she didn't care. The hand that was around her middle pulled her tighter against him. Locking her to him as he thrust towards her. They both moaned then.

"You taste so good," he said when he stopped suckling her neck. She made a mewling noise, rolling over to face him. His eyes were hazy with lust and she knew hers must be the same. His hand under her slid down to grab her ass and ground her against him while his other tangled in the hair at the base of her neck. He brought his lips down to hers hard. Their tongues tangled and their moans mingled. Her hands touched him everywhere. His chest, his arms, his thighs and around to his ass. She couldn't get enough of his skin, the feel of his rough abutting her soft.

They both stopped when a whimper and then a bark sounded in the room. Their attention flinging to Ash who was moving in circles in front of the door before letting out another impenitent bark. "Stop that," she hissed at Ash. Kent let out a playful growl against her cheek and nibbled her jaw. "You too," she playfully slapped at his chest. "Stop it." She was smiling when Kent pulled back to look at her. Kent's sexy lips mirroring her own in a dazzling smile. "I need to let her out before someone realizes she is here." Kent visibly sobered at her words. He kissed her lips, unzipped the bag, and jumped out of bed. She watched as he pulled on a pair of jeans, without buttoning them, and padded to the door. Ash was eager to go out and didn't care who did it at this point, so she followed him outside when he opened the door.

****

Within an hour they were both dressed, packed up, finished their Chinese food from earlier, and on the road again. The sun had dipped and he knew they would be getting in late. He had made a quick call to his brother Reed when he walked Ash outside earlier to check on things and got his voice mail. The man was probably in another meeting so he didn't stress over it. He then called his Gran to inform her of his plan and he had gotten a lecture out of that. He hadn't talked to her since telling her he got back and he knew she would be worried. He just hadn't wanted to go into details and with his Gran, he knew he would have to eventually. She wouldn't be satisfied either way.

The conversation only changed when he promised he would explain more later. Kent wondered where they would be staying when they got there. His old room being taken over by a bouncing little girl named Holly. He was told to use the cottage outback since it was free and already renovated. He agreed and after a quick chat with his brother Austin, he had gotten off the phone. Austin didn't like being on the phone unless he had to, which is one of the reasons they got along so well. Kent never liked to idly chat either. He was more of a get-to-the-point kind of man.

Since getting back inside from walking Ash neither one of them spoke about what they had shared in bed that morning. Normally he wouldn't mind letting it go but something had shifted between them and he didn't know what to do with it. He couldn't deny the way she had felt against him, in his arms, all warm and amazing. She tasted like a dying man's last drink of water to his parched soul but Kent didn't know if Aaralynn felt that way towards him.

Sure, she had responded to him. She had practically thrown herself at him when he kissed her neck, but Kent wanted to know what she was thinking. She avoided eye contact the entire time they got everything packed into the car and even now she was staring out the window. It might be for the best because he didn't know how to talk to her about his feelings anyway.

Taking note of her huddled appearance he assumed she was getting chilled. Her body last night was like ice till he nuzzled in behind her and wrapped her up. *Surely, she wasn't always that cold, was she?* If so, Montana was going to be a shock for her. It normally was cool but in November with the wedding happening on Thanksgiving it would be chilly. He turned up the heat in his car and placed a hand on her thigh. She flinched, practically jumping out of her skin. Concern marred his features. He would never hurt her, and she needed to know that. Mentally adding it to his list to talk about with her later.

"Do you have any warmer clothes?" He asked while turning back towards the road. Removing his hand from her thigh, he placed both his hands on the wheel. She shifted slightly in her seat, sitting up straighter.

"No."

"Nothing heavier then what you are wearing?" He prompted. She had thrown a tee-shirt on over her tank top earlier and still had on her sweatpants. The sneakers on her feet were cute but wouldn't stand up to snow if they got the kind of weather they normally did this time of year.

He sighed, "We will have to make a stop on our way. You will need heavier clothes if you plan on being anything but freezing while we're there." She frowned at him. Looking down at her clothes she seemed to be taking stock of herself and then she looked back up at him. After a minute of not saying anything she shrugged and looked straight ahead.

He was about to turn on the radio when he heard her speak. Her voice so soft and tiny he barely heard it over the engine of the car, "where are we going?" Looking at her out of the corner of his eye, her gaze was still fixed on the road.

"My family ranch out in Montana," he replied.

That caught her attention because she snapped her head to look at him. He turned to her with a grin on his lips that spread even more at the shocked expression on her face. "W..ha..t?" she stammered. He gave a small sympathetic smile.

"Montana. Have you ever been anywhere other than Baltimore?" he asked, his curiosity at her reaction to their location.

She sat, still gaping at him. Blinking a couple of times, she closed her mouth and turned to look out the front window again. "I have been to D.C once and Hershey for a field trip. That's in PA. Other than that, no. Not that I didn't want to go away but I just couldn't." He felt the heaviness of her words. The meaning behind them after what she had told him last night wasn't any more palatable now. His chest burned at the pain in her voice. Wishing he could take it away. "So where are we stopping?" Changing the subject must be something she did a lot when she was uncomfortable. He was OK with that.

"There is a general store closer to home that I am going to take you to. You can pick out some clothes and then we will head to the ranch. We also might want to pick up some food since we will be getting in late." That last statement was more to remind himself than inform her. Aaralynn just nodded beside him. She drew her feet back up, cradling her legs to her chest and rested her chin on them.

"You know, I told you about me. You have yet to tell me anything about yourself." Her words were a statement, not a question. The implication clear, she gave information now she expected him to do the same.

"Well," he scratched the bottom of his chin where stubble was growing again, "I have two bothers. One is getting married to a woman and they have a little girl. Well, the little girl was just hers but

Austin adopted her. My other brother Reed is the oldest of us and you'll be meeting him too." He adjusted in his seat.

"Is Austin older or younger than you?" She questioned.

"He is younger than me." Out of the corner of his eye, he could see her head tilted to look at him. Sharp eyes bored into him. Her cheeks were a tiny pink but he also had the heat on and was attributing it to that. "Our parents passed when we were younger so our Gran raised us. You will be meeting her too. She lives at the ranch with Austin and his fiancé."

"Where do you and," she paused for a moment, "Reed is it?" he nodded, "Where do you both live?" Her pale inquisitive eyes not wavering from his face.

He shifted gears before continuing, "Reed lives in New York. Manhattan to be exact. I have been in Egypt for the past year." Her head popped up in obvious interest. The look of amazement across her face had him chuckling "When I got back, I was staying with him but now I will be staying at the ranch until my leave is up."

"So, you were in Egypt?" a wisp of her hair fell and curled around her cheek. He brought a hand up to tuck it back but she beat him to it. Instead, he just placed it back on the wheel and nodded in response to her question.

"So, why were you over there?" Kent knew these lines of questions were inevitable and let out a rush of air before responding.

"I am in the military. I was a Marine then joined MARSOC." Her mouth formed an O and he grinned. "I did 8 tours and am on leave for a month before I go back. That is if I want to go back. I have the option of retiring but I am not sure if I want to do that yet."

"What is MARSOC?" she asked, her brows furrowing on her face. The look had him almost leaning over to kiss her. Holding himself back by tightening his grip on the steering wheel.

"MARSOC," shifting gears, he took a breath before continuing, "stands for Marine Special Operations Command." He put on the blinker to signal they were getting off at the next exit. Neither of them spoke as he veered them off and started on a regular road.

Aaralynn still stared at him intently, letting out a chuckle as he turned toward her. The smile that greeted him heated his insides. "My unit went all over," he continued his earlier conversation. "I have been to Iraq, Iran, Egypt, Afghanistan, and Africa. All over the Middle East." He stopped to check his rear-view mirrors. "Is there something on my face because you are staring pretty hard." The blush that ran over her cheeks before she turned her gaze back on the road had him getting stiff against his jeans. *Whatever I have to do to keep that blush on her face consider it done*, he thought to himself.

"I just can't believe you did all that." She said to the windshield.

He shifted in his seat again, "Do I look like I can't?"

"No. It's not that," she let out a breath, "That came out wrong. I mean you look too young to have been to so many places and done so many tours." Taking it as a compliment he ran a hand over his head again before replacing it on the steering wheel.

Aaralynn thought he was young. He would love to prove to her how very wrong she was. "I can prove my experience to you." He heard a hard intake of air beside him and he realized what he had just said. In the moment of silent awkwardness, that stretched between them. Kent surmised that he would have meant it, either way, she took it and he wouldn't apologize for his natural reaction to her.

They stopped again to let Ash go to the bathroom before continuing. He never said anything else and she didn't ask any more questions. He watched her out of the corner of his eye while he was driving and noticed her staring out the window. She looked like she was lost in thought. Soft wisps of hair curling around her face. He took in her hands clasped together in her lap just as he turned his gaze back to the road.

After another ten minutes, he glanced over again. This stretch of road went on for a few minutes before they would hit the small town of Crystal Cave. From there the ranch would be about an hour. It was late. The sun had already dipped filling the inside of that car with darkness except for the glow of the dashboard.

When he reached the strip of shops he pulled into a parking spot. After shutting off the engine and stretching he looked at the clock. It said 11:37 PM. The groan of Aaralynn beside him caught his attention. Her arms over her head in a long stretch had his eyes trailing up and down. Her pants fit snug against her, and he couldn't help but watch as her breast push against the fabric of her shirt. Her lips parted with a yawn and the lines of her neck stood out for a moment. He rearranged himself in his jeans again.

****

How tired can someone possibly get? It wasn't like she hadn't slept earlier. In fact, she slept harder than she had in a few weeks. The feel of Kent's body pressed against hers and their shared warmth had willed her into a deep sleep. Now her body ached and cracked when she moved. At least every time her ears heard a pop it wasn't from broken bones like it had been in the past. She considered that a plus.

As she stretched her neck she saw Kent staring at her. In truth, she had noticed him staring at her on and off the whole ride. Her inability to say anything to him should be contributed to the uncalled-for response he gave her earlier but if she was being honest with herself it was because she wasn't sure how she would respond. On one hand, she wanted to give a snarky retort but on the other, she wanted to dare him to prove it.

He shook his head while rubbing his eyes. "I didn't realize how late it was," he said sighing to himself. "I will order us some food." Pulling his phone out of his pocket, he began typing something in. "After I order I will go down the street to the small market and get some things we will need. Then pick the food up on the way back." Finishing what he was doing on his phone, Kent clicked it off before putting it back in his pocket. His tired eyes met hers and held. "Do you need anything? Bath stuff or personal stuff?" The way he said the last part had her smiling. He must've been embarrassed asking but she thought it was sweet he did.

"Isn't bathroom stuff personal stuff?" Aaralynn teased.

Kent gave her a doltish look before rolling his eyes.

"No, I don't need any personal feminine hygiene products." Aaralynn couldn't help the giggle that escaped, "but bathroom products would be nice. I didn't think to pack any. Oh, and if you could grab a tea for me to drink. My throat is dry." The grin he flashed her had her throat going dry and a blush creeping into her cheeks. She gave a dry gulp. With a nod, Kent turned and opened the car door to exit.

Pausing just outside the car door, Kent leaned back in, "keep the heat on and lock the car when I leave." He saw the look in her eye and the corner of his mouth quirked up. "There isn't anyone here that would steal the car, but you never know. It's a small town. Everyone knows everyone. I just don't want anyone accidentally opening the door and Ash getting out."

At the name, the snoring pup in the backseat perked up. "Calm down." Aaralynn made a motion with her hand and Ash laid back down with something that sounded like a grunt.

"I understand." He nodded to Aaralynn and closed the door. After the click of the door shutting, she leaned over and locked the car. Leaning back in her seat; she closed her eyes.

Sharp rapping on the window had her jolting upright. Frantically her eyes flew open and roamed around. Momentarily Aaralynn was disoriented and confused about where she was. A look at the clock showed thirty minutes had passed and she remembered where she was. She must have fallen asleep.

Blinking a few times to clear the haziness, she leaned over to unlock the door. Greeted by his warm smile as she pushed open the driver's side door, his eyes telling her he was tired too. He handed over a brown paper bag and four white plastic ones before climbing in himself. She felt bad for not offering to take over driving but she didn't know where they were going. So instead of mulling on that she put the bags on the floor at her feet.

She made a show of looking through the bags. The loud rustling of the plastic in the silent car echoed, filling the space. "What are you doing," he asked. A hint of inquisitive confusion in his voice.

"I'm looking for the kitchen sink." She made sure her face was as innocent as she could make it before looking up at him. The stunned surprise on his face lasted a second before they both busted out laughing. A hearty, full-bellied laugh that had her sides aching. It had been years since she felt at ease enough to laugh with such abandon.

After catching her breath and his laughter died down, she started looking through the bags again. "So, what are you – "

"Found it!" Aaralynn exclaimed pulling out the tea bottle. She held it up like a prize before tearing the cap off and downing almost half of it. The cool liquid flowed down her throat and she was grateful she didn't spill it all over herself in her haste. That would have been embarrassing.

"Feel better?" His tone had her turning. She was going to say "yes" but the words stuck in her throat. He was still smiling at her. One that went from cheek to cheek and had her smiling in return. The pools of his eyes were pulling her in and even though she could tell he was tired she saw a hint of something else too. She wasn't sure what it was. Lust? Need? Whatever it was had a delicious tremor pulsing down her spine.

Suppressing the shiver that threatened to overtake her she remembered she still hadn't spoken. Before taking another sip of her drink she nodded her head. Kent rewarded her with a light chuckle before shifting forward in his seat. Aaralynn didn't know what to say. Typically, when a man looked at her like Kent did, she would feel dread or disgust because she knew what they were thinking. No woman alive wouldn't know what a man wanted when they blatantly stared at a woman like that. However, with Kent she felt desire at it, wanted it even, and yet she didn't want to react to it at all. Her body was at war with her mind.

Kent turned the car on and shifted the stick to back up. Even his movements seemed lacking motivation. "Do you want me to drive? I mean, I know I don't know where we are going but if you turn on a GPS I can get us there while you take a break." The words tumbled out in a rush.

He was already shaking his head as he turned the wheel and shifted gears to start on the road again. "No. I'm good. When we get there, I'll get us settled in and we can both get some sleep." He yawned then. The movement had the muscles in his jaw stretching and showing off his white teeth. She observed his decent-sized K9s too. She hadn't noticed that before. *Then again what normal female stared at someone's teeth unless they were in the field of dentistry.*

If he wasn't going to let her take over driving she could at least keep him talking. Maybe that would help. "So, tell me about your family and growing up on a ranch. What kind of ranch is it?" She turned sideways in her seat, getting a better view of him.

The side of his mouth turned up and his tone became lighter as he spoke, "it is a horse and cattle ranch but we also do some milk and some crops. Nothing too big." He cleared his throat.

"Do you want the rest?" Lifting the tea toward him in a polite gesture.

"Thank you," he took it and after fumbling with the lid he drank the rest down in one gulp. "Mmmm," he replied. "That was good."

"Told you."

He chuckled again. *Was he always so lighthearted and laughing*? She wished she could be like that. Her demeanor was always on guard with a 'stick to yourself 'motto that kept her safe for so long that she was plain used to it. It felt good to smile and laugh, and not feel like the other shoe was going to drop every two seconds. His voice trailed to her ears and she ascertained that he was still speaking. When she tried focusing on his words, she wasn't sure what he was talking about.

"… to make sure the barn is all cleared and set up before Thanksgiving in a few days. I am not sure what the women have planned since the guys will be throwing their bachelor party."

Aaralynn blinked a few times before shaking her head. "Hold on. I'm confused." He looked at her with a tilt of his head that had her insides warming. Ignoring her body, she cracked her knuckles in her lap. "Why does the barn need to be cleared and set up for Thanksgiving?"

He turned back to the road before responding. Immediately she missed the eye contact. The way he looked at her. It had her feeling special and wanted, and important. She had never felt that from any man before. Sure, Ray and the guys made her feel needed and even Ray felt like a father figure to her at times but normally the guys that had an interest in her had their own motives. Maybe Kent did too, but she couldn't know what. At least not yet, nor did she get a creepy feeling from him either. That on its own was a plus.

Turning down another road Aaralynn tried to take in her surroundings but all she could see was a blanket of ebony. Kent's eyes never left the windshield as he spoke, "The barn needs to be ready for the wedding. It is the morning of Thanksgiving."

Wait? What? Did she just hear him correctly? A wedding? Was it his wedding? "Someone is getting married?" Her voice sounded weird even to her own ears. A knot was forming in her stomach and for a moment she thought she was going to be sick.

"I take it you didn't hear me earlier." His tone was joking and playful. He didn't wait for a response as it was obvious by her question that she hadn't. "My brother Austin is getting married. I mentioned him before."

A rush of air left her lungs and she felt her heart start beating again. It was such a big response that even Kent looked at her for a moment. "Are you ok?" He placed a hand on her thigh and rubbed his thumb in circles. Her response to it being his brother getting married and not him had her reeling. She was relieved. There was no denying it or denying her growing fondness for him.

"I'm fine. I think I am just more tired than I thought." Gently he squeezed her thigh before releasing her and placing his hand back on the stick shift.

"It's OK. I think we both are." They were driving on a dark road and every so often there would be a spec of light from homes off in the distance. They were scattered on the open landscape and reminded her of lightning bugs. She could imagine the happy families inside all cozied in their beds and wished she was one of them.

She turned and rested her elbow on the door. "So, your brothers getting married," she quipped. The sullenness of her mood crept into her voice, but she couldn't help it. It was a complete contrast to the softness of his voice when he spoke.

"He is. He deserves it. He and Annette both do."

"Do you plan on getting married one day?"

"This talk got serious," he grunted. The sound had her head swinging towards him. The light glow of the dashboard gave his face a stern look. The bluish hue highlighting the edges of his jaw and cheekbones. Her lack of a response didn't deter him from answering. "I suppose one day I will. Besides if I stay in the service, I wouldn't want to burden anyone with waiting for me. Especially not with kids. It wouldn't be fair to them." He shifted gears again and she felt the car slowing down.

Pushing her butt back further in her seat to sit straighter, she watched as Kent turned right onto a driveway. It appeared to be new. The consistency is much darker and smoother than the road they were just on. They passed a big metal gate with gold letters on a green sign that said, "Rayne Falls Ranch".

"Yes, there is a story behind the name. I will have to explain it to you some time." The way he said it had her eyes flickering over to him. She hadn't meant to read the sign out loud. Heat rushed through her as her anxiety rose. His chest expanded and fell in a silent chuckle. *Why was he laughing?*

He brushed more hair back from her face. "Has anyone told you you're so adorable when you're surprised?" The smile that claimed his face at her narrowed eyes had her starting to soften toward him. *Damn my reaction to him*, she chided herself.

"No. And I am not twelve. I don't think adorable applies to me" His eyes followed her arms as she crossed them over her chest. Giving her a look that said, 'you were saying' without technically saying it.

****

Chapter 7

Adorable. Plain and simple. As for her response of not being twelve, she was crossing her arms and pouting like a twelve-year-old right now and that just proved how adorable she was. He just smiled to himself as they slowly drove down the long driveway. Taking in the smoothness of the new pavement and trees that lined it. Some updates had happened since the last time he had been here and they were nice. Something like this must have cost a pretty penny.

"So, have you ever thought about it?" He was starting to like catching her off guard. The look of innocent surprise always eased something in his chest.

"Excuse me," a hint of tension in her voice.

He replied as nonchalant as he could without trying to laugh again, "Marriage. Have you ever thought about marriage?" It had been a long while since he had laughed so much in anyone's presence. Normally with his unit, they were serious most of the time. Out in the field, they had to be alert of any real threats, and that usually dulled the mood around them no matter what you tried to do. Now it seemed, he was letting all of it out.

The big white farmhouse from his childhood came into view. The expanse of the porch covered the whole front with such an inviting atmosphere he knew, just like always, that he wouldn't want to leave again. The big red barn off to the side was barely recognizable against the black of the night but he knew it was there. He had played in it so many times over the years he would be able to guide you through every inch of the building. Aaralynn's voice almost inaudible to his ears while he was reminiscing.

"I don't see the point in marriage. Not when stability is only a 9-letter word and faithfulness is just a concept to most. A piece of paper doesn't make people stick around." Her words made his heartache. The way she said it as if the little girl inside her doesn't want to believe her own words. The reality that she has had to live through has crushed the rose-colored glasses, leaving behind something dismal. His insides ached for her.

He parked the car by the barn and killed the engine. Waiting till they both unbuckled their seats, he reached for her, pulling him to her in a tight embrace. At first, her body tensed but then relaxed into him, welcoming the contact. Snuggling her face into his chest, he rested his chin on the top of her head.

Her arms wrapped around his shoulders and squeezed so lightly he almost missed it. One arm cradled her head while the other went around her waist, rubbing her back. The stick shift made the embrace a bit awkward and the way his body had to lean over it was making his muscles hurt but he didn't care. Knowing she needed this, that they both did, was more important than a little pain.

When she pulled back he saw her wipe at the glistening of unshed tears in her eyes. His words spilled out of him unbidden, "I'll always be there." He didn't know why he said that. Maybe it was because he knew something needed to be said or maybe she needed to hear it, or that he couldn't just say nothing, but once the words were out he knew he meant them. He would always be there for her if she needed him to be. Maybe even if she didn't.

Her eyes were raw with emotion when she looked at him and in the next instant, her mouth slammed into his in a harsh, needy kiss. His mind took a moment to register what was happening and just as he was going to pull her tighter she released his lips, sitting back in her seat.

"Sorry. I... I don't know why I did that." The stammer she gave was followed by a hiccup. Ash who had been snoring in the back seat jumped up with alert at the sound. He didn't get to reply because the dog jumped in the front seat to sit on her lap like a giant blanket covering her and proceeded to lick her face. This was Ash's attempt to comfort an upset Aaralynn.

After a few licks, Aaralynn pushed Ash off her and opened the car door. Tail wagging, Ash bounded off her and out the car. He was laughing when he saw her wiping her face and trying to pick pieces of fur out of her mouth.

"There is nothing funny about dog hair. It's not appetizing." Her hands flat against her shirt wiping away anything she could.

"You have to admit it is a little funny and you might hurt Ash's feelings. She went through great lengths to give you her fur. You could at least appreciate it." The half-smile she turned toward him had him smiling at her in return. She swatted a hand at his shoulder in contempt. "Hey," he said without any harshness to it. He was glad she was being playful. He tilted his head in the direction of the open door, "She won't try and go after anything, right? I mean try to eat livestock or anything."

Stilling with her hands on her chest she looked out the window at the darkness. Blinking once, then twice she shook her head. "I don't know. I have never taken her on a ranch before. But she has never gone after any of the other dogs at the park if that says anything."

It didn't, but he wouldn't say that. This was uncharted territory is what she was getting at and he knew he would have to inform his brother of that. They couldn't afford any accidents. Even if Ash was a pet she was still a wolf and her natural instincts could kick in.

"That's alright. We will just have to watch her. Don't need her going after the chickens or cattle or other livestock around here." Aaralynn nodded in agreement. A second later Ash appeared at her open door, jumping back and forth with anticipation. Opening his door, Kent climbed out and went to the trunk. He pulled out all their bags but Aaralynn insisted she take her own. He shrugged and handed them to her.

"The cottage is around the back. See those stones there?" he pointed to a stone pathway and she followed his finger. "That leads to the cottage. Come on," he said hauling his duffel bag over his shoulder, "we can get settled in and then eat before getting some sleep."

"Ssssooouunndds g.g..oo..ood," she said between chattering teeth. He cursed himself for not stopping earlier to get her more appropriate clothing. As it was there was a light smattering of snow covering the ground and it was starting to flurry again. He dropped his duffle bag and pulled out a heavy jacket. He draped it over her. The jacket swallowed her smaller frame but she seemed to at least stop shivering.

Kent picked up his bag again and tilted his head, "come on. The faster we get moving the sooner we can get you warm." She didn't say anything else just followed him. Her light footsteps the only proof she was behind him. When they reached the porch, he opened the screen door to push the front door open. He knew it would be unlocked. Gran said he could just grab the key in the morning.

They both walked in and set their bags down. Ash trotted in. Her nose to the floor, inspecting the place. He moved to turn on the lights, illuminating the space. The smell of wood and fresh paint filled his nose. As he looked around, Kent took in the renovations that had been done. The plush couch and tables filled the living room.

"It's so nice in here." He looked down at Aaralynn. She was looking in awe at everything. She moved further into the room. She seemed apprehensive to move or touch anything. The way she sat down on the couch, trying to remain perfectly still as if she shouldn't get one crease in the material had him understanding a bit more about her. Their lives growing up must have been very different if she felt like she should treat the material things around her like they were more precious than she was.

As if she had been in his head she said, "I won't get anything dirty, I promise." With that, she stood up.

Kent put up his hands, "It's just furniture. If it gets dirty we can clean it. Don't worry." Ash took that moment to walk in from the kitchen and jump right on the couch. Aaralynn whirled around and barked for her to get down.

****

"It's ok," he said in as calming of a voice as he could muster. Ash had already hopped down and sat next to her master licking her hand for approval. The action had Aaralynn instantly petting her head and playing with her ears. She was staring at him with a blank expression on her face and Kent knew she was in her head again.

"Look," he started again but she was still staring blankly at him. He waved a hand in front of her face. She blinked a few times. When he felt she was back with him he continued, "you don't have to worry about it. Just because we are not back in that hotel room doesn't mean you have to tread on glass. This is your place too while you're here. If something gets dirty, we can clean it, or if something breaks we can fix it. And I already figured Ash would jump on things. No need to get anxiety over it. I promise." Kent made a criss-cross motion with his fingers over his heart.

Aaralynn still didn't speak for so long that he thought he lost her again. He began picking up their luggage when she cleared her throat.

"OK."

"OK?"

"OK," she responded again with a nod of her head. Knowing that was all he would get out of her, it was fine with him, for now.

"Good, now follow me and we can get squared away and eat." They both picked up the bags and walked up the stairs to the bedrooms.

He came down the stairs twenty minutes ahead of her. Taking the extra time to start a fire and bring in some more logs from outside. By the time Aaralynn walked downstairs, their dinner was on the living room table and he was bringing out cups of orange soda. His heart thudded in his chest at the sight of her in a tank top and pajama shorts that were almost so short the bottom of her firm butt cheeks were showing. The pale blue of her outfit was so sheer it did nothing to hide the fact that she had no bra on. He audibly swallowed, hard, and averted his gaze. She had to know what an outfit like that would do to a man, right? *She is trying to torture me.*

Ash, who had followed Aaralynn upstairs earlier, trotted downstairs and plopped back down on the couch. He gave a chuckled and placed the cups down on the table. Aaralynn sat down on the floor in front of the table instead of the couch and he followed suit. She smelled of the body wash and shampoo he bought at the general store in town. Without thinking it through, Kent scooted closer to her. His subconscious seemed to have a will of its own.

"Subs?" She questions and he heard her stomach grumble at the mention of food. Mentally kicking himself for not getting something earlier, but Kent just wanted to get home. Tunnel focus was something a flaw of his.

"Yes, hoagies." His response had her turning toward him. A small smile playing on her lips.

"You mean subs. No one calls them hoagies." She playfully slapped his arm. The sensation of her hand on his skin had tingles running up and down his arm. The feelings she provoked in him had him questioning just how long it had been since he had really felt a connection to someone. If what he was feeling kept getting stronger it would be hard to say goodbye when he had to take her back.

"You may call them subs, but everywhere else they call them hoagies." Kent shrugged. He knew he got to her when she made a sound that mimicked a gasp. She proceeded to push her shoulder into his.

He teetered and Ash started wagging her tail. Ash must have realized they were playing and wanted in. "You're a butthead," she commented to Kent and he let out a playful growl. "Butt head am I?" he quipped just before wrapping his arms around her and tickling her.

She fell back giggling and squirming. She was flailing her hands attempting to get him off her at first. When that failed she tried to tickle him back but he was only ticklish in a few places. None of which she was touching.

"Say hoagie," he was saying between breaths. His teasing tone had her giggling more. "Say hoagie," He quipped again. His voice is even playful to his own ears. How long had it been since he fooled around like this? It must have been when he was a kid and even then, he had been pretty serious.

"Stop," she was gasping for air between her bought of laughter. "Stop," he pulled back, bracing his arms on either side of her shoulders.

Her beautiful hair was free of its clip and sprawled around her in waves. Her eyes bright and sparkling with happiness. Her skin glowed with a pink flush that was more prominent in her cheeks from laughing so hard. He wondered if this was how she looked after a night full of sex and the thought had blood rushing to his groin. Getting him instantly hard. Aaralynn instantly stilled and stared into his eyes. Their panting becoming shallower and his insides buzzed with need. He felt alive for the first time in months and he didn't want it to stop.

They laid there, her under him, frozen. His face mere inches from hers. Their breathing started to normalize the longer they stared at each other. Aaralynn wiggled her hips under him, another attempt to get up that had her stilling again when she rubbed against the hardness in his jeans. Another flush crept up her cheeks and he saw the pulse at her neck pick up speed. Her eyes got a darker shade of green that looked stunning to him. The rise and fall of her chest had her breast brushing against his own. That only had him straining harder against the fabric of his pants.

He audibly swallowed as she licked her lips. Those plump pink lips slightly parted and Kent knew he couldn't lay here anymore and just stare at her. His head dipped down to crush her mouth to his. A blending of lips and tongue had a small moan escaping from her mouth. Kent pressed his body further into hers, but still resting on his elbows as not to crush her with his weight.

At that moment, his phone buzzed in his pants, but he ignored it. Kissing her more hungrily had her wrapping her arms around his waist. Kent rubbed his erection against her thigh and another buzz from his phone came through. This time he couldn't ignore it because she felt it too, and began to push against his chest.

When their kiss broke they were both panting hard. Her green eyes searching his, a smile on her lips. "You might want to get that," she said between small breaths. He shook his head but she went on, "it could be important. Besides we need to eat. I don't know about you but I am starving." Kent was hungry but not for food at the moment. She must have read that in his eyes because she started pushing against his chest with her hands and wriggling out from under him, "I am hungry for food. _Not_ that," she replied. Emphasizing the last part.

This is becoming a habit. Kent let out a grumble as he got to his feet. Aaralynn sat in a criss-cross fashion and was straightening her outfit. Brushing her fingers through her hair as he readjusted himself in his pants once again. "I will go grab Ash some food while I check my phone." With that, he walked into the kitchen.

When he got in the kitchen, he headed toward the package of ground beef he placed on the counter earlier. He then pulled out a pot to put the ground beef in. Checking his phone while he was browning the meat on the stove. One message from his brother saying he just got in and would see him in the morning. The other was from Ray. Turning off the stove and draining the meat in the sink he turned back to his messages.

Ray: We have a problem.

Kent read the message twice before responding.

Kent: What's wrong

He took the ground beef and grabbed a bowl from the cabinet. Throwing the meat in the bowl he whistled for Ash to come in. The big black ball of fur strode into the kitchen and smelled the food immediately. She wagged her tail and made some yipping noises. Her teeth snapping together and the clicks that sounded out vibrated in his ears. Just as he placed the food down his phone buzzed on the counter. He sighed and watched as Ash tore into the pound of ground beef like it was nothing.

Taking his phone, he read the next message of Ray telling him to call him. Kent rubbed his face. His face getting scratchy again from the stubble starting to come back. His eyes flicked to the clock on the stove and it read 1:24 AM. Damn, was he ever going to eat and get to bed?

"You coming back in?" The sweet voice from the other room, effectively calming his nerves but making it difficult to concentrate.

"In a minute. Just fed Ash I am going to clean up and make a phone call first. You eat. The remote is on the table if you want to turn on something." She didn't say anything but he knew she heard him. He had spoken louder than she had. Ash licked her lips and sat back on her hind legs looking at him patiently.

"No more girl," he said showing her the empty bowl he picked up. The animal let out what sounded like a low whimper before strutting back into the living room. As he started rinsing the dirty dishes and pot in the sink he dialed Ray's phone. He answered after the second ring,

"It is hard as hell to get you on the phone." Ray's voice cracked with a slight cough as soon as he spoke. "What took so long?" he demanded.

Kent had to give the man a hand, he had some balls. "I was busy, what is so important I had to call you so late?" Kent didn't want to beat around the bush. Get the facts, make a plan, and execute it. That is how he worked. Chit chat doesn't do anything but get in the way.

"Jerry was in here last night and he beat the hell out of Stan trying to get information out of him.

Pu the poor bastard in the hospital," Ray's voice sounded gravelly like he had a hard time keeping his emotions in check. "From what I can piece together all Stan said was that she had left town."

Kent threw the rag down on the counter and blew out a breath. "last night?! And you're just now telling me this?" Kent was irritated and it was showing in his voice.

"I just found out, damn it! Why do you think I was messaging you?" The other man sounded pissed off too. "Stan just woke up about an hour ago and told us what happened. The police are looking for Jerry now but I don't know if they will find him. It's not the first-time people who have made complaints just went missing." The sound of a door opening on the other end had him straining to hear. Some muffled talking could be heard. It sounded like Ray had his hand over the phone. That irritated Kent even more.

Kent yelled into the speaker, "Hey! What is going on over there?!" Odd noises came over the line just before Ray's ruff voice.

"Sorry, was talking to Tony."

"Ray, where are you?" Kent wanted to know. He could hear shuffling and sounds of people talking in the background. Ash rubbed up against his leg and he turned around to see Aaralynn leaning in the doorway. Her expression faltering when she saw his face. She mouthed 'what's wrong' as she crossed her arms over her chest. All concentration lost for a moment as his gaze shifted to focus on her breast.

He inwardly groaned. He would rather be finishing what they started earlier in the living room than standing here listening to bullshit over the phone, but it couldn't be helped. His attention pulled back to the phone call when a loud banging sounded on the other end.

"HELLO! Are you listening?" Ray's deep bellowing voice blasted in his ear.

"Yea I am. So, where are you?"

"I am standing outside the hospital. The police were in his room questioning him when I left him." Kent heard Ray tell someone to hold on. "Look Kent, I am not sure what all he said. He is kind of out of it." Ray blew out a breath, "I am just letting you know in case he did say something and they come looking."

"Alright," he replied. He leaned back against the sink and Aaralynn moved closer to him. Being only inches apart, he could see the look of concern on her face. "Thanks for letting me know Ray."

At the other man's name, her eyes widened and she snatched the phone out of his hand. Kent chuckled to himself.

"Ray," she said all excited. Kent heard some noises from the receiver then, "I am so glad to hear your voice! How is everything?" After a few minutes of mumbling, he visibly saw her face slump and tears start to form in her eyes. "No," that one little word escaped her lips while she wiped at her unshed tears.

His whole body suddenly wracked with the need to comfort her. He practically shook from the intensity of it but remained where he was as she listened. Her eyes leaving his to search out Ash. When a tear ran down her cheek he couldn't wait anymore. He pulled her to him and kissed her forehead. Without protest, her body relaxed into his. Kent reveled in the feel of her against him.

"Sure," she muffled out. The softness of her voice sounded at odds with the gruff male one he heard on the other side of the line. The phone was so close to his ear now that he heard what others were saying.

"Baby, you doing ok?" Tony's concerned voice filtered through Kent's hazy mind. Unable to hide the contempt for the other man, Kent's chest let out a low rumble at the other man's adoring words. Aaralynn didn't seem to respond to what Tony said but instead nuzzled into Kent. The motion had a swelling of warmth spread through him and his arms snaking tighter around her.

"I'm fine Tony. We just got here a little bit ago." A tiny sniffle escaped her and Kent instantly kissed the top of her head again.

"Where is here?" Tony asked and Kent felt himself tensing. Would she tell him where they were? Without pause, his gut told no since he figured they both knew it wouldn't be wise to give away anything. Kent's shirt was getting damp where her tears fell but he didn't care. He could always change later.

"I'm not sure exactly. I know it's Kent's family's home." She took in a few shaky breaths, "I hope Stan recovers. Is it really bad?"

Tony didn't respond to that question. Instead, he simply said, "I miss you, baby. It's been hard without you around."

Before Kent could grab the phone and tell Tony off Aaralynn surprised him. "Look, Tony, I miss you, as a friend should but I don't like you like that. You are like a big brother to me." Tony tried to say something but Aaralynn cut him off without pausing, "You and Stan both are. I really do hope Stan gets better and have Ray call when he has any information but please stop with the pet names. Please." That last word was a whisper of a sound before she pushed the phone up at Kent. He was so proud of her and he had no right to be. She wasn't his. *She sure feels like mine.* They weren't in a relationship. *Yea but you want to be*, the voice inside his head pressed.

\   Ignoring it, Kent lifted the phone to his ear, his other arm still wrapped tightly around the wonderful woman in his embrace. Aaralynn snuggled in tighter and hugged him around his waist. Her face buried into his chest.

"Baby, please. Don't say that. I miss you so bad." The whines and please came across the other end and it had Kent burning mad.

"Look," he started. His rage banking on the edge, "She said to back off. Now put Ray back on the phone." His tone was flat, even and without any leeway.

"Listen here you piece of…" there was a muffled sound and some pushing of buttons before Kent heard Ray's voice on the line.

"Sorry about that Kent."

"No problem here," Kent replied, "I would suggest talking to your man though. Aaralynn is upset enough she doesn't need that shit too."

"Agreed."

"Good."

"I will call if there is anything new. But like I said keep an eye open. You never know what could happen. I'll call if there is an update." With that, they both said their goodbyes and hung up.

****

Chapter 8

After the disturbing phone call early this morning, Kent had kissed her lightly on the lips and ushered her back to the living room. They ate in silence for a long while. Kent had scarfed down his food in mere minutes while she picked at her own. Her appetite had waned, and she just couldn't seem to finish it. Yawning a few times had Kent sending her to bed, telling her he would clean up.

Too tired to argue Aaralynn just nodded before climbing the stairs to her room. She didn't call for Ash, knowing she would follow her to bed. Although, from Kent feeding her meat she may wait around to see if there was more. If there was one thing any K-9 couldn't resist would be meat after all. Aaralynn was so tired she hadn't even bothered brushing her teeth, almost out of energy. All she could do was fall into a comfortable bed. Seconds later she felt Ash curl up behind her. She awoke a few hours later in the same position.

The heavy grogginess was compounded by the tightness in her muscles. A sliver of light filtering through the cracks in her eyelids. Aaralynn wiped at her crusty eyes and stretched out her taut muscles. Ash's body flexed while the animal let out a small yawn against her back. The familiar sound comforting. Aaralynn rolled over to snuggle Ash's back into her. She noticed a blanket that had been draped over them and thought for a minute. Did she put a blanket on? *No, it must have been Kent.* She didn't even bother with covers when she fell into bed. The thought brought a small smile with it and tenderness filled her chest.

He had been strong and sturdy while she cried into him. People get hurt because of her made her feel helpless. Well, that wasn't entirely true if she was honest with herself. She could go turn herself in and stop all this madness, but then what would happen. Ray and Kent had gone through so much to help her, she couldn't just flush all their efforts down the drain. Aaralynn was pretty sure both men wouldn't just let her go that easily either. On the other hand, she couldn't let people keep getting hurt because of her. Being stuck in-between a rock and a hard place was no fun. However, being stuck between Kent and the floor last night was intriguing and had her body heating up again at just the thought.

Her mind shifted and memories of Kent had her heart beating faster. It fascinated her how her body responded to him so eagerly even knowing this wouldn't last forever but she couldn't deny her attraction to him either. Lazily she rubbed Ash's fur and scratched her stomach. The wolf leaned back into her to her silently begging for more. How Kent had taken Ash into consideration had her liking him even more. Her ex Cory never cared about Ash. Cory's affection toward her wasn't there neither. *Why did she stay so long?*

Yawning again, "Oh, I think it is time to brush my teeth." Ash sat up as she rolled out of bed. Quickly locating her bags, Aaralynn pulled out her toiletry bag and padded out of her room to find the bathroom. Stepping out of her room the hallway was hushed. Aaralynn looked around taking in the ample amounts of wood used to make such a stunning home. There was a door directly across from her own and another at the end of the hall. Deciding to try to door at the end of the hall she lazily strolled from her room. Turning the knob, she opened the door to reveal a white tiled bathroom with green accents. Ushering Ash in behind her, she closed the door and began brushing her teeth. When she finished, she relieved herself before washing her hands and stepping out into the hallway once more.

Kent was just coming out of the room across from hers with nothing on but some boxers and a handful of clothes. Her breath caught in her chest. He was stunning. Suddenly she felt like she was moving through a pile of snow. Every step felt heavy and slow. He gave her another half-smile and she felt a tingle race through her. Starting from her toes all the way to her fingers.

"Morning," He said.

"Good Morning to you too," Aaralynn felt like she was talking through a mouthful of cotton but if Kent noticed he didn't let on. He walked past her to the bathroom and stopped just before closing the door.

"If you get dressed we can make it to the main house for breakfast. I will only be a minute. That way we can introduce you and see about getting you some clothes." Without waiting for a response, he gently closed the door behind him with a click, leaving her standing there staring; wishing she was inside that room with him. A minute later she heard the shower go on. Snapping herself out of her stupor. She turned to go into her room, closing her door after Ash strode past her over to the window. Pulling the curtain back Aaralynn saw more snow must have fallen early this morning. The ground was covered in it and she felt the chill of the air through the glass.

A small shiver swept through her and she went to look through her clothes. In Baltimore, it can get chilly this time of year, but this Montana weather was a lot different. She didn't have the type of heavy clothing for this kind of winter weather. So instead, she pulled on the heaviest sweatpants she had and paired it with a layered tank top over a long sleeve shirt. It was the only one she brought on such short notice and she was glad she did. Pulling on her sneakers Aaralynn walked out of her room to go downstairs.

Kent came down a few minutes later. His hair was damp and his skin pink from the fast scrubbing. He smelled of musk and she was instantly turned on. Chiding herself for being that easy, she stood up. "So, you ready?"

He frowned at her after he looked her over, taking in her attire. "Is that the warmest clothes you have?" He asked.

"It's all I brought on such short notice. It's not like you told me where we were going." She reminded him.

"OK. Here," he pulled off his heavy coat and wrapped it around her.

"I can't," cutting her off with a raise of his hand.

"Yes, you can. I have another upstairs. I'll go grab it." He turned around and went upstairs. Taking two at a time with the long strides of his legs.

Aaralynn shrugged into the heavy jacket. It smelled of him. Closing her eyes she inhaled deeply. His scent surrounding her. "Mmmmm." She said to herself.

"You ok?" his voice startled her and she jumped with a squeak. Ash jumped next to her with a bark.

"Yes." She started trying to calm her racing heart, "You scared me." He stood there staring at her intently, scanning her face before turning his attention to Ash. Her face flushed with embarrassment under his scrutinizing eyes.

"Sorry,' he said cautiously. When he was satisfied nothing was really wrong, he went on. "You ready?" After pulled his jacket on he walked to the door and pulled it open for her and Ash. Aaralynn gulped down the lump that had formed in her throat before nodding and walking past him onto the porch.

"You know I never asked but do you have a phone? I never see you use one." His breaths puffing out a white mist as he spoke. Ash walked beside them cautiously scanning the landscape. Aaralynn took in the white snow-covered ground and the fences lining the land. The back of the farmhouse getting bigger the closer they got.

She could understand why he wanted to come back. She was not a snow person by any means but this was beautiful. "No. I used to have one but then it was just easier for my mother to hound me. Now, I simply can't afford it." Her tone was a bit bitter. Most of her life could be described in that one word, bitter.

"Really?" The surprise in his voice had her head turning toward him. "I am not always on mine either but I still have one in case I need it."

"I have never really needed one I guess." She shrugged. It was true. She never had anyone she could call and anytime she needed emergency services other people were around with a phone. There was no reason for her to pay the extra fees for it. "Never really had anyone I could call anyway."

He shook his head as they reached the house. Mumbling under his breath, "we will have to fix that." Her mind was unable to formulate a response. Did he mean the phone or a person to call? Either way, Aaralynn assumed it didn't matter.

The sun was out, and she could hear cows mooing in the distance towards the barn. Just as they reached the stairs and started up them the screen door burst open and an elderly woman came out.

"You're here!" the woman exclaimed. The excitement in her voice had Aaralynn smiling. Kent sported a big smile as well.

"Hi Gran," he said holding out his arms. The woman rushed to him. Kent pulled the elderly woman into him for a fierce hug. His tall frame swallowed her up and Aaralynn could sense the love between the two. A pang of jealousy hit her for a brief moment. The feeling soon replaced with an emptiness she knew would never be filled. A child's need for a parent, someone who is always there no matter what.

"Oh, and who is this lovely creature?" The elderly woman pulled back to turn her bright eyes on Aaralynn. She wiped her hands on her apron and waited patiently.

"Gran this is – "Kent didn't get to finish that statement as Ash bounded up the steps, her tail wagging, and jumped onto Aaralynn to lick her cheek. The woman Kent referred to as Gran shrieked so loud and her hand flying to her chest.

A man came running out of the red barn adjacent to the house at the sound. He charged toward the porch at the same time the front door banged open and three other figures emerged. Aaralynn heard the familiar sound of a gun being cocked back and she instinctively put Ash behind her, blocking her from danger. Ash growled at the sound of the gun but stayed where she was.

"No," Aaralynn got out before Kent stood in front of her, shielding them both.

His hands were out in front of him, palms up. "Austin put the gun down," Kent demanded. "Everyone calm down. There is nothing to get your spurs up about." Aaralynn peaked out from around his large frame and saw the man he was talking to lower the barrel of the rifle. The man had the same grey/ blue eyes and chestnut hair, only his hair was a bit lighter. Aaralynn guessed it was from being out in the sun a lot since his skin was tanner than Kent's. This man was also slightly taller than Kent, but it could be the boots he has on. They were so similar that Aaralynn looked back and forth comparing them as they spoke.

"Kent, what is going on!? And why is there a wolf on the porch!?" The man with the gun demanded.

Kent blew out a breath, running a hand over his head; straightening. His muscles were no longer tense with action. "Nice to see you to brother," Kent's voice was sarcastic and leveling. He wasn't happy but he wasn't exactly mad either. He was just annoyed and alert.

"You didn't answer me," the other man said stating the obvious, "you alright Gran?"

"I'm fine Dear. Just startled is all." Aaralynn turned her gaze to the woman speaking and noticed the other woman had her hand to her chest trying to calm her breathing.

The other people on the porch circled Gran protectively. An elderly man a bit taller than Gran, a slender woman with light auburn hair about Aaralynn's height, the man Kent was talking to and another man taller than all of them but with the same features as Kent. Aralynn guessed he must be related to Kent too.

Kent flexed his hands at his sides as Aaralynn went to move from behind him but Kent bent his arm to hold her in place. "The wolf is here because she is Aaralynn's pet." His statement flat without emotion and she saw everyone turn their expressions of stunned surprise to her.

"Who is Aaralynn?" Austin asked.

With the arm he had around her, Kent pulled her in front of him. "This is Aaralynn and she is my guest. You will treat her dog, Ash as a guest too." He pointed to Ash who sat next to him looking at everyone with interest. Her head turned to the side, mouth open and tongue hanging out from panting. Small droplets of drool dripping onto the floor.

The uncomfortable situation that Kent placed her in had her throat closing up. She didn't do well in the spotlight and he thrust her into it. With a shaky wave of her hand and a simple, "Hello," she had everyone nodding at her in greeting.

Gran came over to where Kent and she stood and she took Aaralynn's hand. Pulling her into a hug and gave her a light squeeze. Gran released her but the other woman's hands remained on her biceps. Both women stood there smiling at one another.

"It has been too long since Kent brought anyone home! Welcome," Gran said in obvious fawning excitement. The other woman's joy was so infectious it was helping to ease some of Aaralynn's anxiety. Taking Aaralynn's arm in hers, Gran led her towards the group of people. Patting her arm with her free hand, Gran nodded her head toward the man standing next to her right, "this is Hugh. He lives on the neighboring ranch." The elderly man tilted his hat to her and Aaralynn nodded in acknowledgment.

"You already met Austin. He's the fussy one with the rifle." Gran waved her hand dismissively toward the man holding the rifle before turning towards the tallest man. "This is Reed. Reed is Kent and Austin's older brother." Reed extended his hand in greeting. Reed's hand was warm in hers. He smiled at her and she smiled back before dropping their hands. "Now this is my daughter in law Annette." Gran beamed at the woman to their left.

"I am not your daughter in law yet Gran. We have a few more days still." Annette turned to Aaralynn, who had her hand outstretched and shook her head. "I don't shake hands," Aaralynn dropped her hand. Annette swooped in and tightly wrapped her arms around her. The hug was welcoming and Aaralynn grateful for it. "Welcome," Annette said as she broke the embrace.

"Thank you," Aaralynn's voice sounded faint even to her own ears. The people in front of her were so friendly and welcoming that it brought tears to her eyes. Turning back to face Ash, Aaralynn blinked them back as best she could before anyone noticed, well almost. Kent took notice and he began rubbing his hand up and down her arm. The motion relaxing the frantic parts in her.

"Now, let's get back inside. I have breakfast out and I don't want my biscuits to burn." When Aaralynn turned back around she saw Gran shooing everyone back inside.

"I'll be in, in a few Gran. I have to finish feeding the horses." Austin said before turning and strutting back toward the barn. The rifle leaning on his shoulder.

When everyone else gathered back inside Kent turned her to face him. Ash hadn't moved from their side and she silently thanked the stars above that nothing bad had happened. She would be lost without that fur ball of hers.

Kent's eyes were solid. Piercing her insides like a silver bullet. He didn't waiver, his gaze roaming her face for any signs of a problem. "You ok to go in?" His tone was light, feeling like a warm blanket to her right now. The chill of the day started to seep into her now that she was coming back to herself. She didn't even notice that she had been starting to shiver until Kent rubbed both her arms.

She wrapped her hands around his, she peeled his off of her arms. With a steady voice, she replied, "Yea. I'm ok. Let's go eat." He nodded and turned to walk inside. His fingers entwining with hers as they went. Ash trotted happily behind them.

****

He wasn't sure if she wouldn't drop his hand, but he was happy when she didn't. Her cold hand eloped in his warm one had tingling sensation running up his arm, and he loved it. Seeing her protectiveness over Ash earlier had him puffing up his chest in pride as his protective instincts kicked in. Out here if a predator comes on the property you take it down. So, he understood why Austin had brought out the rifle, but he also knew his brother wouldn't shoot it unless he needed to.

He saw the shudder of dread just before she shielded the wolf, like she was protecting her child, and essentially Ash is her child. Reassurance washed over him when her fingers laced with his own. Pride bloomed in his chest for his family. They all welcomed her and Ash without judgment. However, Kent didn't miss the reaction she gave to their welcome or their embraces. There was no mistaking that look in her eyes or the unshed tears. It was a mixture of pain, longing, and joy. He wanted to know why but he was smart enough to know the answers would come. He just needed to remain patient.

Walking into his family home, the home where he grew up, a wave of nervousness almost overwhelmed him. *What if she didn't approve of the house or them? Even worse, what if she couldn't stand to be around them?*

The smell of freshly baked biscuits and bread filled the air when they stepped into the entranceway. Ash sat down next to the hallway bench while Kent turned to slide his heavy coat off her shoulders. He didn't miss the way she flinched when he touched her. He felt heat boil inside him at whatever turmoil she must have been through to make her react that way to a simple gesture. The eat was overshadowed by concern. He needed her to understand that he would rather hurt than ever do anything to harm her. She needn't fear him. Something for him to work on with her.

After hanging both their coats, he placed his hand at the small of her back and lead her down the hallway to the kitchen. She examined every room they passed, and he tried to see it through her eyes. Quickly realizing he couldn't because he hadn't grown up as she did. He may not know exactly how she grew up yet but from what he learned so far it was very different.

In the kitchen, everyone stood around the kitchen island, except for Gran who was bending at the stove pulling out the batch of biscuits she made. If Kent knew anything, he knew that wasn't her first batch this morning. Gran placed the hot pan on the counter and turned to face them.

"Sit down you two. Right there," she pointed to two chairs with full plates of food already sat out. Kent pulled out a chair for Aaralynn and waited for her to sit before he sat down next to her. "Oh, poor dear, is that all you have on? You must be chilled to the bone." Gran came to the other side of the counter, already wiping her hands on her apron.

"Let them eat. You can fuss over her later," Reed said. He was standing at the end of the counter to the left of Aaralynn. Leaning over, Reed grabbed a sausage link off a plate just as Gran smacked at his hand. She was shaking her head as he nonchalantly popped it into his mouth. Hugh moved and walked into the dining room off the kitchen. Annette stood on the other side of Reed looking through magazines and smiling at something on the page.

"Well, I hope you two are hungry." Gran turned, pulling out a bowl from an upper cabinet and placed the biscuits in it. Kent eyed Ash as she walked over to where Gran was, to sit staring up at her expectantly. Her black tail wagging back and forth in time with her panting. Kent smiled at the sight. Dogs or cats were never allowed in the house when they were growing up. "Too much of a mess," Gran would say, so the only animals we had stayed out in the barn. He wondered what she would do about this development.

Out of the corner of his eye, he saw Aaralynn staring too but her facial expression was unreadable. Her body, on the other hand, was another matter. Kent had seen people in many situations and knew when someone was ready to jump into action. Aaralynn's body was so tense that when he gently placed a hand on her shoulder she reared back. Her chair skated slightly but none of them missed scraping sound of wood on wood. The noise had all eyes turning to look at them and that is when Gran noticed Ash sitting behind her.

Gran put her hands on her hips trying to feign annoyance. Gran tapped her foot and clucked her tongue, something Gran did a lot when she was thinking. The noise pulled at his heartstrings, reminding him of how grateful he was to be home.

"Now what do you want?" Gran said to Ash tilted her head and closed her mouth at the sound of the woman's voice. Waiting and listening intently. Another bought of clucking before Gran gave an exasperated sigh and threw one of her hands in the air, "Oh, alright." Grabbing one of the biscuits from the bowl, she turned back around, and Ash waved her tail excitedly. "I suppose you want to be fed too," she replied to the wolf as she broke it in half. "Take nice," and Ash gently took the piece from her outstretched hand.

"Hmmm," Gran replied, before handing Ash the other piece. When Ash finished, her eyes looked up at Gran still licking her lips. "No more." The finality of the woman's voice had Ash stretching down in front of her, almost in a bow, then standing up and walking to sit at Aaralynn's feet.

Gran watched until the wolf sat down and saw everyone's eyes on her. Their expressions of surprise, except for Aaralynn, hers was of gratefulness. "What are you all staring at," Gran's voice a bit sterner than her expression, "Eat up. We have things we have to get done today." Gran turned and walked out of the room. As soon as she left, the room broke out in laughter.

Aaralynn sat there eating her food as everyone laughed. Until she understood Gran better, she wouldn't understand what was so funny about what had just happened. When everyone quieted down Kent started eating his food. He said nothing when Aaralynn slipped some sausage to Ash before finishing off her own plate.

Aaralynn leaned in toward him, "Where's the restroom?" she whispered in his ear.

"Just down there," Kent pointed to a hallway beside the staircase. Her gaze traveled from where his finger pointed, back up to his face. Giving a nod she pushed her chair back and stood. Reed stood up straighter, the gentleman he was accustomed to being, and waited for her to move down the hallway.

When Ash began to follow her, she turned, "Stay." Her command firm. Ash immediately sat right back down with a thud staring after her receding form.

"She is lovely," Annette said when Kent heard the bathroom door close.

"Yes, she is," he agreed.

Reed visibly relaxed, leaned over the island, and grabbed a biscuit while Kent polished off his plate. Reed took a bite before speaking, "Where did you find her?" Swallowing down what he had in his mouth, "I leave you alone for a few days and you come back with a girl. Couldn't do this alone?" His eyes were shining with amusement and Kent found himself letting out a slight chuckle.

Pushing back his stool and standing up he slapped Reed on the back, "Well you wouldn't be my date so…" Annette let out a small laugh at that remark while Reed gave a mock offended look. "Really though, it's not like that. I'll explain it later. For now, she is just my guest and so is the furball."

Reed looked like he was going to say something but the noise coming down the stairs had him clamping his mouth closed. A pained look flittered across his face and Kent was going to ask about it but he soon understood why. Kent was surprised to see Molly, his brother's ex-high school girlfriend coming down the stairs with two little girls.

He never knew the whole story of why they broke up, they were pretty serious in high school, but he did know that his brother took a long time getting over it. Kent could never forget the anger that broke into grief for months on end. However, by the look on his brother's face, Reed still hadn't gotten over it. Not long after their breakup, Molly had moved. Kent never did hear why. She was just no longer around.

One of the girls ran over to Annette and jumped on her lap, "Mommy! Mommy!" Annette giggled, hugging her to her chest.

"Yes, munchkin?"

"Can me and Kriss go outside and see the horses?" The little girl's brown hair swayed back and forth as she fidgeted in her mother's lap.

"Please!" Both girls plead in unison.

"Alright, alright," Annette said while laughing. "But I am coming with you." Sliding out of her seat, she grabbed her magazine and closed it.

Kriss was pulling on Molly's hand, leading her toward the front door. "Ok, ok Krissy girl. Calm down." Molly straightened to look at Annette, "You don't have to come if you're busy. I can take them," Kriss was still tugging on Molly's hand.

"It's ok. I could use a break." At that moment Aaralynn walked back into the kitchen and took in the scene.

"Oh," Annette looked at Aaralynn, "Aaralynn? I hope I am saying that right," Annette continued after Aaralynn nodded, "One day you will have to show me how to spell that, but in the meantime, we are going to see the horses with these two darling ladies." Annette gave her daughter's chin a soft caress and Kent saw something in the way Aaralynn watched the embrace. He couldn't put his finger on what it was, but it tugged at his manly instincts. Something deep inside him wanted to pull her into his arms but by sheer will, he stayed where he was.

"Would you like to join us?" Annette queried, looking up at her.

Annette's daughter ran over to Aaralynn and tugged on her hand, "Oh please say yes!" Now Kent

knew what he saw. It was longing. He could see it like
a tiny wish floating from her very being. Unable to
see it, he averted his eyes. His gaze falling on Reed
who in turn was staring at Molly, but Molly was
focused on Kriss. Kent wasn't sure if Molly was
intentionally ignoring Reed or if she was unaware of
Reed staring. Kent decided that either way it was his
brother's business and he knew Reed wouldn't share.
His brother had always been tight-lipped about his
affairs.

Kent faced Aaralynn when he heard the crack
in her voice croak out, "I'd love to." She blinked back
tears while smiling.

The little girl jumped up and down with
giddiness. "My name's Holly, what's yours?"

"Aaralynn."

"Ayrwynn?" The little girl tried to get out.
Holly didn't quite say it right, her nose curling with
the effort. Her little brain trying to figure out what she
said wrong.

"Air-Ah-Lynn," she prompted. Aaralynn
leaning over to be eye level with Holly. When Holly
tried again and Kriss joined in but they both still
didn't get it right Aaralynn smirked and said, "You
two can just call me Lynn." Both girls tried that tittle
and got it right, so they all decided to use that instead.

"Oh, how rude of me," Annette hit her hand on
her forehead, "This is Molly," lifting her hand toward
the other woman, "and this is Krissaline, Kriss for
short." Swinging her arm toward the little girl holding
Molly's hand.

"Nice to meet you," Molly said. Kriss wanting
to just get out the door replied, "We already met."

"Alright girls, you need to put on your coats before going out," Annette instructed as she and Molly ushered the kids down the hallway.

Aaralynn was left standing in the kitchen. She walked over to Kent, "You ok if I go outside?" Her eyes searching his for any sign of a no. He didn't need to give her any approval to go do what she wanted but he liked that she asked anyway.

Gently shaking his head, "Of course. Go have some fun." He squeezed her hand, tilting his lip in a smile. A tightness in his chest eased when she squeezed back, mirroring his smile. Kent placed a quick kiss on her forehead. Aaralynn glanced at Reed. A small blush crept into her cheeks before she turned and walked down the hallway. With a snap of her fingers, Ash got up and followed. *Smart dog*, he thought.

When Kent turned to pick up their plates, he saw Reed staring at him. Questions filled his eyes and he knew a conversation would ensue just before Reed said, "So spill."

****

Chapter 9

So many emotions filled Aaralynn that she wasn't sure what to do with herself. She had felt happy, sad, awkward, horny, helpful, helpless, hopeless, hopeful, scared, nervous and so many other emotions she wasn't sure she could name. In such a short amount of time, her mind and body felt like they were on a roller-coaster caught in a tornado. Now being outside, watching the two little girls interact with the horses she was jealous yet again.

She had always wanted a child or maybe more but to do that she had to have a man. Well, in today's society she didn't have to have one to have a baby, but her personal preference was to have one. She may desire family and stability but, in her experience, she had never been able to obtain it.

It was at least nice to see it, even from afar. Children enjoying their time with their parents and no one was fighting. To her, it was a perfect day. The weather, not so much. Although the dusting of snow on the ground was pretty for the landscape, it was not conducive to her wardrobe. *She was freezing! Why couldn't Kent's family live in Tahiti or somewhere closer to the equator?* A tremor wracked through her when a cold breeze blew down the jacket she wore. It reminded her of the pending shopping trip.

"They really do love dragging us around, don't they?" Molly said to Annette as they walked up to Aaralynn. Both women catching their breath from chasing the girls around the barn.

"I know. At least I never have to worry about a gym." Annette brushed her hair out of her face and turned, smiling at her. "Do you have any kids?"

Aaralynn wrapped her arms around herself to try to fight off the chilly air, "No." She rubbed her arms and shifted her feet. "Ash is my only kid and she really acts more like a teenager than a toddler."

All three women stood looking at the two toddlers standing on a stool to see into Solitaire's stall. Annette explained Solitaire was Austin's horse, who impregnated one of Hugh's mare's as part of a business deal. The two girls were giggling because Solitaire was rubbing his nose against their hands. True to her word, Ash was sitting on the floor next to them watching, wanting in on the action. Tired of waiting, Ash hopped up on her hind legs, her paws resting on the stall door, lifted her nose to lick the horse's nose. Solitaire whinnied and pushed his nose into Ash, effectively knocking Ash over. Both women and children busted out laughing.

"You weren't kidding," Molly said breathlessly.

Strands of hair blew into Aaralynn's eyes and she brushed them away. The smell of hay, dirt, and horse stronger as she took a few calming breaths. "So how old are your kids?"

"Well, Holly is four. She just turned four in August."

"And Kriss is my niece, not my daughter but she is Holly's age. She will be turning five next month."

"Oh," Aaralynn didn't know what else to say to this new information. She was glad when Molly spoke instead.

"My sister passed away two years ago, and I was her legal guardian. I have been raising her ever since." A look of love and devotion as Molly watched at the two girls. Aaralynn felt compassion towards the woman. Her selfless act was refreshing to witness.

"What about your parents?" She knew she shouldn't pry, and Annette still didn't say anything, just watched the girls but Aaralynn couldn't help herself.

Molly let out a long expanse of air. Maybe asking wasn't the right thing to do. "You don't have to answer if you don't want to. I'm sorry. I shouldn't have pried." The words spilled out of her mouth so fast she felt them running through her head even after she had finished. The hum of her voice still in her ears.

"No. It's ok." Molly gave her a brief glance before turning her eyes back to Kriss. "It would just be easier to tell the whole world once, so I don't always have to repeat it, you know?" Aaralynn nodded her head in agreement but she wasn't sure if Molly saw it. Annette patted Molly's shoulder before going over to where the girls were. Ash was sitting down wagging her tail. "My parents were not the happy go lucky kind. They always argued. Even when they would get along, which wasn't often, they would yell at each other." Molly ran a hand through her hair. The motion looked pained and she saw a tear run down her cheek before wiping it away.

Aaralynn was never good with comforting, it always gave her a funny feeling like she was helpless. So, when she rubbed Molly's back it felt odd, but she hoped it comforted her. The shimmering of Molly's eyes tugged at her heart because she also knew what a broken home felt like.

"One night they had another long fight, except this time when dad got in the car to blow off some steam, mom followed him. Dad usually drove around for an hour or so after their fights to calm himself down." Molly was taking in some shaky breaths, but no more tears fell. When their eyes met, Molly quickly looked at the floor. Her focus on something invisible on the stone surface. "I guess they kept fighting and didn't pay attention to the eighteen-wheeler coming down the other lane." The crack in her voice at the end had tears coming to Aaralynn's eyes. She couldn't imagine how hard it must have been to get news like that.

Trying to keep the sullen mood out of her voice and failing at it, Aaralynn asked, "How old were you?"

A small sniffle made her chest ache. The feeling of her heartbreaking a little, "I was 17 and my sister was 15." Molly wiped her nose with her sleeve, "Our grandmother took us in even though she was already pushing seventy-six. I was just glad I was as old as I was because with her health problems there was no way she could have kept up with small children."

"Aunt M," Kriss yelled, "Can I get a pony?"

Already shaking her head," No Krissy girl. Sorry. We don't have room for a pony." The little girl frowned but turned back to pet the pony in front of her. Soon, giggling floated to the two women. For Aaralynn, it was like being wrapped in a warm blanket after being out in the snow.

After their interruption, Molly didn't say anymore and Aaralynn just let the topic drop. She figured it was hard enough talking about it that she wasn't going to ask anything else. All three women walked around with the little girls and let them pet all the other horses before walking back out of the barn. They walked past a pasture with cows and steers dotting the countryside. Soft sounds of mooing came and went.

Annette walked them over to where the other big barn was. Annette explained this was going to be the sight of the wedding. It had been cleared out already and they had people coming in tomorrow to start setting up. The huge red and white barn was open when they walked in. The smell of wood, straw, and hay all mingled together. The aroma was both pleasing and calming. Four big pillars spaced out with a staircase that went up to a big balcony/ loft area. It was a perfect place for a venue.

"There are no stalls?" Aaralynn asked. She thought barns always had stalls for animals.

Annette chuckled, "they don't have stalls in here because this is a livestock or storage barn. They usually store hay, straw, or feed in here. Sometimes they would put livestock like sheep or goats if they needed too but the McPherson's don't use it for that."

"Oh." She had never had a barn before. She couldn't even remember ever being in one before, so this was a new experience for her. The smell and feel of being in one was a welcome unfamiliarity to her. Shrugging her shoulders, she walked around the floor.

She watched as Molly played a game with the little girls. At least she thought it looked like a game. The girls were running around in circles and going up and down the stairs while Molly covered her eyes and counted before bolting after them. Ash was running around them in circles. Barking every once in a while, when they would get too loud.

She jumped and placed a hand over her rapidly beating heart at Annette's voice behind her. "Sorry. Didn't mean to startle you," the other woman said.

"No problem," she got out around a few breaths of air.

"I was saying," she started, "the bar will be set up over there." Annette pointed to the far right of the room. "The stage will be right there," gesturing towards the back of the space, just under the balcony area. "The tables and food will be upstairs. The floor will be cleared for the ceremony and will be the dance floor for after."

"That sounds wonderful. It probably saves you some money too not having to find a place and pay for all their fees." Ash ran over to her and sat down, leaning into her leg. Without thinking about it Aaralynn rubbed her head just like she always did. The weight of the animal got heavier as Ash relaxed into her.

"At least it saved me some headache. I don't like planning these things. Gran has been great at helping. Unlike her grandson. Ugh, men." Annette smiled and rolled her eyes causing Aaralynn to let out a giggle of laughter. "Austin has been no help. He acts like an ostrich as soon as you ask about wedding details. If we lived near sand, he probably would literately shove his head in it."

"Typical men," Molly said as she walked up. The two girls were now chasing each other around in a giant circle. "Sorry, I caught the tail end of that."

"Tail end of what?" A deep male voice spoke over them. The familiarity of it had heat pooling in her stomach and she knew who it was before she turned. Kent walked in with Reed and Austin.

"Daddy," Holly squealed before running over and jumping on the man. He pretended she knocked him over with the movement and landed lightly on the floor. Aaralynn could tell he adored the little girl just as much as she did him and she got a slight pang in her chest at the scene.

Reed strode over to talk to Molly, who turned and picked up Kriss. Before Reed could speak, Molly brushed past him; leaving him to trail behind her. Molly didn't look happy as Reed and she walked out of the barn.

"You didn't answer me," Kent said, pulling her gaze back to his handsome face. *Handsome? Where did that come from?* Oh, who was she kidding, he was downright sexy to her.

"What," her voice soft and breathless like she had run a mile. *Get a grip girl*, she chided herself. She looked around but must have missed it when Annette left her alone. The other woman was now where Austin and Holly were, hugging them both.

"The tail end of what?"

Kent was staring at her, waiting patiently for an answer. Uncomfortable under his assessing eyes, she fidgeted her hands and feet before answering, "Oh. Annette was telling me about the plans for the wedding and Molly had walked over." His smile was making her stomach do flips and she wasn't quite sure she liked the effort this man had on her.

"Mmmm," was his response. Unable to help herself, her eyes roamed over his face. A hint of a shadow showing on his chin and a vein in his neck pulsing rapidly. Getting a sudden urge to lick it. Her eyes snapped back to his face. What she saw had any embarrassment fading and her breath catching. His eyes were deep pools that look like the beginning of a storm. The irises seem to have gotten darker and he twined one of his hands with hers. His thumb rubbing the back of her hand in lazy circles.

His eyes fell to her lips. She wondered if he would taste as good as the first time, he kissed her. Her tongue darted out to lick her bottom lip before sucking it into her mouth and releasing it. *Did he just growl?*

"So," she began but the words cut off as his mouth descended on hers so fiercely, she forgot how to breathe. She leaned into him without thought, deepening the kiss. He felt so right that she could stay in this moment with him forever and the thought terrified her so much she abruptly pulled back. Kent looked stunned. His face searching hers. If he was hurt by her retreat, he said nothing about it.

"So, what are you guys up to?" Attempting to veer the conversation away from the now awkward situation. There was no way she would be able to explain it when she was not sure of her own reactions.

Kent cleared his throat. His hand, still holding hers, was warm and clammy. The feeling of being linked to him easing her tension and holding her back from releasing him. "I was coming to ask if you were ready to go into town? Austin is going to the feed store with Reed and I got asked to take the women into town to do some wedding shopping. I figured I would bring you along and we could go to the store after."

"Sounds good to me." The smile she was getting used to seeing was back on those wonderfully delicious lips of his.

He tilted his head towards the doors and said, "Come on let's go." Nodding she whistled and Ash stood up with a bark. Tugging on her hand, she let him lead her out, back into the cold air with Ash leading the way.

****

The ride into town was full of chatter that her head hurting by the time they reached the town limits. Not paying attention to the conversation she merely closed her eyes to try to dull her aching head. She sat up front next to Kent. He hadn't even asked her to, he just pulled her around to the side of the car and opened the door for her. Giving her no other option but to slide into the passenger seat. She would have rather of given it to Gran, who was slow getting in and out of the car but that was not Kent's plan. Ash got left behind at the cottage. At first, she thought Ash would've had a fit. Instead, she just curled up on the couch and fell asleep. Seems her pup was even more comfortable at the place then she anticipated.

The more time she spent in the family's presence the more she knew it would hurt when it was time to go. She was liking these people and leaving didn't seem like it happened often. Her life wasn't in Montana though. It was in Baltimore, at least right now and she didn't see that changing anytime soon. Kent leaned over, squeezing her hand just as they pulled into a parking spot in front of a bridal shop. She belligerently opened her eyes. Blinking a few times and rubbing her temples. The small quaint town was built around a strip of storefront shops. All the shops were either stone or looked like old-fashioned houses. It was adorable and colorful.

"Alright ladies, we are here." Kent turned off the engine and got out. He came over to her door before she could open it and did it for her, extending his hand to help her up. "You enjoy your nap?"

"Yes. Thank you." She wasn't used to anyone helping her out of a vehicle and it felt off but nice. She wanted to melt into the smile he gave her. Instead, she moved out of the way so he could close the door before going to the next door and helping out Gran and the other females.

"Kent, we will call you when we are ready to leave," Annette said before turning to walk on the sidewalk. The other women following behind.

"Ok," he said after her, "Are you ready to go shopping?" Kent said to Aaralynn.

"Ye-" she began to reply but Annette cut her off.

"Aren't you coming with us?"

Was she supposed to? This was a planned wedding trip and she didn't think she was included in that. Not sure if she could handle mere chatter. Her headache was receding, but she also didn't want it to come back. "I was planning to go get some suitable clothes with Kent." Aaralynn waved her hands up and down in front of herself, "I didn't know you expected me to come with."

"I need all the input I can get," Annette walked over to her, ignoring her awkwardness and looped her arm through Aaralynns', "You can go shopping once we are all done in the bridal shop," Annette said without any room for an argument. Before she could try to protest, Aaralynn was being pulled towards the sidewalk and the bridal shop.

She mouthed "sorry" to Kent as she was dragged away. "Now you go do what you need to. We will call in a bit."

Kent just nodded his head at Annette and gave Aaralynn a sly smile and disappointed look with his eyes before she was pulled into the group of women already walking into the shop. The shop was filled with dresses. All kinds. From outside it looks like little houses, but it turns out that two houses were combined into one shop, with three floors. Annette explained that the first floor had casual, evening, and bridesmaid's dresses with accessories. The second floor was the bridal dresses. Although, Aaralynn thought the first floor should have had those. Bridal dresses weight a ton in her opinion and having to drag them up and downstairs must be grueling. The third floor had tailoring. Next door was the hairdresser, which is where the bride was going next. Aaralynn figured she would go shopping while the group of women went to do that.

Annette said they were not having bridesmaids or best men. Only Holly, who was going to walk down the aisle with the rings as they said their vows. Annette wanted the wedding as simple as possible and she didn't have any family to have their anyway. Aaralynn could relate to that too. The women chatted amongst themselves in hushed voices as they filed upstairs for the last fitting appointment before the seamstress finished and she could pick up her dress.

All the women sat around in a semi-circle on the top floor waiting for the curtain to be drawn back so they could see the bride. Gran was talking to Molly about Kent and if he would be moving back home or not while she was flipping through a bridal magazine.

"I thought Kent was on leave?" Aaralynn questioned, still flipping through a wedding magazine but not paying attention to it anymore. Now she was more interested in what the two women were discussing.

Gran clucked her tongue, "he is," she confirmed, "but he could also retire. He has been serving for almost two decades now and I would like it if my boy got to settle down soon. He is always on the move, taking care of everyone else. I think it would do him good if he took care of himself for once."

Interesting, she thought to herself. *Apparently, Kent was more of a gentleman than the men she had been around from the sounds of it.* "So, he could get out if he wanted to?"

Molly said nothing. She looked to be half-listening; half distracted. Lost in her own world.

"He could," Gran agreed. "If he had someone waiting on him, other than me," she added, "he might stay around. Lord knows I have asked that boy over and over why he doesn't stay home but he just says his men need him." Her tongue clucking again.

"You think the girls are ok with Hugh and Cliff while we are gone?" Molly interjected out of the blue just as the curtain drew back. Revealing a stunning Annette. Her ivory lace wedding gown was an off the shoulder drop waist fit with bell sleeves that had cut-outs on the shoulders. The hem fell to about her mid-calf. The seamstress was walking around her repeatedly to make sure there was nothing else wrong with the dress.

"You are gorgeous," Aaralynn said in awe.

"Absolutely stunning," Molly stated. Aaralynn noticed shimmering in the other woman's eyes. Tears that glimmered with something she couldn't place.

Aaralynn nodded her head, "Austin won't know what hit him." Turning her focus back to the bride.

"You ladies took the words right out of my mouth," Gran chimed in last.

Annette just giggled and beamed as she looked down at herself. "Thank you, ladies. You think it will look ok with my boots on?" Without hesitation, all the women agreed in unison. Molly wiped away at the tears that slipped. A concerned look on her face that Gran and Aaralynn noticed.

The older woman patted Molly's leg, "The kids will be just fine. I am sure they will be feeding them lots of junk food and wear them out by the time we get back." Molly eased back in her seat and turned her attention back to Annette. The concerned look no longer on her face.

"Agreed," Annette said after her. "I bet we will have a mess to deal with when we get home."

"I will give you all a minute while I go check on another order real quick." The seamstress said before standing up and backing out of the room.

All three women stood up to watch as Annette turned this way and that in front of the tall mirror. Each one giving her compliments and encouragement. Aaralynn wondered if this is what it felt like to be a part of a family and have siblings because if it was, she loved it.

"You will be a beautiful bride," Aaralynn said as she watched Annette do another twirl.

"Thank you," Annette said taking her hands. "I am glad you are here. From what I have heard Kent has had a hard time and he needs someone around that will make it better."

Aaralynn gave a halfhearted laugh, "I don't think I make it better or easier for him, and I am only here for a short while." Aaralynn was highly surprised when Annette took her in her arms for a big hug. The other woman's smile didn't falter at all.

"Either way, I am still glad you are here. And I know Kent is by the way he looks at you." They both pulled apart and Aaralynn could see the sincerity in the other woman's face.

"I agree with her," Molly spoke up this time, "He does look happy. Almost like he did when we were younger."

"I bet he is like that with a lot of people," Aaralynn responded shyly. Not sure if she was more uncomfortable or excited at the thought that she had an impact on the man she had begun to have deep feelings toward.

"No." Gran's voice was sad but hopeful.

"The last girlfriend he had; he wasn't happy with?" confusion lacing her voice.

"I haven't heard of him seeing anyone in years. He barely comes home and when he does he is alone." Gran clucked her tongue again, "I haven't seen him with a girl since high school, come to think of it."

Aaralynn blushed slightly, as her heart fluttered in her chest. Excitement overcoming the unease of the conversation. "Oh!" Annette suddenly squeaked. "I have an idea."

"Uh-oh," Molly replied as Annette grabbed Aaralynn's hands.

"You need to get clothes which means you don't have anything to wear to the wedding." The other woman was so excited that she was practically jumping with joy, "you can get a dress while we are here. Everyone else already went shopping. This way we can spoil you, I get to play dress up and who knows maybe we will surprise Kent too."

All the women murmured their agreement. Chatting around her before she could even protest. Not that she would know how to protest but the idea of surprising Kent had her a bit antsy, hopefully in a good way.

****

Chapter 10

Kent had already gone to the store, put the bags in the car, and was at the feed store with Austin and Reed. The men were going over how much the feed prices had gone up and how the negotiation part of crops was not like it used to be. He wasn't much of a numbers man, being more of a man of action, he tuned out their conversation for the most part. One person he couldn't tune out was Aaralynn and it made him uneasy. He couldn't understand how in such a short time the woman had caught his undivided attention. He wondered if he had the same effect on her. Sometimes he thought so by how she would smile at him but then others she seemed to pull back. The woman was an enigma.

But what did it matter? He was leaving in a month. Going back to his job, his life, and he wouldn't see her again. Wasn't he? Wouldn't he? This paradox of feelings wasn't something he was used to. He made a plan and stuck to it even if the circumstances changed. Besides, she wouldn't want the mess he had become. He barely sleeps and when he does it usually was filled with reenacting nightmares of what went wrong with Jason, his best friend, and brother in arms. Kent blamed himself, only wishing he could make it right. Aaralyn didn't need him. She deserved better. She deserved a man who would be there and do right by her.

He was rubbing the scar of a bullet hole on his shoulder, trying to forget the past when his phone buzzed. Pulling it out of his pocket he read the message from Annette saying they were finished. His brothers debating when he strode over to them. Quickly he told them he had to go pick up Aaralynn and that the girls were wrapping up. His brothers gave him an odd smile like they knew something he didn't. Instead of wasting time trying to get it out of them, he just shrugged and walked out the door. Kent didn't care what their opinions are.

Aaralynn was waiting by herself outside the bridal shop. She was holding open the door for an elderly couple and what he assumed was their granddaughter. The door shut with a soft click when he reached her. The brightness of her smile radiated to his very core and made him almost trip. *Maybe she could cure his demons*. Kent shook his head side to side. *No, that was nonsense*, he told himself.

"You ready to go?" His voice was off even to his own ears. Un help what this woman did to him.

"Yup. The girls are at the hair salon now. Annette wanted to try out a few more hairstyles before she picked one." A few strands fell out of her ponytail and were dangling in the cool breeze. She brushed the strands back out of her eyes. "Do you think it will snow again?" She rubbed her arms through the fabric of the coat.

Holding out his arm to her, "Most likely. It snows more often during this time of year." Taking his arm, he walked her down the sidewalk and across the street to the Dames and Duds clothing store. It wasn't fancy but they had everything a sensible person would need, and their prices are fair. Aaralynn didn't say one word till they reached the doors and he held one open for her.

"I don't have a lot so maybe just a pair of jeans and a sweater."

"Don't worry about it. I got it." He placed his hand to the small of her back and eased her inside.

She stopped before passing him and said, "I am not letting you buy me a ton of clothes Mr." The firmness of her mouth and the furrow of lines around her eyebrows made her more attractive to him.

"I brought you all the way out here. The least I could do is make sure you have the right clothes." He began walking in after her, effectively easing her inside all the way too. She went to protest again but he held up his hand. "Not another word about it. If you won't pick out clothes, then I will just have to do it for you."

She blew out a frustrated whoosh of air in answer and Kent knew he had won this debate. He wasn't sure how shopping with her would go but he wasn't prepared for it to be easy. He had shopped before with his cousin and his Gran, but they had been very picky. Compared to those women Aaralynn might prove to be simpler and even a bit of a tomboy. She didn't try on tons of clothes, nor hang out at the makeup or bag section. She walked right over to the jeans, the only article of clothing she tried on, and then over to the sweaters. He went to look at the belts and hats giving her some time.

Aaralynn didn't seem to like company while she was shopping. She seemed to do better when she was on her own and he didn't mind. She asked his opinion on two different shirts and that was the extent of his input. After twenty minutes, she had a basket full of sweaters, shirts, and jeans. The cart squeaked as she strolled over to where he was.

"I like that on you," she pointed to the charcoal grey cowboy hat he had on, "It looks sexy." The wiggle of her eyebrows had a laugh escaping his lips. *Damn*, she made his insides explode with warmth.

"You think so?" He pulled her in his arms and tilted his head down to hers. Her eyes became the size of saucers at the unexpected embrace, but he felt the moment she relaxed in his hold.

"Yea," her voice almost a purr.

"Uh, huh" his eyes lowered to her lips. He was just about to ease down and claim them when her hands came up. Pushing against his chest. He released her but didn't back up.

"Such a tease Kent."

"I don't have to be darling." He drawled, knowing she would react to it. He wasn't disappointed. A flush crept to her face almost immediately and she averted her eyes.

He took the hat off his head, teasing it into the cart too. Aaralynn pulled a deep burgundy red one off the rack and slid it on her head. The cowboy hat fit her perfectly. Her bright red, almost orange wavy hair a beautiful contrast to the deep red of the hat. It made her green eyes stand out with such brilliance that Kent couldn't look away.

She twirled around in front of the tiny mirror on the hat stand, "Beautiful," he spoke breathlessly.

Aaralynn hands came up to move the hat to different angles on her head. The way she moved had him watching more closely. The lines of her legs and her curves had a bit extra. He liked how she filled out everywhere. He wasn't into stick figures and knowing she was comfortable with who she was, only attracted him to her more. She may not always be confident in her self image, he noticed she faltered sometimes, but he didn't mind that. No one was always happy with themselves one hundred percent of the time. He knew he wasn't.

Satisfied with the hat she took it off and added it to the pile in the basket. Kent watched as Aaralynn tried on a deep green crochet beanie and threw that in the cart too. Walking over to the belts, Aaralynn following close behind him. Kent inspected a few and she pulled down two to place in the cart. He was still browsing when she took a belt that matched the hat, he tossed in the cart earlier and held it up to his waist. The buckle was big and had a big bold letter K surrounded by swirling designs.

"This one," she said simply. Like it was the easiest thing.

Her beautiful eyes looked up to his. His body unable to suppress the goofy grin that dawned his face. He couldn't say no to this woman. It just wasn't possible. The next thing he knew he nodded, and she was placing it in the basket. Looping a finger through a belt loop, Kent adjusted himself in his jeans. *What happened to his backbone?* He guessed he longer had one when it came to her.

"I think I am all done." A slight tug on her hand when she turned to go to the register had her swinging back around. That was when she noticed his fingers entwined with her own. "Nope. You need a coat." His hand unlaced from hers to slide up her arm. Lightly gripping her bicep, he attempted to walk her to the coat section.

Aaralynn dug her feet into the wood floor as best she could, and he turned to face her again. "I already picked out one earlier." Quickly, she sorted through the basket after he released her arm and she pulled out a thick suede coat with a sheepskin and wool inlay. *Nice.*

Smiling she turned back towards the register and he followed with the cart. Kent told her to wait by the door while he rang everything up. He just didn't want to hear her protesting when he asked the clerk to also ring up another jacket and three more pairs of pants for her. He didn't pay attention to what she had bought or the total price, he just knew he didn't want her to run out of anything she may need. Adding a few extra pairs of socks and a pair of gloves that matched the coat. He waited patiently for his total. When it was all finished and paid for, he took Aaralynn to his vehicle and dropped all the bags in the back.

Gran and the other two ladies were on their way back to the car just as he shut the trunk. Annette was all smiles while they chatted about different flowers and color schemes when they came up to them.

"Kent dear, me and the girls are going to the store to grab some things for dinner. Do you mind waiting a few more minutes?" Gran asked.

"Not at all. I was just going to ask if you minded we take a few more minutes," he waved his hand towards Aaralynn, "I need to get this lady some boots still."

From the corner of his eye, he saw Aaralynn whip her head in his direction. He could imagine the look she gave him. Smiling to himself, he figured she had forgotten. "Perfect," Gran said and he granted himself a look beside him. Aaralynn had a frown on her face and her eyebrows drew together. She was looking at her shoes and back up at him. Her body tense. Her gaze set on Gran when she said, "she will need them. Lord knows around here those sneakers on her feet will freeze when they get wet."

The two other women both mumbled agreements. He heard a release of air beside him and knew she had given up under their discussion of her shoes. Kent grinned when he heard "fine," come from her tight lips.

The women left them then, on their way to the general store down a few buildings. Kent took hold of Aaralynn's hand and twined their fingers, pulling her towards the Rust and Dust Boot Outfitters. The smell of hides and leather mixed with metal was always a greeting to his senses. Next-door was an armory and outside of town, they had a military surplus store where he got his first rifle when he was 16. Well, he didn't buy it. Gran had taken him. The memory of Reed helping him pick it out always brought nostalgic feelings.

Aaralynn looked like she felt out of place in this store. She was shifting from foot to foot and playing with the hem of her shirt. She was moving the zipper on the jacket up and down seemingly lost in thought. He would be amused at her childish demeanor, but she didn't look like she would find his amusement funny. So, he bit his tongue.

"Well," he began, "We should probably get you a pair of heavy boots or sneakers. Oh, and a pair of riding boots." He started walking towards the aisle of boots for women but he stopped when he realized she still hadn't moved from her spot at the door. Kent held out a hand to her, waving her over but when she still hadn't moved, he walked back over to her.

Bringing his face down to hers so no one else could hear, he gently asked, "Are you ok?" When she failed to reply, he remarked, "Hey," Trying to soothe her slight trembling by wrapping her in his arms. "It's ok. It's just a shoe store." Resting his chin on her head he breathed in the scent of her hair. She smelled like flowers and honey.

He felt it when her muscles relaxed, and she leaned into him. Her arms came up to grab handfuls of his jacket and he heard her sharp intake of breath. His own body getting tense over her emotional response. *What in the world had caused this reaction from her?*

"Sorry," she whispered into his chest. Her voice a bit muffled from her face buried against him.

"Nothing to be sorry about," he pulled back. enough to see her. His hand slid under her chin, tilting her head up for him to look at her face. "Are you ready?" He cooed. His voice dropping an octave and smooth as honey.

She nodded without a word and placed her hand in his. His lips brushed against her forehead in a gentle caress. Dropping his hand from her chin Kent lead her down the aisle of shoes. He crouched down in front of her, staring at her wonderfully full legs, as she pulled a pair of boots off a shelf and sat on a stool. The boots are grey and red, a perfect color for her.

Minutes of her not meeting his eyes passed before she finally spoke to him. "Sorry about earlier," her hands gripping tight around the top of one boot, trying to push her foot in. "I didn't mean to have a breakdown. Just had a bad memory."

Aaralynn stood up when she got her foot in all the way. Standing she took a few steps and turned back to sit back down. The whole time she never met his eyes and he never moved from his position next to the stool. Giving the boots a hard stare, Kent wanted to know what was going through her head. He didn't know what to say to her confession and he figured the best thing to do in that situation was not say anything.

"My ex-boyfriend, Cory, worked at a shoe store." Her voice was devoid of emotion. The flatness of it made it seem like this was just an everyday fact she was talking about and not an interictal part of her life. "I was with him for three years! That whole time I didn't notice that he was just using me." Kent's jaw clenched, as he ground his back teeth. Aaralynn looked like she wanted to cry and hit something at the same time. "I was so stupid." The words came out so softly, he knew she was saying them more to herself than to him.

Aaralynn slowly pulled off the boots and put them back in the box. "He had cheated on me so many times it was ridiculous. Thank goodness I always used a condom with him," her green eyes shot to his with her confession and surprise etched her features. Kent shook his head and tried to relax his jaw because if he didn't he was going to break some teeth. "He always talked about me losing weight and how to eat. He would talk to other women with me around and appraise them. I never said anything because I thought that was just how he was. I was very naive and young."

She blew out a breath and handed over the box with the boots in them. Kent took them but wasn't moving to get up and neither did she. A glimpse of unshed tears shimmered in her eyes just before she turned her focus to the shelves of shoes.

"One day he came into the bar, drunk, with another woman. I was unaware of this when I went to wait on his table. I walk up to see his hands on her ass, her on his lap, dry humping him through his clothes." Kent felt his body shake and tremble with all the rage he produced. The urge to hit something coming in bucket loads now. How could a man do that to a woman? He had seen some of the men in his unit get crushed by their significant others cheating while they were deployed and he had also seen some of his men do the same with nurses while they were deployed, but he had never once thought of doing it. *Why cause someone pain? If you care about someone, wouldn't it also cause yourself pain too?*

"By the time he saw me, he just smiled and started to give the woman a hickey on her neck." He heard a sniffle and lifted his eyes. She was still looking at everything but him, only now there were tears silently rolling down her cheeks. He wished he could find Cory and kill him. Maybe he would. "Ray saw and he hauled him up out of his seat. Tony took him outside and beat the crap out of him for it," a slight smile hit her lips. Well, he would have to give Tony some props but that is where his likeness of the man ended. "I didn't tell Ray all the things he said when he saw me the next day though."

Her eyes fluttered to meet his then. All the air in the room was sucked out of him at her forlorn expression. Her jaw tightened, and she seemed to be chewing on the inside of her cheek. Those streaks down her cheeks left blotchy red marks. Kneeling in front of her, his hands came up and cupped her cheeks. She closed her eyes and leaned into his touch.

"He was an asshole." Knowing the words is not going to solve it but he had to state the obvious. "It was his loss. You are better than what he deserves."

The slight smile she tried to bring to her lips failed. His thumb caressed her cheek as she sniffled. Even with her eyes shut, red streaks marking her flushed cheeks, and her hair falling from its ponytail she was still the most stunning human being he had ever seen. He was sure he was falling for her or maybe he already had.

"I'm not worth anything more than what my body can give. That was even *shotty*, in his opinion," her fingers air quoted the *shotty* part. "He also mentioned he got that woman pregnant and he had been with her for months before I found out." The tears had stopped rolling down her cheeks and she took in a shuttered breath. "As if dealing with my mother wasn't hard enough, it also turned out that he had slept with her when she visited my apartment. He was horny and she needed money. He rubbed it in my face that she was able to do things I wasn't. my own mother!" When her eyes opened, she looked so crestfallen and alone.

****

Aaralynn didn't know why she felt the need to explain her problems right here in the middle of a shoe aisle for everyone to overhear. She just knew she had an urge to explain, to get it off her chest. Her reaction earlier had stirred up old emotions that she thought she had gotten rid of but must have just been buried. By the way, Kent was breathing so harshly, and clenching his jaw like he could chew nails had her wanting to tell him. She needed to tell someone. And now that she had, now that tears had spilled, she felt relieved to get it out.

Kent's hardened face and steel grey eyes were telling her that he wished he had been the one to take Cory outside. Knowing that he would protect her from it all if given the chance had her warming to the idea that she was having deeper feelings for him then she first thought.

"I do not know your ex or your mother, but I will say they are obviously off their meds. There is nothing wrong with you." She felt the sincerity in his words. He was one of a kind. Kent leaned in to brush his lips across hers before placing another kiss on her forehead. His fingers, strong and sturdy, at the back of her neck, felt nice. He brought his forehead down to touch hers and their breaths mingled. The deep baritone of his voice resonated through her with firm softness. "You should wait for a man who would be willing to take on the world for you. You deserve it," he drawled.

The deep twang in his voice mixed with the meaning of his words had her insides coiling. Her body hummed with the need to pull him into her. To melt their bodies together. She couldn't do that though. They were in the middle of a store and it would be highly inappropriate.

"Come on," he said when she didn't speak. "Let's get your boots." His arm wrapped around her shoulder when they stood. His other arm holding the box she had handed him. After another Thirty minutes of trying on three pairs of heavy-duty boots, she chose a black pair that was for all seasons. He paid and they left. Kent holding the bags in one hand and her hand in the other as they made their way, down the sidewalk.

It felt right having him next to her, but she couldn't get the thoughts out of her mind that this was just temporary. Her heart craved for it to be longer, telling her this was the beginning of something, but her mind was trying to be practical. *He wouldn't want you anyhow*, her mind chimed in, *surely not after everything you just unloaded on him. And that wasn't even all of it.* To give him credit though he didn't shy away from what she had said. Maybe he would stick around.

"You two get lost?" Annette said when they reached the car and all the women were standing around waiting.

"Sorry ladies," Kent said while opening the trunk of the car again to put the groceries and his bags in the back. "This one right here takes a while picking out shoes but you ladies should know what that is like. Isn't it a prerequisite to being a woman?" At his teasing tone, Molly and Annette batted his arm, while Gran clucked her tongue and Aaralynn gave him an amused look. She was trying hard not to laugh but failed when he turned to her with a playfully pained look on his face from being swatted.

"You are incorrigible," Molly joked.

Annette was still trying to be mad, "Don't make me sick Austin on you."

Gran stopped clucking her tongue to voice her opinion, "If you are done messing around my old bones would like to get out of this chill."

With that statement, Kent rushed getting the rest of the things in the car and helped Gran into the car to warm up. He waited for the other two women to slide in before closing the door and opening Aaralynn's. He was a gentleman; she would give him that, but he also seemed to not be able to stop touching her. The hand on her back, the rub of his thumb on her cheek before he closed her car door, the way he rubbed her thigh before he put the car in reverse to back out, and the way he entwined his fingers with hers when he switched it into drive.

She never had someone need to touch her like this. Normally she was the one who always initiated or sought out affection. It was different, uneasy at times, but very nice. The ride back to the ranch was quiet. Not an uneasy quiet but comfortable silence. The women in the back seat had bouts of hushed chatter but nothing that reached the front seat where Kent and she were sitting in muted bliss. It was like they were in their tiny bubble in the front row of the car. They would steal tiny glances at each other every so often and he would squeeze her hand in response. Once he brought her hand to his lips and she knew she heard a muffled "Oh," come from the backseat but she ignored it and just stared out the windshield.

They were greeted with two very tired looking men walking down the porch steps when Kent parked, and they all shuffled out. The two men looked like they have been awake for days with the lines under their eyes. It was confirmed by the next words coming out of Hugh's mouth.

"Those rascals are a handful," he said exasperatedly.

Cliff stood next to him with his hands out, ready to take some bags, "They would wear out the crazy bull in the pasture if we let'em."

The two women were giggling and mumbling agreements. Cliff and Hugh hauled in all the grocery and shopping bags from the other women, leaving only Kent and Aaralynn's bags in the car. Gran decided to get dinner started while Kent and she took their things to the cottage and got cleaned up. She was not going to argue with that because by now she wanted a hot shower and to change out of the clothes she had on.

The stroll to the cottage was made in silence. The closer they got to the front door the more nervous she felt. She wasn't sure about being alone with Kent again. Mostly, she wasn't sure she could trust herself and what might happen. So, when they reached the porch steps and opened the door, her whole body was vibrating.

Kent pulled the door open and waited for her to go in. She did and smiled as she passed. The smile felt a bit forced but she couldn't help it right now. Ash practically ran her over when she walked in. An assault of licks descended upon her. Giggling, she watched as Ash left her to run circles around Kent. Finally tiring, Ash sat in front of them, waiting. Her tail swished back and forth with restrained excitement and Aaralynn knew it would not be tempered anytime soon. Sighing, Aaralynn opened the door to let Ash outside.

As Aaralynn stood there watching Ash sniff the ground, Kent picked up the bags and went inside. The sound of pots being banged and running water reached her. Kent walked into the Livingroom with a bowl of ground up food. Just as she let Ash back inside.

"I bought some of that real food dog food. Figured her being a wolf she prefers this to dry dog food." Aaralynn drew her eyebrows together in a furrow and Kent shrugged in response. She couldn't argue with that. It was better for Ash, but it was also expensive. She would have to say something to him about how much he was spending on them later. Kent placed the bowl down on the floor and Ash ran over to eat it up.

"Well, she was hungry," Aaralynn said with a clap of her hands.

"Yup."

"So, have you heard anything from Ray?" Her mind racing to think of something else to say before she had time to sort through what was or wasn't going on between them.

Kent frowned when he pulled his phone out of his pocket, "Looks like my phone died." He put it back in his pocket. "I'll charge it while we get ready and check it before we go for dinner." With a wave of his hands, "Now get upstairs. I'll bring up the bags."

She would have protested but he was already picking up bags when he started talking. Conceding, Aaralynn just turned and walked up the stairs. Heavy footsteps trailing behind her.

****

Chapter 11

Kent heard the shower switch off and waited a few minutes before knocking on the bathroom door. He needed to take a leak and he couldn't wait anymore. He contemplated talking to Gran about putting in another bathroom, having only one in the house; one was not convenient at all. When he got no response, he knocked again.

"Hold on," the voice from the other side said. A moment later the door opened a crack and Aaralynn's wet head popped thru. "Did you need something?" Droplets of water dripped off her hair onto the floor.

Hell yes. "Umm," he cleared his thoughts, "I need to use the restroom." *Yea. That was it. Keep it on track Kent.*

"I'll be out in a bit." She smiled at him and was about to close the door again, but he stuck his foot out preventing it from closing.

"I really need to go." He had both palms propped on the door frame. "Please," he added, leaning in close. He could smell the soap on her skin and the scent of her shampoo.

With a frustrated breath, she stepped aside and let him into the bathroom. Squeezing past, her he took note of her naked body wrapped in a green bath towel. Wasting no time, he lifted the toilet lid. At this point, he couldn't care if she was watching or not.

"Do you always drop your pants with women in the room?" He couldn't tell if she was joking or being serious. The rise and fall of her voice left no hints.

"Only with you," he joked.

"I don't know if I should feel offended or special?"

He zipped up his pants after shaking off and flushed. He laughed and turned to wash his hands. "What do you think?"

An odd noise came from where she stood, "with my track record…" she let the last of it slip. Like the rest of it should be obvious to everyone. Well, he wasn't going to agree with any negative comments she had towards herself.

He turned from the sink just as she was moving to go past him, and they collided in the small space. He grabbed her bare shoulders and she steadied herself by placing her hands on his forearms. "Whoa," he said, just as much for her as he did for himself.

He was so close to her, could see her pulse beating from the vein in her throat. The smell of honey and flowers floated around him teasing his senses and making his hands itch to hold her close. She shivered under his hands and he instantly felt himself getting hard. She looked up, their eyes locking, at the same moment her towel came unwrapped and dropped to the floor.

She stilled and her eyes locked on his. He knew he shouldn't look, screamed it in his head over and over, but he was just a man after all. It was as if his hands had their own mind. Keeping his eyes on hers, his hands caressed up and down from her arm to her hip. Aaralynn's hands came together in front of her chest. Her hands palm out, resting against his chest. The feel of her breast heaving against his chest was arousing him even more. His pants were becoming painfully tight and his breathing picked up coming out harsher.

Her breathing sounded raspy. When she shuddered and licked her lips, his hands slid from her hips to her back. Her skin searing his everywhere she pressed against him. Causing his hold on her to tighten. Eyes roaming further down to glimpse the tops of her full breast sandwiched against him. An agonizing groan escaped him.

"I think I need a shower too." The words came out hoarse as they flittered through his lips.

"Is that so," her voice smooth as cream to his ears.

"Mmhmm." He replied, his hands sliding down to cup her rounded ass. She let out a mule. She was perfect. "I think I'll need some help."

She opened her mouth to speak but Kent was faster than her words. His mouth descended upon hers ferociously. A mingle of teeth, lips, breath, and tongues as she met his vigorous claiming, lick by lick. Her hands slid up his arms and held onto him like she was clinging onto life itself.

He was surprised to find that she needed him as much as he needed her. Maybe she always had, and he was just holding them both back. Either way, he was going to push through his uncertainty and indecision about their lack of a future and live in this moment. Life was full of moments and he wanted to remember every single second of this one.

Hands grabbed the hem of his shirt and yanked it upwards. Helping, he stepped back and pulled it all the way off. The sharp intake of breath, her eyes raking over his skin, had his painfully hard erection twitching in his jeans. He grabbed her wrist to pull her arms apart so he could get a look at her too, but she held tight to her position, shaking her head.

"Baby," he started, wiping any expression off his face, "there is nothing about you I would change. I want every single sexy curve of you, and you got to see me. Now it is my turn." She visually relaxed at his encouragement. Her body going soft and swaying slightly into him.

Her eyes fell to the floor as she dropped her hands to her sides. Stunning, every inch of her, but he wasn't satisfied. She began to coil into herself with all her inner self-doubt. Kent hated how she wasn't sure of her body and he silently promised himself he would show her how beautiful she undeniably was.

"Beautiful," the word came out gravelly and deep. Her eyes remained fixed on the floor as he cupped his hand under her chin and lifted her eyes to meet his. Those bright, glittering eyes that were holding back unshed tears were an odd contrast to the radiant smile on those luscious lips. "Don't cover yourself up around me. Ever."

She shivered and he cupped her cheeks with his hands and lowered his lips to hers again. This kiss was less rushed. He took his time devouring her mouth. Licking and sucking her bottom lip before diving his tongue in to meet hers. One hand moved around to her neck while the other snaked down her body to grab her bottom and haul her against him once again. His hard shaft budded into her belly through his jeans and he couldn't stand it any longer.

He pulled apart, she gave a small whimper and he started unzipping his jeans, pulling them down and shucking them into the corner of the room followed by his boxers. He stood there, naked as the day he was born, and let her eyes sweep over him. Her slow assessment of his body had him humming with pent up desire. When seconds ticked away, he started getting worried she wasn't as into him as he was to her. She hadn't spoken, hadn't said a word but turned around. He watched the sway of her long hair, now free of any constraints, a dark red from being so damp. It flung tiny droplets of water around when she turned, and it stopped just above her plump bottom that he didn't know what he wanted to do more. Run his hands through her hair or grab at her ass. *Definitely, grab her ass.* She bent over to lean into the tub.

He heard the shower being turned on and she looked over her shoulder. A sly grin pulled at her mouth and her eyes were practically glowing at him with mischief. Standing up she climbed into the shower. Her movements were graceful like a poem to his soul.

A finger wiggled at him, "I thought you wanted to get clean," she said as she stood under the spray. This woman would be the death of him if he let her.

"Yes Ma'am," he drawled before climbing in behind her.

Her hands brushed back her hair and he took that opportunity to run his fingers up and over her rib cage to cup her breast. They were full and fit perfectly in his palms. He stroked them, feeling her press against his palms for more traction. He rubbed them leisurely. Felt their weight in his hands before moving up to tug on her nipples. Those sweet dark nipples he had the pleasure of seeing.

She arched her back, pushing her ass into his lower abdomen. Her head fell back to rest on his shoulder and her arms wrapped around his neck as she

let out a soft moan. His lips fell to her throat suckling
and licking the tender spot while tugging lightly on
her nipples. Her sharp intake of breath told him she
enjoyed the pinch of pain. Her lower half vigorously
ground against him. By now every part of him was
standing straight up.

"Mmmm," she murmured when her hands
slipped from around his neck. He stopped suckling her
neck as she grabbed for the sponge and soap.

His hands left her breasts to rub down her
stomach. "What are you doing," he asked as she
began to put soap on the sponge and mix it in. The
sponge became full of bubbles.

"You said you needed a bath. And wasn't it
you who said he needed help?" She turned around and
put the sponge to his stomach. "Now turn around."

"You don't have – "he began but she cut him
off.

"Turn around."

"Bossy," he muttered but complied.

The sponge wiped over his back in slow
circles, before moving up to his shoulders. Wiped
down each arm. Then made the way back to his back,
dipping to his ass. When he tensed and was going to
move around, she pushed him back. "Don't move,"
she stated.

He looked over his shoulder to see her bend
down on her knees and inwardly groaned. *Can he turn
around now?!* He turned back to the wall and stared at
it. Paying close attention to every detail. She soaped
up each cheek and then nudged him to spread his legs.
She scrubbed up and down each leg. Picking up his
feet one by one to soap them as well. This is one thing
he had never done with a woman before. Sure, he had

taken showers with a woman before, but they never wanted to do intimate things like washing each other. Even his last girlfriend never took the time to intimately care for him like this and it felt raw. He felt exposed and uncomfortable and in a way that told him, Aaralynn really cared about him.

Kent was still lost in thought as she nudged him around. His eyes falling to the top of her head while she was busy washing up the front of his legs. She moved with purpose. Making sure she didn't miss a spot. Tentatively she cupped his balls as she scrubbed them too.

****

Aaralynn had never washed a man off before but she felt a compelling need to do it. She wanted to touch him and see him, and what better way to do all of that then help him wash as he had asked. His balls were heavy and from the look, he had given her, she had guessed he hadn't cum in a while. The red tint of them got worse the longer she cleaned him. He gave a sharp intake of air before a whispered, "Damn," came out. Her head snapped up to meet his dark stormy eyes. Their eyes locked in a sensual embrace.

Her attention shifted to washing his hard shaft. His impressive size even more mouthwatering being up close in her face. Now, her hands wrapped around the thick massive member, stroking it lightly as she washed him. Their eyes never wavered as she stroked him. Up and down. His shaft seemed to get thicker the longer she took, and his breathing became ragged.

"Baby," he rasped, "if you don't stop I will cum in your hand and I don't want to do that." A guttural moan escaped his lips and Aaralynn felt her cheeks flush at his words. "Baby," he repeated pleadingly.

She stopped stroking him and she heard a rush of air being released. When her hands released him, his cock bobbed in front of her face. His eyes shut and she took a moment to admire what was right in front of her face. He was all man. Muscles everywhere but she assumed that was standard for a military man. His erection was an impressive muscle, in her opinion, as well. Thick and long. Pulsing and teasing her.

"Are you..." His whole body goes still when she suddenly took him in her mouth. "Fuck," he yelled out. Aaralynn wasted no time teasing and licking him first. She just wanted him, all of him. He stretched her mouth with his thickness, and she could feel him pulsing against her tongue.

"Mmmmm," she vibrated around him.

"Oh. Damn." His hands twisted in her hair. "Do that again." Loving that she pleased him, she did it again. He growled low and deep. She knew if she wasn't already wet, she would be now. The sound sent heat right to her pussy.

She pulled him out and licked the tip. Swirling her tongue around the head. Her eyes looked up to meet his as she swallowed him whole again. His face was all hard, restrained lines. His hands gripped her hair; slowly guiding her. He was pacing himself, she realized because she was moving slower than before.

"I need to taste you." His hands tugged on her hair, freeing himself from her mouth. "Now." He left no room for arguing. He bent down to pull her up, the soapy sponge is forgotten on the floor. Aaralynn didn't know what to say so she remained silent.

Her arms prickled as the water started to cool Kent noticed. He reached around her, while rubbing her arm, and turned up the water temperature. When the water heated up again her skin smoothed out. "Better?"

"Much," she croaked, licking her lips seconds before his mouth came down on hers. He squeezed her biceps, pinning her to the cool shower wall as he assaulted her mouth. Unable to move she gave in to the onslaught. Her soft skin against his rough lines. He nipped her bottom lip several times before releasing her.

"Sooo good," his drawn-out murmured played against her swollen lips.

She sighed as he began to kiss his way down her middle, lowering onto his knees. Now it was her turn to feel. Parting her legs, he exposed her to his greedy eyes. He slid a finger between her wet lips and dipped in, then out. Aaralynn let out what she hoped sounded like a moan. It was low and breathy but got higher at the end with her need rising. He looked at her. His smile reaching high with his approval at her reaction. "Kent," her breathless voice had her body pulsing with unbidden need. His fingers slid in and out of her a few more times, pumping faster, coupled with her moans of pleasure. She wasn't far from the edge, the pressure building almost unbearably when suddenly he pulled out of her. The feeling of unsatisfied emptiness not lost on her.

Her frustrated whimper was cut short by the first flicker of his tongue against the right sensitive bud between her thighs. At the jolt of pleasure, her hands braced the wall behind her, her back arched and her legs spread open even more. "Oh God," the words slipped from her mouth without thought. His hot mouth against her mixed with the warm water beating down on her skin, had her body getting rigid.

"So, beautiful," he hummed against her wetness.

"Don't stop," her hands fisted in his hair, holding him in place. Aaralynn ground her hips into his face, searching for her release. The lashing of his tongue became more persistent and her panting more clipped. When she came it was so hard that she saw a glittering of white sparks. Aaralynn cried out, one arm bracing herself against the shower wall and the other in his hair, holding him to her.

When she got her breathing under control, she released her hold on his hair and stood on wobbly legs. He wiped his mouth on the back of his hand with a chuckle. Her heart was still hammering against her ribs when he got to his feet, towering over her.

"What is so funny," she demanded to know. The water was becoming cold again and she hated the feel of it against her heated skin. The last tremors of her climax now dissipating.

"You almost suffocated me, but I would have gladly died with you on my lips." She slugged his arm, "hey" he said rubbing the spot.

However, her shoulders were quacking with silent laughter too and she had a peachy grin across her face. She was happy and joking. It had been so long she almost forgot what this felt like. And all because she had climaxed. Go figure.

****

Kent could still taste her. Her honey sweetness was still on his lips and the faint smell of her climax on his face. He was hard still, and the cooling shower wasn't stopping it. He delighted in the look of the woman standing naked in front of him. Her cheeks all flushed, her hair wet and clinging to her face. She came undone by his mouth and now he could see she was more relaxed then he had seen her this whole time. Amazed and proud he could do that for her.

He reached around her and turned off the shower. If he was going to do this, it wasn't going to be in the freezing cold. He kissed her again, hard. Pushing her body against the shower stall. Not wanting her to think it was over, he silently promised to keep her wanting more. The way she came apart at his touch and wiggled against him had him thinking of all the things he wanted to still do to her. If this was going to be a short-term thing, he would make sure it was the best experience for both of them. Rubbing his hard erection between her thighs, he felt her soaking wetness there.

Their moans mingled together. Charging his libido even more. Mentally he held himself back. *Whoa boy, patience.* Still kissing her, he wrapped his arms around her legs and lifted her. Straddling him she let out a squeak in surprise and he moved his mouth from her lips to her neck. Nipping and licking her tender flesh. He moved from the side of her neck to her collarbone, and then to the base of her throat. Her breast bounced as he moved them out of the tub and fiddled with the bathroom door handle. Her hands wrapped around his shoulders and her legs clung to his waist.

He finally got the door open, moving his mouth back to her red swollen lips. His stride was long and rushed to get them down the hallway into his bedroom. Not bothering to close the door since no one else was in the house. He loved that she didn't protest once. Just melted into him. He leaned over the bed, gently easing them both onto it.

Her hands gently push him back, her questioning green eyes meeting his. "Do you have a condom?"

Without faltering he nodded and leaned over the bed. Without moving from between her legs he unzipped his duffle bag and pulled out a condom. The silver package glinted in the darkening room. The sun was dropping, casting shadows about the room. Her silhouette reminding him of a Greek Goddess lying there. Her flame-red hair splayed around her pale naked body, with her pale green eyes shining up at him. "Simply delectable."

He hadn't realized he spoke out loud until she giggled. Actually, giggled like a schoolgirl. The sound had Kent's insides tingling and a warmth spread through his chest. His erection pressed instantly against her opening. He could feel her moist and ready for him. Not ready to tempt the Gods of Fate just yet, he shifted and tore the condom open with his teeth. Quickly he rolled the condom on with one hand. When he got it on, he rolled back on top of her. Her legs fell open wide, ready for him.

"You sure?" He questioned. Holding his breath for her reply. What if she said no and he had to go finish himself? He didn't get any protest from her so far, but he was on the edge and he hoped she wasn't rethinking this.

"Positive." That single word, giving him the green light, was all the encouragement he needed.

He took her wrist in his hand and lifted them above her head. Exposing her full breast to him. Her eyes got wide at his abruptness, a devilish grin spreading across his face. Bracing his weight on his other arm, so as not to crush her with his weight, he pushed just the tip inside her. She whimpered under him.

"Spread them wider," he demanded, and she obeyed. Opening her legs wide for him with a silent invitation coupled with the most innocent doe eyes he had ever seen on a woman had him almost exploding. "Good girl," he cooed, settling himself between her hips just before slamming his cock fully inside of her.

If air could be painted, Kent swore the room exploded around them in a sea of colors marveling a rainbow. Aaralynn let out a broken cry at his swift and intense intrusion, that she writhed beneath his body. Her body wriggled beneath his grasp, but Kent held her firm. Thrusting in and out of her in fast strokes. Her legs, still apart, lifted for deeper access and he ground into her harder. "Fuck baby," he said between exasperated pants and rough thrusts. Kent noticed his words must be arousing her if the pool of wetness creaming out of her was any indication.

"Your so wet for me," he mumbled between clenched teeth. It was becoming immensely hard to hold off his orgasm, being as it had been so long since his last one. He didn't want to release this early yet.

"Yes." She gasped between her moans of pleasure.

"You like me talking dirty to you? Telling you just how sexy, delicious, and savory you are to me?" Shivers broke through him as her nails raked down his hardback. "Does it make you more excited to know I love the feel of your wet pussy around my cock?". He felt her pussy tighten around him and knew his words were working. She must be close to orgasming again and he wanted her to do it while he was buried deep inside her.

"Yes," her voice barely audible, her breaths shallow. By now covers were discarded and pillows were strewn around about the room from their feverish lovemaking.

He bent over, tracing a line from her throat to her ear with his tongue, stopping to suckle on an earlobe. An "Oh" escaped her lips, that had him grinning as he pulled back just enough to say in her ear, "Cum for me baby."

****

Her second orgasm within minutes had rocked her. The feeling of her limbs shaking under her, like Jell-O before it is completely molded, was a new sensation to her. For a brief moment, she wasn't sure she could breathe. Her pants came in bursts from her sore throat. Kent released her wrist to wrap his strong muscled arms around her waist. Awash with content satisfaction, Aaralynn could have laid there forever without having a single complaint. Before she knew it, she was being flipped over onto her stomach.

"Wh…what"

"Shhh," she heard from behind her as her bottom was being tugged upward. Aaralynn looked over her shoulder to see Kent gripping her waist and staring down at her exposed openings. He looked like he was going to eat her up, piece by piece, and still ask for more. A shudder of excitement ran through her and she wiggled instinctively.

A growl, guttural and carnal rose from him and his eyes locked on her face. He shifted behind her, looming over her, and slid himself between her legs. His cock rubbed her swollen lips in a rhythmic motion. Back and forth, back and forth. Never entering her. Teasing her so she was boarding on frustration. Aaralynn heard the smooth, slick sounds their bodies were making and her arousal only peaked higher.

After a few minutes, she was not sure she would be able to handle it anymore. He had her body on fire. His calloused hands slid down her back and came around to cup her breast, stroking and needing them in his rough palms. The trail of kisses his mouth left down her back had her dreaming for more moments like this.

With his breath hot on her skin she begged, "Please." Her mouth expressing what her body needed, "please. I need you." Hating the neediness of her voice but there was no room for prideful preservation in their intimacy.

Biting down on her shoulder, he slammed his cock into her wet folds. She screamed out, "Oh yes," and pushed her ass back into him, meeting him thrust for thrust. His movements getting more frantic with every breath he took. Aaralynn could almost see the sparks of electricity emanating between them. There would be no denying that this encounter will change their relationship, but she pushed those thoughts aside for now.

Kent leaned back, pulling her to sit up. His hands still cupping her breast, his mouth now sucking on the juncture between her shoulder and neck, as he thrust into her harder. Over and over he rammed his hard cock into her and Aaralynn had never felt like this before with a partner. No one had ever claimed her like this. So, feral and predatorial. So, ferocious and raw. As she heard him release her neck to cry out his release, his hold tightening on her almost painful, she knew she would never be satisfied by another man like she was right now.

They sat there like that for a while, her form curled into his, both of them catching their breaths. Kent pulled her with him as he sat back on his feet, never breaking their connection. Kent slid his hands from her breast to her stomach, sending delicious shudders through her and his head fell to her shoulder. Cradling her to him, he nuzzled her neck.

"Damn perfect," she heard him mumble against her warm skin. She couldn't even argue with him because he was perfect. From the soreness on her neck, she knew she would have a nice size hickey tomorrow.

He pulled out of her, breaking their connection. "We need to get changed. Dinner will be ready soon." His tone and words felt like a bucket of ice being dumped on her, waking her up from a haze. Nodding, Aaralynn climbed out of bed wrapping herself in a blanket. Kent frowned and walked towards her. She backed up and bumped into a nightstand. "Baby," The sensual drawl of the word making butterflies in her stomach as he tugged the blanket away from her, "don't ever cover up from me." The sentence ending in a manner that had her head swimming with different thoughts.

"I…"

"You what?" he let out a frustrated huff of air, "there is no reason to hide yourself from me." His hand came up to cup her cheeks, "You are downright sexy, and if or whenever we do this again you don't need to cover up." He kissed her. His soft lips met hers with tender recognition. Slowly pulling back, he dropped his hands and stared down at her, "now, go get ready." His words came out husky and he cleared his throat. We will leave in a half-hour." With that, he smacked her ass that had a loud clap ringing out. Aaralynn squeaked and gave him an "I'll get you back for that later" look. His chuckle fading as she strode out of the room.

Alone in her room, with nothing but the soft noises of the house creaking against the chilly weather outside she had time to work through what just happened. The only problem with that was she wasn't exactly sure what had happened. They had sex of course, but the way he held her and tended to her; had her thinking it might be more. He didn't say they were an item and with her pending departure, did she dare hope there was something more than just an attraction? His demanding demeanor during sex, coupled with his compassionate and attentive side had her head spinning in thought.

His considerate behavior threw her off. She had been around her fair share of demanding men and even some women before. Always telling, never asking. Physically forceful at times but she had never had a man who cared about her needs. Thinking back Kent had shown his protective side from the start but always with her needs in mind. She liked it. She could get used to it and that scared her because she wasn't even sure he was sticking around, let alone if she would either.

****

Chapter 12

Dinner turned out to be a normal affair. Warm greetings like they were old friends, welcomed Aaralynn and Kent when they arrived at the main house. Scrumptious smells of food filled the room as Gran served dinner to everyone at the table ten minutes after they walked through the door. Aaralynn sat next to Kent at the table, at Gran insistence - of course. He knew Gran was trying to play matchmaker, or maybe she saw something between them, either way, he didn't mind. After what they just shared, he wanted to never leave her side again. And that had him doubling back inside his mind.

In the deafening stillness of his room after she left him, he rethought his plans for retirement. He could put in for retirement and move back home. His family wouldn't complain. Gran was always asking him when he was going to be done. Her subtle pursuit for him to settle down and finally come home to roost. However, what would he do after the military? He had no idea and that was unnerving. He always had something to do. Someone commanding or giving orders to go somewhere. With the prospect of it possibly being over, he didn't know how to feel or what to do next. Kent knew he couldn't ask her to stay for a man who had no stable income. It wouldn't be fair to her. No, he needed to give this more thought before breaching the subject to her about it.

His mind was racing during dinner, but he hid it well. Between the girls and Gran, Ash got more than her share of scraps. It was amusing to watch Gran, who never wanted animals in the house, pamper this pooch. Aaralynn's fondness for the older woman obvious.

He had his own fondness for his family and now for the redheaded beauty sitting next to him. Unable to help himself, he kept sneaking small glances her way and rubbed her thigh a time or two. The overwhelming need to feel her skin was intoxicating and he wanted to do so much more, but she kept jumping and nudging his hand away. At first, he thought she didn't want his touch, but then she would blush and smile at him after she moved his hand. Kent chalked it up to her being shy in public instead of her not wanting his touch. There were small bouts of chatter at dinner, mostly about the upcoming wedding. Austin mentioned needing to get the cattle tagged for the butcher next week and subsequently asked Reed and him for help with that. Reed informed them he was to be returning to New York next Saturday since he had several meetings he couldn't miss.

However, they both agreed to help while they were there since Austin was down two men. One left to go further East and the other retired. Austin mumbled something about the man's wife wanted to go where she would never need a sweater ever again. "It was a sight to see her heft all those piles of clothes to light them all up in a bonfire pit before they left." Austin laughed as he regaled them with the scene he witnessed.

Molly barely spoke to anyone but Kris. Kent noticed Molly and Reed looking at each other everyone in a while. The looks they shared were odd and seemed pained. Minding his own business, for now, Kent turned his attention elsewhere. He suspected Hugh had been courting Gran, with as much as the older man had been around. Kent didn't mind that, seeing as how they were both widowed and he knew the older gentleman was honorable.

During dinner, the group was all filled in on how Annette and Austin met. Gran enjoyed relaying her part in the matching making. The older woman's tale of rescuing a distressed girl and her young child, only to have the two falling in love. Apparently, Annette and Austin had a scare with her ex-husband and the result was the ex-husband ending up 6 feet under. According to Gran's tale, it would seem he missed a lot in the last few months.

Catching up was just what he needed. He had been smiling and laughing more than he had in a while, or maybe it was just the woman stealing his attention next to him. In all the family dinners he had been to before he couldn't remember ever feeling this relaxed. His attention never fully focused on the people around them. He heard bits and pieces of comments but truthfully, he focused on the redhead sitting to his left. Her smile, her smell, her laugh, her voice, her eyes, her lips, and every other part of her had him at full attention.

After dinner wrapped up, he excused himself to go check his phone. The ladies cleared the table and congregated in the kitchen to chat while they cleaned up. The men went to the Livingroom to relax. When Kent got to the cottage, he unplugged his phone and turned it on. On his way back, his phone began to buzz instantly. After waiting for the buzzing to cease, he checked it. *Eleven messages and fifteen missed calls!*

Two of the messages were from one of the men in his unit, wanting to know if he could come for a visit while he was on a two-week leave. He quickly texted him back telling him he had no problem with it but he would have to check with the family to make sure. He would also need to figure out where he would be sleeping. He noted at the end of the message that he would need to find a nice outfit for the wedding too.

The other nine messages were from Ray. He stood there in the dark looking over message after message. At first, it just said everything was fine and he wanted to know how she was doing. Then it got more urgent saying that Billy and his goons came back looking for her. They didn't stay long because the police were looking for them for what they did to Stan. Stan was still in the hospital with a bad concussion. Ray had gotten several nasty threatening phone calls and business seemed to slow down for him. Numerous messages were of Ray demanding Kent call him. The last one said it was urgent and Aaralynn may be in trouble.

Concern and rage churned in his gut causing his hands to start shaking and his heart pumping so hard he thought it might come out of his chest. He pulled up Ray's number and dialed. It rang once before he picked up.

"Where the fuck have you been! I have been trying to reach you for hours. Where is our girl? Is she safe?" Ray's voice boomed so loud it rang in his ears, sending Kent's body on alert and his mind on the defensive.

"My phone died." Pausing, Kent took a few breaths of air to calm his feelings of rage. *She is ok*, he reminded himself. "She is fine, we are still on my family's ranch. What the hell is going on?" Kent barked out.

Ray's ragged breathing filled Kent's ears. The sound more strenuous than calming. "Fuck man," he began and Kent instantly tensed.

"What." An edge of caution to his tone.

"Billy has still been looking for her. Driving my business down the last few days."

"And that is an emergency?" Annoyance oozed off his words.

"No, but Tony will be a problem."

At the mention of the other man's name he reflectively clenched his jaw and ground his teeth together. "What the hell are you talking about?" Kent bit out.

He could hear the clicking of keys in the background and guessed Ray was in his office. "Tony had been asking me if he could call her. I kept telling him no, but he wouldn't drop it. It was getting to him, I could tell." More clicking of keys, "Well, long story short he is probably on his way there."

"What!" Kent bellowed so loud he waited to see if anyone in the house would come out. He was standing on the side of the porch now. After a few moments, when no one came out, he turned his attention back to the call.

"What do you mean he is on his way, Ray? I never told anyone where I was going." Kent clenched and unclenched his fists trying to relax.

"He got your number from my phone when I left it on the desk." Ray sighed in frustration. "I guess he also hacked into my computer and pulled up the information I checked up on you about. It wasn't hard to pinpoint your family ranch after that."

"Fuck," he said to the darkness. Cursing to himself just as much as Ray.

"I know man. I could say I'm sorry, but we have more pressing matters.," Ray cleared his throat, "I don't think Tony will do anything to her. Tony isn't my main concern anyway. Fred, my new bouncer I just hired, he said when Tony left one of Billy's men was following him."

Kent's veins ran cold. He couldn't believe what he was hearing. "So, you mean to tell me that he is going to lead them right here?" His tone was clipped and menacing but who could blame him? He was pissed off.

"Uh-huh."

Kent pulled the phone away from his ear and yelled "FUCK" again before running a hand through his short hair. The phone rested back against his ear, but he was only half-listening to what Ray was saying. So many thoughts and scenarios ran through his mind. His first priority would be to tell his brothers to expect company.

"...Doubt it will take them as long to get there." Ray finished saying when Kent tuned in again.

"Right. Look, Ray, I'm gonna have to let you go. I have to get things situated." Kent's mental list must have been a mile long by now.

Ray made a grunting noise in response. "Just have her call me in the morning. I will be at the hospital checking on Stan if she wants to talk to him." Kent promised he'd have her call before saying his goodbyes and ending the call.

Frustration still rang through him when he walked back into the house. He tried to push it back as best he could, giving himself time when he sat to take his boots and jacket off. Kent could hear the women in the kitchen still talking as light giggles floated down the hallway. Knowing it was going to be an awkward discussion he decided to go around up his brothers and inform them before talking to Aaralynn about his phone call. With a blank expression plastered on his face, he blew out a breath of air, hardening himself as he walked into the Livingroom.

The room was dim and the smell of logs burning from the fireplace filled his senses. The scent bringing back so many childhood memories. He inhaled the scent reveling in it for the briefest of moments. Kent found Austin, Reed, and Hugh all sitting around the fireplace. Austin had his head tilted back and his eyes closed, while Reed was looking at his phone, and Hugh was sitting in the lounge chair staring at the flames in the fireplace. Clearing his throat had Austin opening his eyes and all three men sat up to look at him.

"We need to talk about something." He began. "It involves why Aaralynn is here." He came over to the other chair next to Hugh and sat down with a thunk. His whole body was still tense, and he needed to try to relax before he went out to go search for the men himself. All three men just sat there staring at him, their gazes locked on him, waiting for him to elaborate.

It took him a whole fifteen minutes to go through everything that had happened in the last four days. As he explained his brothers listened intently. Their expressions getting more livid when he got towards the end. Kent was surprised none of the women walked in as he spoke, instead, they remained in the kitchen. He would hear bouts of laughter every so often that had his nerves relaxing just a fraction.

"So, you are telling me that I might have trouble right before my wedding?" Austin didn't sound happy and Kent couldn't blame him. This was horrible timing.

"Sorry man. It wasn't like I planned for this to happen." Kent ran a hand over his neck. Things seemed to get more and more complicated.

"Damn Kent. I mean, is this girl worth it?" It was Reed who asked but it could have been any of them from the way they stared at him.

With a nod, Hugh leaned forward and took stock of his face. He must have seen something because he responded with, "You got it good, don't ya boy?" The man's gravelly voice scrapped at something inside him. He couldn't argue that Aaralynn had become important to him in the short time they have known each other.

Pushing down the strange and new feeling she was provoking in him for the time being, he tried to focus on his brother's reactions. Austin was up and pacing the room, going back and forth in front of the fireplace. Reed was still sitting on the couch and Hugh was staring at him intently from the chair.

"Damn." Reed said again when he didn't respond to Hugh's statement.

"Yup." Was all Hugh said as he leaned back in his chair again.

"Alright," Austin stopped pacing to stand in front of all of them. "If she is that important to you, she can stay." *Like her leaving was even in the cards* Kent said to himself, "but we will need to be on alert. I will tell my other ranch hand in the morning and we will look to hire another hand or two as soon as I can." Before he could go on, Hugh interjected.

"You can borrow a few of mine in the meantime. You don't want to hire someone and risk them being shady."

Austin mumbled an agreement. Kent sat there, silent. He had caused this trouble by bringing her here. Now he needed to make sure no one got hurt because of him. Not to mention, the wedding went off without a hitch.

"We can't let the women walk around unsupervised until these men are dealt with." Not that it needed to be said but Kent voiced it out loud anyway. The men all nodded in agreement and Kent stood.

"I am going to go see if Aaralynn is ready to go now. I will talk to you more in the morning." He knew the next few days were going to be chaotic, but he wouldn't spoil this happy time for his brother if he had any say in the matter. He also wouldn't let anything happen to the woman he now knew he was falling in love with. Silently, he encouraged himself, turned, walking into the kitchen and towards the one person he wanted a future with.

****

The moment Kent walked into the kitchen she could tell something wasn't right. He had a scowl on his face and seemed lost in thought. His whole body looking tense and on alert. She was watching the toddlers jump around and get licked by Ash who was in the corner wagging her tail. The women stopped talking when Kent barked out, "Are you ready?" They all turned to stare at him. The questions came out more of an order and it had the hair on her neck deliciously standing at attention.

Before she could respond he walked up to her with her new jacket and held it open, waiting. She was stunned at how rude he was being to his family but instead of saying as much, she kept her mouth shut. The tight line of his mouth and the flexing jaw muscle told her he wasn't in the mood to discuss anything right now. Aaralynn stood and took her time putting her arms in the sleeves. She felt the light brush of his fingers against her neck when he pulled up the jacket. They lingered a little longer than necessary. Her skin tingled but other emotions twisted in her stomach from his attitude.

"Tomorrow we will have a girl's day. I promised you two a tea party," she said to the two toddlers. Bending down she opened her arms and both of them ran over to hug her. Both gleeful with anticipation for tomorrow.

"Alright, you two, upstairs. It's time for pajamas and teeth." At Molly's words, both gave soft grumbles. Kris stifled a yawn as they trudged up the stairs with Molly following close behind, mumbling a quick goodbye to Kent and her.

"Hold on," Gran said while turning and pulling a bag off the counter. "take these to snack on. There is nothing in that cottage and I figured you might need something." The older woman handed over the bag to Aaralynn.

"I already did a little shopping," Kent informed her.

Gran clucked her tongue a few times and gave him a stern look. It made Aaralynn giggle to see Kent feigning a hurt look. "You might have picked up a few things, but I doubt you got comfort things." Gran made a show of putting her hands on her hips and

Kent gave a defeated sigh. Gran went on as Kent made a display of rolling his eyes. "Good, now you two have a nice night. If you need anything else dearies call up to the house. I'll be up for a little while still."

Aaralynn saw Kent go over and hug his Gran. She could tell how close of a family unit they were by the playful bickering between them and it made her envious. *This is what I have been missing,* she silently thought to herself. Annette came over to Aaralynn and wrapped her arms around her, "Tomorrow we will have girl time. That way we can get to know each other and maybe you can give me some pointers about the wedding."

"Ok," she said hesitantly, "I don't really know much about weddings, but I'll help if I can." A light squeeze and Annette let her go. She knew the other woman was just trying to include her and she was grateful for it.

Gran walked over and hugged her too. Pulling back, Gran lightly cupped her chin, "I'll see you tomorrow," she said before turning her in the direction of the hallway leading to the front door where Kent was waiting on her.

Heat rose to her cheeks at the way Kent stared at her. His eyes leisurely roamed her body before resting back on her face. Her blush deepened at the tilt of his lips. Aaralynn's eyes fell when he turned to lead the way out, a tired Ash trailing behind them. Once they were on the path leading to the cottage, she blew out a whoosh of air she had been holding. Kent gazed at her over his shoulder.

"Are you ever going to tell me what is bothering you?" Her voice came out terse and rude, but she couldn't stand it anymore. The silence and the air around him radiated with something she couldn't quite name and it made her uncomfortable. There would be no way she could deal with this odd energy all night.

His head turned back around lazily, and she got the feeling he was anticipating the question. He kept silent for so long that she wasn't sure he was going to talk at all. He rolled his shoulders. The tension in them making a cracking sound. Just as they started up the steps he said, "I am not sure how to start this, but I got a phone call a little while ago." Her senses perked up at the steely tone. She knew something was wrong and now she could sort of guess why.

"Ray called to update me." He knocked his boots off on the porch before opening the screen door, then the main door. He held it open for her. She passed him with her eyes focused on her feet. She couldn't look at him because she knew if she didn't like what she saw she might break down and that is something she couldn't handle right now.

When they were both inside, he continued, "He said Stan is still in the hospital. They are still checking him over before releasing him. I am to have you call tomorrow morning." *That wasn't bad news*. It was still bad that he was in the hospital, but it wasn't anything worse. Questions filtered through her head and she started chewing on her bottom lip. She dared to look at him then and her lips turned into a frown. She knew there was more. His face was tight, and she watched as his jaw clicked. "Apparently Tony wasn't happy that you left and weren't talking to him. The man went off his rocker and hacked Ray's computer and phone to get information on me."

"Information on you?" Her voice going an octave higher. Not able to hide the concern lacing her voice and the queasy feeling in her stomach. Tony had always been close by when she was at the bar, but she had never thought of him to be that clingy. She saw him more of a protector type and maybe a big brother, but this was a bit crazy, even for him in her opinion. If what Kent said was true, he may be more of a threat then she thought.

The faint sounds of scratching came from the door and Kent leaned over to open it. They must have forgotten to let Ash in, and she growled as she stepped through. The door slammed shut with a bang that had her jumping and Ash hastily turning around to face the door. What sounded like a mumble came from the pooch. They both watched as Ash turned back around and went to lay on the couch, like a grumpy old lady.

"Yea," Aaralynn shook her head. Attempting to clear her mind and pull her attention back to their conversation.

Kent ran a hand over his hair and down his face. "and that isn't even the worst of it." He grumbled something inaudible, showing his frustration. "He wanted to know where you were. Ray wouldn't tell him, so he searched for me. Ray thinks he figured out where we are and left to come here." Aaralynn gasped at that. Kent moved a little closer to her, having removed his boots while he was talking. He stopped inches away and crossed his arms over his chest.

He seemed to peer into her eyes, assessing her. His next words came out slow and measured. "It is a problem he is coming here to probably start shit, but the bigger issue is Billy's men were seen following him. So, they are probably on their way here too."

She couldn't have heard that right, could she? Her hand flew to her mouth to cover a sob. The air felt thin and it was getting harder to breathe. *Am I having a panic attack?* Her chest grew tighter. She knew this wouldn't end well and she should have just gone with Billy at the start. *They will take me*, her mind screamed loudly in her head.

"No," Kent said sternly, "it wouldn't have solved anything, and I won't let them take you. Not ever." She must have said that last part out loud. Her brain rattled with a million thoughts and she couldn't focus. Spots danced across her eyes as her vision began to blur. Was she having a panic attack? She asked herself for the second time.

She bent over at the waist and Kent was right there with a hand rubbing her back. He bent in front of her, but she couldn't focus. He was saying something to her, but she couldn't understand him, while she focused on breathing in and out, but it was hard. Ash got up from the couch to lay next to her on the floor.

A second later, her knees hit the wooden floor. Her palms slapped against the unforgiving surface. Catching her. Ash began licking her hands trying in vain to comfort her. One-minute Kent was gone and the next he was in front of her, keeling and handing her a glass of water. "Drink," he demanded, "drink baby." He couldn't hide the worry she saw in his expression and she couldn't blame him. She had never had this feeling before.

Slowly, she sat back on her heels and tried to take the glass, but her hands were shaking too much, and she sloshed water onto the floor. Kent took the glass, eased it to her lips, helping her take a sip. The water in her mouth a cool contrast to her heated skin. She took a few deep breaths before taking another sip. Her pulse slowed and her breathing began to calm down. Ash sat up, tilted her head, and stared at both of them. Loudly, she sniffed the air and pulled her tongue back into her mouth.

"There you go," Kent cooed. He rested his forehead against hers. "Don't scare me like that." One hand rubbed the back of her neck, as his other rested on her thigh. The contact centering her nerves while she focused on her lungs. In, out, in, out. A rhythmic motion relaxing her, until she felt like she was able to get up. Lifting her head, Kent straightened.

"You OK to stand?"

She was already nodding and pushing up before he finished asking. He stood, taking her hand, and helped her to her feet. She swayed a bit at first. "Whoa." Ash jumped up and was making circles around them. Unsure if her legs felt weak from the effects of the panic attack or the blood rushing to her head, but she started getting dizzy again. Her hand flew to her forehead as she swayed. Kent caught her and lifted her in his arms. With her legs flung over his arms and her head resting against his chest, he started climbing the stairs. The black wolf trotting up the stairs behind them.

Aaralynn nuzzled into him as he cradled her. His warmth seeping into her and helping to keep her brain grounded.

"Sorry," Aaralynn got out as he nudged her bedroom door open with his foot. His breathing stable as if she was light as a feather. Ash rushed past and jumped on the foot of the bed, paced in a circle twice, and laid down.

"Don't be. Gives me just another reason to touch you." When she turned her eyes to his face he looked down and gave her a wink. A small smile touched his lips before his brows creased with concern again. Laying her down on her bed, he pulled the covers back up and felt her head, his brows furrowed deeper. "You're warm." The coolness of his hands was welcomed on her skin. Disappointment instant when he pulled back. She missed his touch.

"It's nothing. I think I had a panic attack."

"Do you get them often?" He sat on the side of the bed searching her face. His eyes tracing every curve to rest on her lips. She felt heat rise and knew she must be blushing. Her tongue darted out to lick at her dry lips.

"No. Never." Shrugging, she shook her head slowly. "But what else could it have been?" His eyes lingered on her mouth a few seconds before snapping back up to hers. A glint of hunger deepening their color and it had her breath catching in her throat.

He cleared his throat, "Well, just to be sure, you are going to stay in bed while I go grab you some soup." He looked at her mouth again and for a moment Aaralynn thought he was going to lean in to kiss her. Her breath held. She wouldn't have minded it if he had but instead of doing that, he pulled back and stood. She released the air from her lungs. "I'll be right back," were the last words he said before turning and rushing out into the hall. Ash leaped off the bed to follow him.

****

Chapter 13

The soup heated up on the stove while Kent leaned back against the counter. He hadn't expected Aaralynn to react that way to the news but then again, he wasn't sure what he had been expecting. He was still livid that Tony was putting her in danger yet again and being an annoyance on top of it all, but he had bigger things to worry about. Starting with Aaralynn herself and his feelings toward her. He wanted to talk to her about it, see how she felt too but now wasn't the time. The added stress causing her to hyperventilate earlier and now feeling warm to the touch. No, he would let her rest and then talk about it tomorrow. Hopefully, by then, she felt better.

"What am I going to do about all of this?" He mumbled to himself just as much as the wolf chomping on the food he put in the bowl by the fridge.

He didn't expect a response, but he kept talking anyway. "We will need to take precautions girl. Your mama could be in even more trouble these next few days." Ash looked up at him and blew out a huff as if she understood what he just said. Then, she went back to finish up her food, dismissing his concern.

The soup started to bubble, and he stirred it after turning off the stove. He poured the soup in the bowl and checked the bag Gran had given him. Tentatively, he pulled out the contents and set them on the kitchen table. It consisted of a carton of homemade chicken soup, a loaf of fresh bread, a Ziploc bag of cookies, a Ziploc bag of pastries, and a carton of ice cream. Yea, Gran knew him. He put the soup in the fridge and the ice cream in the freezer, leaving the rest out on the table.

Sloshing sounds had him turning his head to see Ash making a mess of the water bowl. He swore under his breath before grabbing a dishrag and wiping up the floor. The beast was messier than he was. "Dang animal," grumbling under his breath.

Ash strode out of the room without looking back and he assumed it was either to go lay on the couch or back to bed. Grabbing a spoon from the cabinet, Kent picked up the bowel, heading back upstairs. The heat from the soup seeping through the bowel, warming his hands.

Kent thought as he walked about how scared Aaralynn had looked before she had her attack. Her skin had paled. The iris of her eyes dilated, and she had broken out in a sweat. A mixture between a deer in headlights and a rat caught in a corner by a tomcat. He hated witnessing how afraid she was. The need to hold her, shield her, and protect her was so strong he practically could feel it oozing off him in waves.

He reached the landing and strode down the hallway. His back straightened when he reached her door and nudged it open with a creak. "Hope you're hungry."

"Hmmm, it smells good," she sniffed the air after he entered.

"It's chicken soup with dumplings." He walked over; Ash was already at the foot of the bed snoring. "Now, I want you to eat and I will give you some Tylenol when you are done." The food sat down on the side table with a click. Leaning over he kissed her forehead, feeling it was still a bit warm and went to go grab the Tylenol from the bathroom.

He walked back over, placing the pills in her small palm and handed over a mug of water. In one gulp she swallowed the pills and placed the water on the side table. Aaralynn pulled down the covers and turned, moving her legs off the side of the bed.

"Whoa. What are you doing?" Concerned, he placed a hand on her shoulder to hold her in place.

"I want to get in pajamas at least. I am still in the clothes from dinner." Waving a hand over herself to prove a point.

He frowned and then she mirrored him. "I will get them for you."

"I am perfectly capable of getting my own clothes."

Aaralynn pushed up off the bed and then swayed a bit before plopping back down on it. He looked at her face and she was staring blankly at the floor. The sounds of her breathing coming a little too fast for his liking.

"What's wrong?" Worry pouring out in his tone. It unnerved him the way she blankly stared, with that odd look on her face. Like she wanted to throw up and fall over. Her skin got even paler too.

"Sorry." She shook her head and tried to stand again, but he put both hands on her shoulders this time to make her stay on the bed. "I got light-headed from standing too fast."

"Oh, no you don't. You don't look good darling and I am not having you faint on me. Tell me where the clothes are, and I'll get them."

She didn't respond just kept shaking her head and gave him a hard stare. He knew she had her undies in a bunch over him helping and being told no, but he was only thinking about her.

"Stay." He barked. "I mean it."

With a huff, he straightened. When he was sure she wouldn't move, he turned and walked out of the room. A few seconds later he was back carrying one of his big black long sleeve shirts that said "Brother's forever. Blood spilled we forget never." It was a gift from one of his men in his unit.

Her eyes followed his movements as he came back to stand in front of her. He laid the shirt back down on the bed, not even giving notice to the glare she was giving him. "Lift your arms." His tone coming out harsher than he had meant for it to be. The daggers she shot at him proof she didn't like it either. "Take off your jacket and shirt or I will do it for you." He leaned back folded his arms over his chest and waited.

Their eyes locked in a silent battle. Kent was used to this game and wasn't backing down. Eventually, she huffed out a breath of pent up air and unzipped her jacket. Her gaze never leaving his. The intensity in her eyes had his heart skipping and he mentally reprimanded himself because her being mad shouldn't get him worked up but for some reason it did. Maybe he did prefer his women hard-headed.

After removing her jacket, Aaralynn lifted her hands above her head. Thick locks of her hair fell around her face and shoulders, her eyes stern and not wavering. She was waiting on him to help and he felt a pang of something in his chest. He unfolded his arms and bent at the hip. Grabbing the hem of her shirt, he bunched it up and tugged it up over her head. She sat there on the bed, her arms still above her head, naked except the grey lacey bra she wore that barely contained her. Her full breast and hips had his mouthwatering.

The cream-colored skin of her stomach looked soft and lightly puffed around the top of her pants. Kent drew in a sharp breath. His need to hold her and run his hands over her almost overwhelmed him, but he forced himself to hold it together. Now wasn't the time to do any of that. Grabbing his shirt off the bed he pulled it on over her head, tugging it down around her. Then he knelt to take her boots off.

"You don't have to do that." She protested.

"Be quiet" He gritted out before grabbing each boot and tugging them off in one swift motion. The look of surprise had him smiling. "Now the pants."

The blush that filled her cheeks warmed his insides. He thought she was going to argue again but instead, she leaned back on her elbows, her face softening a bit as she unbuttoned her jeans. With his help, she shimmied out of them and he kissed her thigh before standing back up.

"There," he said grabbing her clothes. She gave a smile that didn't reach her eyes and eased back onto the bed. He pulled the covers back up onto her lap. "I'll put these in the laundry with my clothes and I'll be back to check on you." She nodded and as he was leaving, he saw her grab the bowel. Dipping the spoon, she brought it to her lips. The feeling of being needed made his chest tighten. He wanted to be that for her. A man she could count on to be there and take care of her. Now, he just had to figure out which was a priority to him. His unit or her.

****

The sun was peeking through the curtains, basking the floor with an orange glow. Aaralynn felt heat against her back and a weight along her middle.

Her head was pounding, and she felt off. A light breeze fanned her neck and she instinctively knew Kent was laying behind her. She realized she must have fallen asleep at some point and he stayed in bed with her. The last thing she remembered was eating some warm soup.

A vision glittered in her mind of her hair being caressed and strong arms wrapping around her. She could swear she heard Kent's voice, low and sweet whispering to her but she couldn't quite make out what it was saying. *It must have been a dream*. She blinked and tried to sit up, which was hard for two reasons. One, her pounding headache seemed to get worse with the movement. Two, she couldn't move the arm on her. Her limbs felt so weak. Maybe she was getting sick. She hoped she wasn't getting sick, but she couldn't deny the way her body was reacting.

She shifted to face him. Their noses almost touching. He was dreaming. His breathing sped up and slowed down in a methodic rhythm. His eyelids were moving back and forth in a jerking motion. Slowly, her eyes traced the lines of his face. Starting at his hairline following his smooth skin, further down to the scruff making a shadow of a beard on his jaw. Aaralynn loved the light shadow look but she wasn't a beard person. She loved that he always shaved his face clean.

Her hand gently pulled the covers back to reveal an almost naked man before her. His muscled chest and tight stomach made her mouth go dry. The top of his boxers hung low on his hips. He had one of those V lines that always made her sigh with desire. He laid on his side and his muscled arm was twitching from time to time. She used her hand to caress his shoulder, easing her hand to his face when his features changed.

Kent seemed to calm under her touch. His breathing slowed and the twitching calmed slightly. Aaralynn allowed her eyes to move from his face, trailing down his neck, to land on the scar at his shoulder. Her fingers gently ran over it, tracing a circle around the white edges. *It must have hurt*, she thought to herself. Her eyes flitted up to look at his when she felt fingers running up and down her spine.

Kent's eyes were open, watching her and he had a big grin splayed across his face. Her hands snaked up around his neck and ran through his hair. He let out a low sexy groan and it vibrated through her. His hand ran down her spine and cupped her butt, pulling her closer against him. She could feel his arousal against her stomach, and she purposefully wiggled. He sucked in a breath, loving the effect she had on him.

"You think that's funny, do you?" He swiftly moved his hand from under his head and the other tightened on her bottom when he moved to his back, effectively positioning her to lay on top of him. Aaralynn gave out a small sound. A mix between a gasp and a giggle.

"That's better," he sweetly said in her ear.

The movement made her a bit dizzy and she tried to ignore the headache that seemed to be spreading from the back of her head to her temples. She would have retorted back if her effort to ignore her pounding head actually worked. Sadly, it did not.

He frowned. "What's wrong."

"My head," she sat back on him, cowgirl style. Kent made a hissing sound as his hard member pressed against her sex from the position. Attempting to ignore the dizziness at the movement, she frantically rubbed her finger over her temples. Her eyes slammed shut and she just rubbed, trying but failing to get the headache to go away.

"You might be dehydrated," His hand touched her forehead. She let out a, "Mmmmm" at the feel of his cool hand against her hot flesh.

He wiggled his hips and helped her to slide off him. Aaralynn sat on the edge of the bed squinting her eyes to see him. All the dizziness had her nauseated. Through the slits, she saw him go to the bathroom and come back out. He stood before her and handed her a glass of water and four pills.

"Take these," he ordered.

"What are they?"

"Migraine medicine and Tylenol cold and flu." He placed them in her hand. In one gulp she swallowed them down, wincing at the feel of them sliding down her throat. She took the glass and took a few sips to help push them back down. When she tried handing the glass back he held up his hands. "You are going to finish that whole glass. You are probably dehydrated. When you are done, I will help you to the bathroom. Then I will go and get breakfast from the house and bring it back. You need to rest today before you do get sick."

Aaralynn had never been waited on before and it felt weird. Nice, but weird. She stared at the man before her, well she probably looked more like she was glaring from her lowered eyelids, but she couldn't help it. She was thankful for him being here right now and she wasn't going to complain. Her stomach gurgled and she tried to hurry as fast as she could to finish the water. Her need for a shower, some alone time, and food getting the better of her.

****

Thirty minutes later Aaralynn was settled in the shower, while Kent went downstairs. He knew she wasn't feeling well yesterday, and she still wasn't today. She had been going nonstop since he had met her, and he figured it was catching up with her. Not to mention, the climate in Montana was a bit different than Maryland. Ash had followed him downstairs and he opened the door to let her out. He turned to put on his boots, intending to go to the main house but then hesitated, remembering last night. The way she reacted coupled with the possible threat coming, he wouldn't feel comfortable leaving her in the cottage by herself. He wasn't sure who or when the other man or men would show up. Instead, Kent went to the phone on the wall and called up to the main house. Chuckling lightly whenever he had to use the old cord phone from his youth as it brought back so many memories. No one hand these anymore and it was vintage in his mind.

After two rings the woman he wanted answered the phone. "Hello."

"Hi, Gran."

"Oh, hi sweetie, what do you need?"

"Gran, Aaralynn isn't feeling too well. I am letting her rest. I don't want to leave her alone."

"Yea no problem sweetie. I will have one of the boys bring over breakfast. The poor dear. Hugh told me all about it this morning. I hope everything will be alright."

"Of course, he did," Kent mumbled into the phone. He couldn't blame the older man, but he did want them to tell the women together. Oh well. "Oh Gran, something else."

He heard clucking coming across the line and knew his Gran was waiting for him to go on. "My friend Tanner, one of the guys from the unit, is off for two weeks. Do you mind if he comes over and goes to the wedding too?"

"Not at all, honey. The more the merrier! I don't have anywhere else to put him unless he sleeps in the loft in the barn." Kent heard the clucking again and knew she was thinking.

He lightly chuckled, "I will let you know if that is necessary. Thanks, Gran. Love you."

"Love you too sweetheart. I'll have them bring over two plates as soon as I get them together. Let me know if the poor dear needs anything else."

"Will do," and they both hung up.

Scratching at the front door had him turning to let Ash back in. Stopping over the threshold she shook off white powder, getting it everywhere, before continuing into the kitchen. It must have started to snow again and his was confirmed when he took a look outside to see about two inches of fresh snow covering the ground. If it didn't stop soon no one would be going anywhere. He looked over by the fireplace and saw there were only a few pieces of logs left to burn, so he pulled his boots on and jacket to go outside to check for more wood.

He searched the porch and then the side of the cottage with no luck. Then he remembered they used to put it on the back sunroom and turned back inside to go check. In the sunroom, there was a closet and when he opened it, he saw it was full. Hauling out some logs, he filled the tray by the fireplace. Sitting down he yanked at his boots and jacket, placing them by the front door before starting on making a fire. Finishing up, Kent sat back on his heels and rubbed his hands, trying to get the debris off them.

Out of the corner of his eye, he saw Aaralynn walking down the stairs. Getting up he met her at the bottom. Her long damp red tendrils fell from a loose cup and her skin appeared freshly scrubbed. The pink flannel pajamas clung to her so tight that when she breathed, he could see the outline of her nipples. He cleared his throat, preparing to say something when a rapping at the door stole his attention. Turning, he opened the door already knowing what it was about. Aaralynn was behind him trying to catch a peek at their guest.

"Hey you two," Molly said. She was all bundled up and Kent noticed Reed was standing behind her off the porch. His brother stared at Molly's back like he was looking through her. Kent didn't know what was up with those two and right now it wasn't the time to ask. Reed gave a smile and Aaralynn said from behind him "Hi! Come on in."

Kent stepped to the side giving them both room to enter. Molly held up three plates and said, "where do you want these?"

"In there is fine," Aaralynn chimed in before he could, pointing to the kitchen. Ash leisurely trotted in from the kitchen and gave a halfhearted barked.

"You're a little late, aren't you?" Kent replied sarcastically and all the people laughed.

Ash let out a huff of air in reply and went to lay on the couch. Her head still up watching everyone as an uncomfortable Molly and a just as uncomfortable Reed walked past them into the kitchen.

Aaralynn turned to walk away but Kent grabbed her hand and tugged her back towards him. He waited until she met his eyes. "How are you feeling?"

Her smile didn't reach as high as it normally did but he was grateful for it, nonetheless. "I'm better. The shower helped a little. I still feel a bit off from the migraine last night, but I'll be ok once I get some food in me."

He nodded just as he heard a commotion coming from the kitchen. He dropped her hand and she turned her gaze toward the noise. The curve of her neck enticing him to plant a kiss there, but he held himself back. A moment later Molly and Reed came out of the kitchen. The sight of them both trying to fit in the doorway at once was comical to him, but he didn't dare laugh. After a few attempts and pained looks from both of them, Reed held out a hand signaling for Molly to go first, which she did.

"I hope you feel better. I also brought a packet of lavender bath salts in case you need a little downtime." Kent watched as Molly wrapped her in a hug and Aaralynn squeezed her lightly back before letting go.

Reed held out a hand to him and he shook it. "I'll let you know if I hear anything."

"Same here," Reed tilted his head toward Aaralynn, "you just make sure she is ok. We don't need any sick people around here, wedding or not."

Kent gave a chuckled as they all said their goodbyes and he watched as his brother and Molly walked back out the door. Kent turned around to say something but Aaralynn was already gone. He wondered where she could have gone but he didn't have to wonder too long when he heard rustling in the kitchen. With Ash still on the couch there was only one other person it could be.

Before going into the kitchen to make breakfast he shot a quick text to Tanner.

Kent: Hey, you can come to visit. Do you need to crash here, or will you be staying in town?

Kent pocketed the phone while he waited for a response. Striding into the kitchen, he leaned against the doorjamb just watching as Aaralynn pulled out one plate from the microwave and put another one in. Pressing a few buttons, she started it and turned to him, freezing in her tracks. The surprised look on her face had his insides warming and he smiled.

"So, you think that is funny," her tone of voice as she went to sort through a drawer told him she was joking with him.

"Uh-huh."

She let out a strangled noise he couldn't quite make out before she closed the drawer, she was in. Her nose crinkled. "Where are all the utensils?" The irritating way she asked reminded him of a toddler. The microwaved dinged and the phone in his pocket buzzed.

He grabbed his phone as she went for the microwave. "In the drawer by the fridge," Kent motioned toward the other side of cabinets at the fridge.

He heard her say "Oh" as he looked down at his phone to read the message.

Tanner: Cool brother. I will be staying at a hotel, so I don't impose. I just need your address man so I can google places.

Kent text back the address before clicking his phone off and putting it back in his pocket. Pushing off the doorjamb he walked over to where Aaralynn was. She had the plates on the small kitchen table and was putting ketchup on her eggs. *Hmmm, interesting.*

"You are going to eat and then go rest. I want you in bed till you feel better. I think you have been too stressed lately." Kent grabbed both plates when she went to put the ketchup back. Turning back around, she went to grab her plate but then placed a hand on the chair instead, leaning over it.

"You ok?" he inquired.

Kent watcher her shake her head, back and forth, then side to side before lifting her head. Her gaze pinned on him. "I got dizzy again but I'll be fine. I just need to eat." She pushed off the chair and stood up straight. "I'm not an invalid you know. I can handle thigs myself." She snapped.

"I know," was all he could say. He knew she could handle herself, that she had been, but he wanted her to know she didn't have to do it alone anymore. For whatever reason, he felt adamant about him being the one to help.

"Maybe I have been under too much stress, but it never seems to go away. You would think my body would be used to it by now." She gave a halfhearted laugh and it tore at his heart a little. From what he understood she had been through so much and he had barely heard the tip of it. He knew a lot involved her mother and he wanted to know more.

"So," he began, taking their plates into the Livingroom and depositing them on the coffee table. "Tell me how you got Ash. It isn't every day you come across a wolf."

He waved his hand for her to sit and she crisscrossed her legs in front of the coffee table on the floor. She looked so cute and vulnerable at that moment, sitting on the floor Indian style in her flannel pajamas. He would be a fool to believe she was a vulnerable child, but he knew that at times she felt like one. He had seen it on her face briefly more than once.

He turned back towards the kitchen, "Hold on." He hurried to grab two cups of milk from the fridge and placed them back down in front of their plates on the coffee table. Aaralynn gave Ash a piece of sausage and bacon as he sat down next to her on the floor. He assumed she had forgotten his earlier question but as he took a bite of his biscuit, she cleared her throat.

Turning from Ash, she stared at her plate, pushing food around with her fork. "The story of finding Ash isn't all that exciting. I was walking through an alleyway and this man had a box that said free on the side. He had on a black trench coat and messy hair but what bothered me the most was he looked to be messed up on something. He was twitching and talking to himself. I wasn't going to even stop but something told me to. I saw him drop the box and heard a thunk, then a tiny squeal. I stopped in my tracks when I saw him pick up this tiny puppy, or what I thought was a puppy by its hind leg. He let it dangle in the air while he lit a lighter and started singing off fur. I think he was going to try and eat it. I don't know if there were any more puppies ever in the box or if he just took the box or what, but I was not about to let him harm that poor creature.

Emotion welled up in Kent. A burning intensity. Clenching his fist at his sides, he held his tongue and let her continue.

"The squeal alone had my heartbreaking and I just couldn't watch it. So, I barreled into him. I think it surprised him just as much as myself since I normally don't act that way, but he dropped the puppy back into the box and yelled at me. Called me a demon and hissed. Actually, hissed at me." Aaralynn chuckled at that and Kent had a burst of pride in his chest. He knew if push came to shove, she would always do the right thing. "I told him he was right; I eat souls and I will eat his if he ever harms another living creature. He yelled when I leaned in towards him and whispered that maybe I would do it now."

Aaralynn gave a sad smile and shook her head at the memory. "I didn't know she was a wolf pup. I don't even know how you would find one, but I picked her up in my arms and took her home. I took her to the vet the next day and thank goodness, I knew the vet. She used to date a friend of mine. She agreed to say she was a mixed shepherd and after her vaccination and health clearance, I kept her. I have had her for three years now."

Kent watched as Aaralynn turned around to look at Ash, who was laying on the couch. Her head was down, her big black eyes intently watching the two of them. It was almost like she knew they were talking about her and maybe she did. Kent saw the smile lazily spread across Aaralynn's face while she looked at Ash. Gently, she pets her head before turning back around to face him.

"You going to eat?" She asked, using her fork to point at his plate.

"Yea. I was just listening to you." Kent turned back toward his plate and began eating. They ate in silence. Neither one of them speaking the whole time. The only noise was the crackle of the fireplace. The soft glow of the flames mingled with the smell of burning wood was relaxing and not uncomfortable at all. Kent's phone buzzed again, and he pulled it out of his pocket.

Tanner: I booked a place in Crystal Cave. I will be there tomorrow after I check-in. See you soon brother.

Kent: Good, see you then.

"Your woman messaging you?" Aaralynn inquired.

"Yea I practice polygamy. You didn't know? I have five women already. You want to be number six?" That was answered with a smack to his shoulder. He rubbed his arm, not that it hurt but just for show. "Geeze woman. Women don't know how to take a joke."

That comment landed him another smack and a giggle. She took her empty plate and cup into the kitchen with Lent following close behind her. She took his plates too and began washing all their dishes, drying them, and handing them back to Kent. Kent put them back where they belonged.

She leaned against the counter watching him put away dishes. He liked giving her time to look at him. He made a show of putting the dishes away.

Flexing all his muscles in his arms as he leaned over the counter to reach the top of the cabinet.

"It was my marine buddy on the phone. He is coming to visit for a little while." Kent liked the feeling of her watching him. The heat radiated through him and pooled down towards his growing erection.

"So, your buddy is coming. Is he staying here?" He tilted his head toward her, not missing her questionable look. He grinned.

"No. He is staying at a hotel in town." Relief swept over her features so profoundly that it almost had him chuckling again. Maybe she didn't want anyone intruding on their space and that thought made his already warm body tingle with even more heat. *Maybe she wanted him to herself just as much as he wanted her too.* Kent finished putting away dishes and wiped his hands on the dishtowel.

Aaralynn pushed off the counter and went over to grab a bowel for Ash's breakfast. Kent's arm shot out in an instant when she swayed just trying to stand back up with the bowel.

"Whoa there," his hands cupped her hips and pressed her back against him to steady her. "What happened?"

"Sorry," she had her arms held out to her sides to center herself. "I got a bit dizzy." She shook her head and turned to face him. Her eyes wide and her face flushed. "I am starting to feel like a horse with you saying whoa all the time."

A small laugh escaped him but then frowned again when she swayed into him. Her body collapsing against his chest. Her cheek rested on him and her hands flew to his shoulders. The bowel fell with a clang to the floor. Ash heard the noise and ran into the kitchen. Her nails making tapping noises as she moved.

Kent wrapped one arm around Aaralynn and held out the other to Ash. Ash stopped and sat down. "It's ok girl. Your mama's fine." He pulled her head back with his free hand to look at her face, "we are getting you to bed. No arguing" he said when she opened her mouth. "I told Gran and everyone you are staying in to rest and that is exactly what you are doing. Now that I fed you it is off to bed little lady." She pushed against his chest. He reluctantly released her and watched her move to go upstairs but she swayed again after a few steps. Swiftly he walked over to her to scoop her up in his arms. She gave out a soft squeak of alarm before relaxing into him.

Once upstairs, Kent deposited her into bed. He made sure she had water before closing the curtains. He placed a light kiss on her forehead, brushing her hair from her flushed face. She had already started to doze. Her eyes were closed, and her breathing was slow. One last kiss on top of her head and he left her to go back downstairs. There he fed Ash, who was so grateful she licked his hands afterward. Then, he let her out for a bit. While Ash was outside doing her business, he leaned against the porch railing and text Ray to let him know he hadn't seen anything yet and that Aaralynn was in bed not feeling well. He would have her call to check-in and to talk to Stan later today if that was fine.

It wasn't long before Ray replied. Nothing had happened on his end yet. Ray hadn't heard anything from Tony. He wasn't answering his phone and Billy's men hadn't been back into the bar yet. That didn't sit well with Kent however there was nothing else to do but wait. Kent knew the girls were planning to do some wedding stuff today and his brothers were going to go pick up Austin's tux in town. Kent wouldn't be missing much today.

When Ash came back onto the porch, she shook off a light dusting of snow, spraying it all over him. He cursed under his breath. He had been so distracted that he didn't realize it had started snowing again. The weather this time of year was colder than this time last year. He made a mental note to make sure the house stayed warm. They didn't need any pipes freezing up. It happened more often than he would like to think. Shaking his head, Kent followed Ash back inside to check on the fireplace.

****

Chapter 14

Aaralynn had woken up with a start. Blinking the dryness from her eyes she tried to focus on where she was. Her skin felt flush and the pillow felt damp. She sat up straight and pushed her back against the headboard. The air in her lungs felt heavy and she tried to calm her breathing. *In and out, in and out. That's better*, the voice in her mind said.

She heard scratching coming from the door and a low whimper sounded on the other side. Sounds of heavy footsteps were coming from outside the door, accompanied by a muffled noise. She just remembered where she was when the door opened, and Ash came bursting through with Kent. A worried look on his face. Ash hopped onto the bed and wiggled up to her, licking her face. Aaralynn pushed her back just as Kent reached her side of the bed and sat next to her. His hand felt warm against the skin of her forehead.

"How are you feeling?" His tone was gentle and comforting.

"Better than earlier but I feel sticky." She cleared the dryness from her throat. "I think I need a shower." He grabbed the cup of water on the nightstand and handed it to her.

Taking it gratefully with both hands, she swallowed down a few big gulps. Letting the liquid cool her dry throat. She handed it back to him with a small sigh. A shiver traveled from her toes to her head and she felt goosebumps pricking her skin.

"Let's get you that shower and then you can try to eat something." Kent stood and pushed the covers back. "Can you stand?"

Aaralynn didn't say anything, just nodded and flung her feet over the side of the bed. She wasn't going to show weakness if she could help it. She had taken care of herself all these years and whatever was going on with her right now was not going to keep her down. She pushed off the mattress with her hands and stood. Her legs felt wobbly but she didn't fall back down. She took that as a positive sign. Kent held out an elbow for her and her hand wrapped around his arm for support.

"What time is it?" She couldn't tell from the drawn curtains but she couldn't believe she had been asleep that long.

Slowly they made their way down the hallway to the bathroom. "It's five-thirty. I let you sleep while I made a few calls and cleaned up."

A tiny gasp escaped her and he shot her a concerned look. She couldn't believe she had been asleep so long. Her head felt weak. It must be the after-effects of the migraine she had before she fell asleep. Her body, on the other hand, was a mixture of relaxed and tense. When they reached the bathroom, Kent turned on the shower. After checking the temperature, he sat on the toilet in front of her. Without asking he began slowly unbuttoning her top, pushing it off her shoulders. The material falling to the floor in a puddle of fabric.

Unable to miss the look of desire in his gaze or the way they darkened while lingering on her breast. She felt herself flush for a whole different reason this time and went to cross her arms over her chest. His lips thinned in a straight line but he didn't say anything. The look of disappointment plain as day.

Kent loosened the light tie on her pants and grabbed at her hips with both hands to pull down the flannel. Her underwear came down with her pants and she stood before him fully bare. The sound of the shower in the background the only noise as she stood there, frozen in that spot. Nervously, she bit the inside of her lip, as his eyes roamed her naked body from head to toe, lingering in a few places, then back up again to latch onto her eyes.

The dark grey of his eyes had flecks of blue in them tonight and she was fascinated by it. His breathing seemed to pick up but then he shook his head and stood. Confused, Aaralynn just watched him as he leaned into the shower. She guessed he was checking the water temperature before turning back to her and cupping her cheeks in his hands.

"I am going to let you get a shower." Her hand came up to rest on top of his and she saw him close his eyes, shuddering at her touch. She didn't want him to leave and didn't understand why he would either. "I will be downstairs making dinner." The roughness of his voice made her stomach clench. His hands never leaving her face, but his features seemed taut like he was holding himself back.

"Stay."

His eyes flew open searching her face. "What?" His voice low and questioning.

"I want you to stay." Her tone soft but firm.

His eyes searched her face for the longest time. They stood there listening to the water running and the echo of their breathing. She felt everywhere his eyes roamed, almost as if in a caress. His thumb began lazy circles on her jaw and after what seemed like an eternity, he bent down and kissed her. This kiss was soft and inviting, like an unspoken promise. One of his hands moved down to cup her bottom and pull her against him. His arousal straining through his jeans, rubbing against her causing her now damp panties to rub uncomfortably. His other hand ran from her face to the back of her head, locking her to him.

She relaxed into him, her hands clinging to his biceps. The feel of his mouth claiming hers had her sex needing release. A tiny whimper escaped her and he slid one of his thighs between her legs. His jeans becoming wet where she ground against him in abandon. The shower was all but forgotten as they both sought their release in each other. She loved the feel of his fingers digging into the sensitive skin of her ass. He was all but lifting her off the ground to grind her against him harder. Heat building that made her ache to have him inside her.

A pounding came from the door downstairs, causing them to jump. Kent tore his mouth away from hers. They were both panting and she could see his jaw had clenched, his body going tense. He let out a curse and pulled her away from him. She could see the wet spot she had made on his jeans. His eyes followed where hers were and she saw his lips tilt in a grin.

"Damn, you're so fucking hot." His words were so blunt that they sent a tingle throughout her body. He reached for her again just as the banging repeated. "Fuck!" He jerked his hand back.

"Who is that?" Aaralynn asked. Her voice coming out harsh due to her building frustration.

"I don't know sweetheart but they better have a good reason for interrupting." He walked past her and smacked her bottom. She jumped at the contact, giving a light squeal. "We will finish this." He hollered over his shoulder as he walked out of the bathroom and closed the door. Leaving Aaralynn naked, horny and alone.

After her shower Aaralynn rushed to her room to throw on a pair of jeans, a tank top, and her new jean jacket, leaving it open. After running a brush through her hair, she made her way downstairs to see where Kent had gone.

Kent, Reed, and Hugh were standing in the Livingroom with Tony, who was sitting on the couch. Ash was scratching at the door to be let in. All the men turned toward her as she descended the staircase. Her nerves on edge at their expressions.

"What is going on? Tony, why are you here?" She knew that the last question was probably a stupid one but she wanted everyone to start explaining what was going on. Reaching the bottom step, she moved to the front door and let Ash in.

The wolf came in and sniffed her twice before turning toward the men and growling. She heard the familiar click of a gun being cocked and her gaze searched the room. Hugh stood with his shotgun at his side. Ash growled again.

"Put that gun away!" Aaralynn all but screamed as she stepped in front of Ash.

****

Kent hated the look on her face when she was trying to protect her pet. Quickly, he moved over to Hugh and put his hand on the loaded gun. "Put that away, Hugh." He flicked his eyes from the man to the animal. "She doesn't like it." Hugh gave him a challenging stare for a brief minute, but then huffed out a breath and uncocked the shotgun. The older man shifted his feet and turned his eyes toward Aaralynn.

"Anyone going to tell me what the hell is going on?" The aggravated and grateful look she gave him had Kent's insides warming again and he knew he would be hard in seconds. His body just couldn't help it.

"This man was trespassing on the property," Reed said before anyone else spoke. He leaned over and hauled Tony to his feet. Kent saw the moment Aaralynn noticed Tony's hands were tied behind his back. "He told us you were expecting him." Reed's accusing voice had Kent tensing. In his mind, he knew his brother understood what was going on but he still didn't like the way he had said that. *It isn't her fault, so don't make it sound like it is.*

"I needed to make sure you were ok and to bring you back home," Tony said. His lip bleeding and Kent could see he would have a black eye in the morning.

Kent held his breath, waiting to see what Aaralynn would do. He knew it would tear up his insides if she went to him. He wasn't normally a jealous man but he had already claimed her in his heart. He didn't like it when other men touched what was his. It turns out, he didn't have to worry. Aaralynn never moved. She never even tried to. He watched as she blinked, took in a few deep breaths, and shook out her hands.

Ash, sitting down, leaned into her, and Aaralynn's hand immediately went to her head, rubbing. He figured it was a calming gesture and he was grateful for the beast then. Reed shook Tony by the ties bounding his wrist when he went to move toward her.

Aaralynn held up a hand." You mean to tell me you drove all the way out here, left Ray alone, to find me?"

"Yea." Aaralynn's hand stopped stroking Ash at the lack of remorse in his tone.

"How did you find me, Tony, because no one knew where I was." Aaralynn dropped her hand and stared at Tony. Kent's back stiffened as he moved to stand next to her.

Tony looked confused for a minute. Shaking his head and rolling his shoulders back before he focused his eyes on her. "Does it matter?" He responded, "I found you. Now I can take you home."

"It does matter." Kent felt her shiver so slightly beside him that he wasn't sure if he imagined it. "You knew why I was out here Tony. There was no reason to come find me. I know Ray told you I was fine." Her arms folded in front of her.

Tony's eyes hardened as he looked between Kent and her. Kent saw the other man's jaw clench and unclench. "Fine!" his voice rang through the small space and he saw Aaralynn flinch. His arm flew around her to rub her shoulder. He felt better when she didn't shrug him away. "Oh, so you'd rather he protect you than me? I have known you for a long-time baby. Why are you doing this?" Kent instantly tensing at the term of endearment. Tony's voice was almost pleading now and Kent would feel bad for the other man if he had it in him to do so. As it is, Tony was the reason that they soon would be Billy and his men, if they weren't already here.

Aaralynn shook her head at him while rubbing her forehead. "Tony, I already told you, I don't like you, like you, like me. We are friends or were. That is until you put me in more danger."

Tony's eyes laser-focused on her face now. The other man searched her face slowly and when he saw something in them, Kent didn't know what, he slumped back down on the couch. "I love you," he mumbled under his breath and Reed let out a frustrated grumble.

Hugh gave a hearty, "Ha!"

Kent ran a hand through his hair and kissed Aaralynn's temple. He wasn't sure what to do about Tony but he wouldn't be their problem much longer. Kent knew Reed called the deputy to report a man trespassing and he would be at the ranch soon.

Aaralynn shrugged out of his hold and moved to kneel in front of Tony. Her expression softened and she laid her hands on her knees. Kent's stomach churned at her nearness to the other man but he didn't say anything. Ash moved closer to him and they both watched as Aaralynn and Tony talked.

"Tony, look," she let out a breath, "I don't have feelings for you like that. You are like a big brother to me. I adored you as one, but romantically I have no feelings. Besides that, you all but lead Billy's men to me. Ray said they were seen following you when you left and now, we believe they are coming here." Tony's eyes, now full of unshed tears, looked at her. The man looked broken and, at that moment, Kent felt bad for the man.

"I didn't know." His response low. Kent almost missed it. Reed and Hugh came over to where Kent stood. Both men just observed the same interaction. A broken man with a broken heart. Kent didn't know what he'd do if Aaralynn ever told him she didn't like him as he liked her, but he knew he wouldn't go stalking her. *Would he?*

The sound of sirens approaching caught all of their attention. Reed went over to Tony. "Alright, time's up." He pulled Tony to his feet. "Deputy is here to talk to you." Tony looked scarred and planted his feet.

"What?" he choked out. "I didn't do anything!"

"You were caught trespassing my friend," Reed said, "and around here that is a criminal offense." Reed yanked Tony to follow him out the door. Hugh nodded his hat at Aaralynn before lifting the shotgun over his shoulder and heading out the door too.

Aaralynn stood and rushed over to Kent, "Don't let them lock him up. I know he was wrong and this is a big mess but he isn't a criminal." She grabbed his shirt and tugged him toward her. "Please." Her words were like lava in his veins. He would do anything this woman asked even if it went against his better judgment. Grabbing both her arms he nodded and bent down to claim her mouth in a chaise kiss. Releasing her, Kent spun to head out the door. *Damn him and his lack of common sense.*

✱✱✱✱✱✱✱✱✱✱

Chapter 15

Two hours later Kent watched the deputy follow Tony's car down the driveway to make sure he left town. Kent believed Tony meant Aaralynn no harm but he wasn't taking any chances with his obsession over his woman. Yes, his. He already claimed her and he wouldn't be letting any harm come to her. Earlier, Kent used the time that Aaralynn was asleep to contact his next in command. Informing him that he would be retiring instead of returning. Now Kent only had to turn in his official forms and make plans for what he would do next. The deputy had mentioned they were starting a new K-9 program and needed someone to run it. Maybe he would go in and talk to him after the wedding to see if it was an option. Either way, he needed to figure out how he was going to talk Aaralynn into staying because if she didn't he would follow her instead.

Walking into the cottage, he spotted Aaralynn sitting in a chair at the dining room table playing with something black. She was so focused on the object that she was oblivious to him walking up and pulling out a chair. He noticed the black object was a camera that she seemed to be adjusting.

"Where did the camera come from?"

Her green eyes turned up to him and he saw they were red-rimmed and shining with tears. His heart clenched and it took everything in him not to pull her onto his lap to soothe her. She wiped her face with her sleeve before turning her attention back to the camera.

"I have always had this camera. It was in my bag with two other ones."

"So you like photography?" Keeping her focused on other things would help him learn more about her. Something was obviously bothering her but he wouldn't press her about it right now.

"Yes. I got my first camera when I was ten and I loved being able to take photos." Her eyes glanced back up to his face. The shimmer in her eyes had his attention, as the corners crinkled with adoration at what she was talking about. "There is something to be said about looking back at a photo that brings you so many emotions and memories. It is a wonderful way to relive times in your life or being able to share them with others." Her smile had him catching his breath. He leaned over and took her hand.

"Have you ever done it for work?"

She shook her head and pulled her hand back to fidget with her camera again.

"Why not? I bet you'd be great at it."

She gave a half heart laugh at his response. "You have never seen me take pictures. How would you know?"

"Just a hunch." Shrugging his shoulders, he went on, "If you are as passionate about taking pictures as you are at talking about them, they must be amazing." He knew it sounded like a line but he did mean it. "Besides, you have the time to do it while you're here. You might as well take advantage of it. I can take you around and you can get some shots." He added.

"Maybe," her voice cracked and he took her hand again to make her look at him.

"What's wrong?" His thumb lightly rubbed the outside of her hand in an attempt to relax her and help her feel more comfortable to share. She sat back in her chair breaking their connection. Wanting her to open up to him he remained silent and waited for her answer.

Unable to take his eyes off her, Kent watched as she took in a few deep breaths. Her chest rhythmically rising and falling. The camera turned in her hands a few more times before she sat it down and looked at him. Her eyes displayed the effect of her worry of the evening. Her tired expression made him itch to be able to take all her problems away.

When he thought she was done talking, he pushed his chair back, ready to get up, when her soft whimper reached his ears. She had started crying again. *What has her so upset*, he wondered.

"I should leave." Three words had him up out of his chair and kneeling right next to her.

"You are not leaving." He stated without giving any room for further discussion. She would never be leaving him.

"But- "

"No. You are safest here with me and my family."

"But they are in more danger with me here."

The camera trembled in her hand. He plucked it from her fingers and laid it carefully on the tabletop. Turning back to her, he shifted her chair so she was facing him. Firmly, he gripped her upper arms and without any hesitation spoke.

"You are safer here with me and my brothers. No one will harm you as long as you are here."

"What about the rest of your family?" The sound of her sniffling had his insides twisting.

"They all understand what is going on and they are not shy about protecting themselves or the ones they care about." Snaking his hand up to cup her chin, he made her look at him. Her eyes, those beautiful green eyes, looked at him with such fear and concern.

"Why?"

He tilted his head to the side and furrowed his brows. "Why what?"

"Why do this for me? From the first day you met me, you have been trying to help protect me. Now you are putting your family in danger trying to protect me. I just don't understand why."

Kent stood, pulling her up with him. He moved himself to sit down in the chair, sliding Aaralynn onto his lap. Cradling her to him, he laid her legs over his and held her close. Her head rested on his shoulder and she sighed. Her breathing slowed to a normal pace and he felt her body relax against him. Lightly, he brushed a kiss over her temple and swept a lock of hair behind her ear. This woman, he realized, was one of the most important people in the world to him and she needed a reasonable explanation. She deserved the truth, but he was unsure if he could reveal his true feelings. He was still figuring them out himself.

He rubbed up and down her arm, leaning his head to rest on top of hers. "If you want a rational explanation for my protectiveness over you, I don't know if I have one." *Honesty. Just give her honesty.* "I think at first I saw someone who needed my help and I was able to supply that. But, the longer I was in your company the more I wanted to *be* in your company. Does that make sense?"

Her head jerked in a nodding motion under his chin and he smiled. "I knew I had strong feelings for you early on. I can't say exactly when, but I can't deny it either. After being with you, really being with you, I can't be without you." She placed a hand on his chest and pushed herself back some to look at his face. So many questions swirled around in her eyes.

"What does that mean exactly?"

"Just what I said. I can't be without you. Let me ask you this, how do you feel about me? Is this just one-sided or do you feel something between us?"

His hold loosened on her when she shifted more to get comfortable. Kent was also glad because she was beginning to press him through his jeans and that would have been more of a distraction. He was going to drop his line of questioning and move on when she suddenly spoke. Her eyes roaming over his face as she did so.

"I didn't want to feel anything. After my ex, I figured being single was better than anything else. And well, you know a little bit about my family background. It wasn't like I grew up with the best examples." A tear rolled down her cheek and Kent wiped it away with the pad of his thumb. "I…" Her eyes left his face and moved to her hands that were now clasped together in her lap. "I like you. A lot. I care about you and just knowing that scares me."

Hope bloomed in his chest but he still wasn't sure what to make of that. "Why does it scare you?" Her fidgeting with her hands seemed to be an anxiety relaxer for her but it was beginning to get on his nerves because she wasn't answering him. After a few more seconds he repeated his question.

"Why does it scare you?"

"Because it means I could lose you!" Her high-pitched voice rang in his ears but he didn't care.

She was worried about losing him and that made him happy because it meant she cared about him a lot too. Even if she wasn't ready to say the words, he knew she felt it.

"Why are you smiling?!" Indignation was written all over her features.

"Sorry, but I am happy."

"You're happy because I'm scared? Or you're happy because I could lose you?" She pushed off his lap and stood. Every woman's signature moved when they are mad, hands-on-hips, and eyes narrowed.

Kent held his hands up in surrender. "Hey, I didn't mean it that way." He stood up too. He rubbed his hands on her shoulders, "I meant I am happy you care about me. So much so, that you are afraid of losing me." Her shoulders slumped.

"I do care but I hate feeling this way. Don't you understand? I hate being scared and worried. It's better not to be involved with anyone. Less drama."

"Less happiness too." He quipped.

Her eyes turned downward, suddenly interested in her toes. He cupped her chin and forced her eyes back to his. He could feel the heat from her body and it reminded him she had been feeling ill. Kent needed to get her back into bed. The wind had picked up outside and he could hear the rustling against the house. Whistles floating in through the window panes and Aaralynn's body trembled slightly.

"Look, we can finish this conversation later but one thing is for sure. I am getting you back in bed and you are going to eat and rest. No more talking about leaving." He held a finger to her lips when she opened her mouth, "I mean it. You are putting no one in danger but yourself if you leave and then I will have to follow you anyway. Do you want my brother and Annette mad because we missed the wedding?" He didn't like having to guilt her but he knew his point got across when she clamped her mouth shut so hard, he heard her teeth clank. "Now, turn your fine ass around and go to bed. I will be up after I feed Ash and get your dinner." With a low growl, she leaned over and grabbed her camera gear, and turned around.

Kent couldn't resist smacking her bottom as she walked past him to go back upstairs. The little squeal she let out had him adjusting his jeans and blood rushing to what felt like steel in his pants. That woman would be the death of him.

****

Sitting with all the women at the dining room table in the main house Aaralynn was starting to understand why she never wanted a big wedding. Her body was still a bit tired from her emotions of yesterday and now her head was hurting from listening to Annette and the other two women chatting about what still needed to happen for the wedding. Austin went with his brothers to get last-minute items and to pick up their tuxes that had been tailored. While they were away, Hugh was at the house, sitting in the Livingroom. All the men still on edge over the impending arrival of Billy or his men, or all of them.

To be honest, her anxiety over the whole matter was shot and she couldn't bring herself to worry anymore. Austin had slept next to her last night after she ate her soup and she loved how he cuddled her. Still feeling the flutters in her stomach at the thought, she shifted in her seat attempting to calm herself.

"I don't know if everything will get done," Annette was saying to the room while she added more candy to little bags that she was making for the guests as favors. How Aaralynn got roped into doing this free labor, she will never understand.

The women all murmured their responses of, "It will get done" and "Don't fuss over it", while she just sat there lost in her thoughts. Looking at the clock she realized she had been there for over four hours already and she hadn't let Ash out once. Finishing the bag, she was working on, she pushed her chair back and excused herself. The women barely acknowledged her retreat as they tried to finish the task of their bag making.

Aaralynn found Ash playing tug of war with a stuffed bear in the Livingroom. On one end was Ash and on the other was Holly. Kris was sitting on the floor watching as Hugh was reading the paper. A whistle got Ash's attention who dropped the bear and trotted over to her, sitting in front of her waiting for further instruction.

Hugh put down the paper and looked at her inquisitively. "And where are you going, young lady?" The two girls watched the exchange with a mix of boredom and anticipation.

"I am just letting this girl outside for a minute. I promise I won't go anywhere." Aaralynn made an X symbol across her heart.

"OK. But no going off the porch. I don't need anything else happening this week." The elderly man grumbled and proceeded to burp before turning back around and opening his paper. The two little girls giggled as they got up to go into the dining room and a small laugh escaped her lips before she could help it.

Aaralynn let Ash outside, turned to grab her jacket, and a scarf hanging on a hook before following Ash outside. The cold November air hit her lungs and assaulted her face. She pulled the scarf up over her mouth and nose to keep herself warm. She hated the cold but this wasn't normal cold for her. With the wind, it felt below zero, and back in Baltimore, it was at least warm enough for only a sweater. Here, it seemed, Mother Nature had other plans. Snow dotted the landscape and she could see the green contrast of some pine trees in the distance. The wooden fence barley stood out but the two red barns were defiantly noticeable from the soft blanket of white it has been covered in.

Ash walked around and did her business as Aaralynn leaned against the porch railing. Puffs of smoke floated around her from the dropping temperature. The sun doing nothing to warm up the day. Noises of laughter and muffled chatting could be heard coming from inside just beyond the door making her thoughts travel again.

Last night she was able to call Stan and make sure he was ok. Talking to Ray had them both emotional, but the hard as nails boss hid his feelings well by clearing his throat a few times. She was glad they were both ok and had not heard from Billy since they were seen following Tony. That bit of nerves, however, had a knot forming in her stomach at the implication of what was to come for her but she pushed it down, just like she was doing now at the reminder. Austin, his brothers, and even Hugh had taken it upon themselves to make sure she was safe and she knew she would have to trust that they could.

Stan had sounded horrible to her ears, all gruff and throaty but he assured her he was doing much better from when he first arrived. He initially tried to say it was nothing but she knew better than that. A high pitched "Hey!" brought her back to the present and she heard giggling once again from inside.

This was a family. One she would love to be a part of but she wasn't sure she should have the luxury of. She was a responsibility, as her mother drilled into her, and that meant she was a burden. She didn't want to be anyone's burden, which concluded her to being alone. She tried to explain that to Austin last night, it wasn't just about losing him, but he didn't want to hear any of it. His mind made up that she would stay.

A rush of chilly wind swept up her neck, rustling her hair and making her shiver. She looked around for Ash ready to go back inside before she froze but she was nowhere to be seen. Cupping her hands around her mouth she yelled out for her.

"Ash! Here girl!" Aaralynn let out a low whistle.

Nothing moved. No noise came. That was not like Ash. Normally she ran right to her and if she was further away, she would make barking or chuffing noise to alert her of where she was. For her to do nothing was odd.

Aaralynn whistled again and then cupped her hands to her mouth. Again, she yelled out. Once. Twice. When she did it for the third time and the yard was still silent, she got worried. A ball seemed to form in her throat and she felt like she couldn't swallow. Anxiety lacing through her in seconds, beginning to build to a panic. She moved off the porch to go look for her without thinking. Aaralynn tried tracing the faint paw prints in the snow but they were so erratic from Ash running around that it was hard to decide where to go.

One set leads off towards the barn where they had set up for the wedding. Setting off in that direction she looked around as she walked but still saw no sight of Ash. The sun was falling and an orange glow began to cover everything around her. The door to the barn was slid open a crack and the paw prints showed she went inside. Pushing open the door enough for herself to slip through, she instantly heard faint growling noises.

"Ash?"

After calling out she felt the hairs on her neck and arms rise. Something wasn't right and her whole body was on alert. She couldn't see anything; the interior was pitch black except for the sliver of orange glow coming in through the doorway. Moving toward the growling sounds she called out again. A faint whimper came next followed by a door slamming shut.

Aaralynn jumped, covering her mouth from the cry that escaped. She knew she would have to be quiet now, something was very wrong and all she could think about was Ash. She didn't want her to be in any danger either, but unarmed and out of her element, she felt helpless.

The faint rumble of a truck engine approaching had her heart skipping a beat. *The men must be home! They would know what to do!* Just as she turned to head back out of the barn door, it slid shut completely. Her heart pounded in her ears while her eyes fought to see, anything, in the darkness. If she wondered before about being alone, she knew she wasn't now.

Her ears strained to hear. At first, nothing seemed to be there, but then she heard boots moving in front of her. Her harsh breathing and pounding heart thrummed in her ears. The sound of a truck door opening and slamming shut momentarily stole her attention. Sounds of men talking loudly gave her some hope someone might hear her. She opened her mouth and began to scream but it was cut off by a large hand. The hand-pulled her against a hard body as another wrapped around her middle.

Her eyes got wide and her breathing became rushed. Panting against the hand covering her mouth, Aaralynn only hoped what noise she did make someone had heard.

"Shut your trap," the man in front of her said. "Or else that beast of yours will get sliced up into steaks." Something sharp ran up and down her upper arm and she realized the man must have a knife.

"You ready to go? The boss is waiting outback." The man behind her said. His hot breath swelling of whiskey and cigarettes. Immediately she knew who they were referring to. It had her heart pumping so hard she thought she might faint.

Suddenly, she picked up her foot and stomped it hard on the man's foot. She took a chance that if she couldn't see, then neither could either of them. The man swore under his breath and loosened his hold on her enough that she was able to get her arm free. Quickly, and with as much force as she could make from the odd angle, she elbowed him in what she thought was his stomach. His grip on her completely gone as she felt him bend over.

"What the hell bitch!" He bellowed behind her just as the blade of a knife grazed her chest and arm. Letting out a scream from the cuts she backed up tripping over one of their feet. As she was falling the barn door slid open with a big screeching noise.

Her eyes slightly adjusted to the tinted glow to see figures rushing in just before her head slammed into the wooden floor, causing her to let out a breath and blacking out.

****

Chapter 16

Kent got back to the house in a good mood. His brothers had teased and quizzed him on his female guest attempting to figure out what exactly was going on between them. He had told them only that she was special to him and as far as he was concerned it was a permanent type of special. Now he only hoped she would see it his way. His tux fitting took a bit longer since he couldn't make it yesterday for the final fitting, as he was taking care of his girl. The tailor understood, which was a relief, and finished his while they did the rest of their last-minute shopping.

Kent was happy that his brother finally found the woman he was meant for. As corny as it sounds, he finally understood the songs that talk about finding your missing piece because he felt he had finally found his too. His brother Reed contributed to the conversation too, but every time the subject of women or Molly came up, he fell silent. Kent knew that the two had history and that they had ended it long ago, but he sensed something else must be going on for Reed to act this way. He only hoped his brother Reed would find his own peace when he could.

As they all pulled the bags and suites out of the truck, Reed turned his head towards the barn and pasture. He stopped walking and just stared.

"Did you hear that?" His chin lifted in the direction he was looking and we all stared, focusing our attention that way.

"Hear what?" Kent didn't know what his brother was referring to, not having heard anything except their joking since they shut the truck off.

Austin said nothing as he searched the area. The sun was falling and it would get harder to see since they would have limited lights around the property. Austin turned to Reed and shook his head.

Reed shrugged, "must be nothing. I don't hear it now."

"Unless it was Austin letting one go again." Getting a slug to the shoulder for that comment by Austin, Kent just chuckled. "Hey, you did it twice in the truck. Had to roll the windows down and just about get frostbite. It was either that or pass out from the smell."

Reed just bellowed a laugh as he turned to walk up the porch steps. "Can't argue that," he threw over his shoulder.

Austin hit Kent on the shoulder one more time before smiling and following Reed. Kent just rolled his arm back a few times as he made his way up the stairs and into the foyer. All three men unloaded their bags in the kitchen before going in search of the women.

A running Kris collided into Reed's leg just as Holly hopped onto Austin. Both men about fell over at the impact. A lot of hugging and giggling ensued as Kent left the room to find the woman of his thoughts. Walking into the living room, Kent found Hugh tending to the fireplace but no Aaralynn insight.

"Hey, where is Aaralynn?" Hugh turned towards him and something flickered in the other man's eyes.

"She took Ash outside thirty minutes ago," Molly said as she came into the Livingroom. Annette, Austin, Reed, and the two toddlers all crowded into the room behind her.

"We didn't see her outside," Austin said as he let Holly down from his arms.

"Has anyone seen her?" Unable to keep the worry from his voice. When no one answered, Kent pushed past everyone and grabbed the shotgun from the fireplace. Checking if it was loaded, he grabbed another box of ammo and shoved it in his pocket. "I'm going looking for her."

Without another word, he rushed out the door onto the porch. Both his brothers and Hugh rushed out after. All the men stomped down the steps towards the truck just as a high-pitched noise rang out.

"It's coming from the barn," Austin said just as Kent began running that way. Reed pulled out his phone and Kent heard him asking for the sheriff.

Kent reached the barn first and forcefully pulled the sliding door open. It slammed open with a loud screech and vibrated when it hit the end. What greeted them had Kent seeing red. Two men stood around Aaralynn who was falling to the floor. She hit the wood with a thud, her head bounced when it hit with a sickening cracking noise that had his stomach rolling.

Kent pointed the gun at the two men just as Austin pulled out a pistol from his belt. Kent was glad his brother was always carrying.

"Don't move." The order clipped out. The soft sounds of growling could be heard coming from the back of the barn and Kent knew they must have stashed Ash back there. Right now, Kent was more worried about the woman, his woman, lying on the ground seemingly lifeless.

"The Sherriff and deputies are on their way," Reed informed them before putting his phone back in his pocket. When one of the men shifted, Kent heard

Austin ring out a shot. The man moving shouted and dropped a knife.

"I wouldn't move if you know what's good for you," Austin replied and Kent saw blood dripping from the other man's hand. *Nice shot.*

Kent moved a little closer but he didn't want to get too close in case he had to pull the trigger. "Hugh, can you take this? I want to check on Aaralynn." Hugh moved to Kent's side and carefully took the loaded gun.

Everyone froze as the sounds of a car being fired up came from behind the barn. A second later, screeching tires were heard rushing away. Reed turned and ran out the door to see what was going on. Kent went to the unmoving Aaralynn on the floor. Reed came back in the barn laughing as sounds of sirens filter through the air. Staring at Aaralynn, Kent didn't share his brothers' good humor.

"Well, that didn't work out too well for the driver. They just surrounded him."

Kent barely paid any attention to what Reed said as he slowly turned Aaralynn over onto her back. His breathing ragged as he saw the cuts on her chest and arm. His hands roamed her slowly to see if there was anything else wrong. His muscles gradually relaxed as he didn't find anything else on her. Her breathing was steady but she still hadn't opened her eyes. Anxiety surging that something else could be seriously wrong from her hitting her head as hard as she did.

When he swept the hair off her forehead, he heard a soft moan escape her lips. Letting out a silent thank you that she was going to be ok. Kent took in a much-needed breath. The sounds of car doors came from outside and a moment later there were four men in uniforms stepping into the barn. The lights flickered on and for a brief moment, Kent was blind until he waited for his eyes to adjust to the light.

Within a matter of fifteen minutes, the two men were packed into a squad car along with their boss, Billy, and hauled away. EMT's were on scene and politely pushed Kent out of the way to secure Aaralynn's neck and place her on a straight board. They informed him they would be taking her to the hospital for observation and asked if he would like to ride in the "bus" with them. He was torn. One hand, he wanted to go with her. He never wanted to leave her side, but on the other hand, Ash was still locked away somewhere and she would need to be looked after. The decision was made for him though when Gran came outside, in her robe. She had been getting a shower when all this happened and after being clued in, she ordered him to go with Aaralynn. She promised him she would go get the animal and bring her inside.

With that, he followed the EMT's as they wheeled Aaralynn out and placed her securely in the back of the ambulance. Sitting on the bench next to her as instructed, he took her hand in his and whispered in her ear, "I've got you, sweetheart. I'm not going anywhere, ever." Kent placed a kiss on her knuckles as the door closed and they began to move. One of the EMT's sitting across from him began checking the IV line and monitors. Kent sat back, still holding her hand, and prayed that the woman he had given his heart to would wake up so he would be able to tell her just how much she meant to him.

****

Kent rubbed his hands over his face and sat back in the waiting room chair. After the nurses informed him that they were taking Aaralynn for an MRI he could do nothing but think. Thinking was the last thing he wanted to do. When left to his thoughts he became restless for not being able to fix this situation. He was used to being useful, making things right, and protecting those around him with his life. He couldn't help feeling he failed in this scenario and blame was beginning to weigh him down.

Never good at waiting very long, Kent rose and paced around the waiting room. His brothers had kept him in the loop via text about what was going on with the sheriff's department and at home. Gran was feeding Ash and trying to keep the depressed animal busy with the two little girls. Kent smiled to himself at the image of Gran doting on any animal, let alone a wolf. His Gran, who never wanted any animal in the house, was now catering to a wolf. Shaking his head in disbelief, Kent didn't hear the person who came up behind him until he got smacked hard on the back.

"How is she doing?" Austin's voice boomed around them. Austin didn't look any better when Kent turned to look at him. Concern and worry clouding his brother's features.

"I don't know. They took her for an MRI." Kent replied, wishing he had a better answer to give. Turning toward the door as Reed walked into the room with a familiar figure close behind him.

"I found this man snooping around the ranch. He said you were expecting him." Reed patted him on the shoulder just as Austin had done.

Tanner stood just to the right of Reed and with a tick of his jaw, he studied Kent's face. Kent knew his friend would have so many questions but he wasn't in the mood to answer any right now. Kent nodded his head in acknowledgment.

"Sorry I didn't meet you when you got there, man." Kent held out an unsteady hand. Tanner took it, pulling Kent in for a brief hug.

"Yeah, man. I was worried when I was greeted with shotguns aimed at me. Haven't had that since being back from overseas." Tanner replied when he released Kent and stepped back. Reed and Austin cleared their throats in embarrassment.

Kent gave his brothers a look of disapproval but then he shrugged. He realized he would have probably done the same thing after having other men already show up on the ranch trying to raise trouble. "It's been a hectic day, to say the least." His response engulfed a whole complicated mess he wasn't ready to unleash on his friend.

Tanner had a lightness in his eyes at the response but then they narrowed on his face. "I heard about the little lady. Is she doing ok?"

"No one knows." Kent shook his head and ran a hand through his hair. It was getting later. Kent rubbed at his prickly chin and knew he would need a cut and a shave, but that would have to wait. He couldn't leave until he knew what was going on with Aaralynn. "Last I heard she hadn't woken up and they were taking her for an MRI. She hit her head hard."

The memory of her smacking her head on the ground had his stomach clenching. He felt his blood boil in rage. His hands balled up in fists and he had to slow his increased breathing. Too much coiled-up tension for a hospital. Silently, he swore to whoever was listening, that he would protect her until his last breath if she would wake up and be ok. Nothing else matters at this moment.

"Hey." Austin nudged his shoulder for Kent to look at him. "You are stressed too tight." Austin's observation of Kent's physical state was correct. He was stressed.

"You want coffee?" Reed interjected. "I think we all need some. It might be a long night. Gran and the girls will be demanding an update." Reed grinned as he looked around the small circle of men that had formed. He knew his brother was trying to break some of the tension while giving him some space and he loved him for it.

Kent nodded his head, "Yea. That sounds good."

"I'll come with and call the girls. I need to check on them anyway." Austin followed Reed back out of the waiting room. Instead of following, Tanner walked over to a chair and sat down.

Sighing, Kent rolled his shoulders, taking in every crack of protest his joints gave, before walking over and taking the seat next to his friend. He rested his elbows on his knees and his head fell to his hands. Kent rubbed at his temples as Tanner spoke.

"So. All this over a girl, huh?"

Kent let out a noise that even he wasn't sure what it was supposed to be. Feeling restless and agitated at himself for so many reasons, and there wasn't a damn thing he could do about it right then.

Tanner let out a whistle that seemed to echo in the sterile room. "You got it that bad." The sarcastic tone was not helping Kent's mood. "I thought I'd never see the day someone got Closer Kent to bend to their will."

The nickname his unit had given him brought a sense of nostalgia to his worn-down mind. He lifted his head to see Tanner grinning at him from ear to ear. Kent's mouth tilted up at the corner too.

"Well, now all that's left is to close this deal." Kent leaned back in his seat, his mood sobering. "If only she would wake up for me to do that."

Tanner frowned. Tanners features becoming solemn and Kent didn't like that one bit. "Sorry man." His friend replied giving voice to what Kent already knew he was feeling. "I wish I had been there to back you up."

"Don't man." Not being able to handle someone else feeling bad about something he should have been able to take care of himself. "Just don't. There was nothing else you could have done. I have been running around in my own head playing the 'what if' card since this all started and I can't take it if someone else joins in with me."

"Alright." Tanner nodded. His mouth in a straight line. "She will be ok man. I know it."

Kent and Tanner sat there in silence until Reed and Austin came back with coffee. Austin said he got ahold of Hugh and the women are doing as well as could be expected. They were worried of course but nothing else they could do, except hope and pray that Aaralynn would be alright. Something Kent had been doing a lot of already. Reed walked away to answer his phone. Kent thought it was about his work but the way he jumped up to answer his phone had Kent wondering if it might be a little more personal than that.

Austin and Kent exchanged looks as Reed left the room, but both of them just shrugged at the behavior, since neither of them knew what was going on with their brother. Besides, Kent had other things to focus on. Like how long till someone came out here to give him feedback on what was going on with his woman. Kent had been in this waiting room for over two hours, over an hour since he was told she went for an MRI and still he hadn't gotten an update. He was just about to get up and walk over to the nurse's station when a man in a white lab coat walked out from behind swinging doors and called his name.

"Is there a Kent McPherson here?"

Standing, "That's me, Sir"

The dark-haired man with a slightly crooked nose walked over to Kent, Tanner, and his brothers. All of them standing shoulder to shoulder. The man looked over the group of men with a critical eye and Kent wondered what the other man was thinking. He didn't have to wonder long though.

"Is everyone with you Mr. McPherson?" Kent couldn't help but focus on the Doctor's nose. He wondered if he had gotten it broken from a fight or an accident and just never fixed it. "Hmmm," the man said and it pulled Kent back to the conversation they were having.

"Oh, sorry." Kent shook his head. "Yea they are all with me. What's going on doc?" Kent folded his arms across his chest, waiting for the man to speak.

"Yes, well Mr. McPherson, it seems that Ms. Gravella has a mild concussion." The doctor cleared his throat. "I am Dr. Larson. I have been assigned to her while she is here and I wanted to speak to you about her status since you are the one who brought her in and filled out her paperwork." Dr. Larson was shuffling around a clipboard full of papers before moving his eyes back up to Kent's. "I need to get more information on her health history."

Kent was a bundle of nerves and at first, his mind was circling around all the other questions he wanted answered himself. "Look, Dr. Larson," he started and the Dr. flicked his head slightly to move his black hair out of his face. "I don't know much about all of her health history. I honestly am unsure if she has ever even been to a doctor," He would sure as shit find out all about her background when he could now though. "She has only been staying with me and my family for a few days. I do know she has been perfectly fine, no sickness, before this."

The Dr. blew out a breath of frustration and looked down at the chart in his hands. He flipped a few pages back and mumbled something under his breath, before taking a pen from his coat pocket and jotting down a note on the paper. Kent followed the man's movement, shifting his feet a few times. Kent hated beating around the bush and wasting time. He wanted to know what was going on and if there was anything he could do.

"Well, I will have to find out- "

"Sorry, but now you have me more worried about what is going on. You came out here to see me. Why? Is everything ok?"

Dr. Larson looked up from the chart and gave an awkward smile. The smile had Kent feeling uneasy, but he pushed that feeling back down and waited for the man in front of him to answer. Dr. Larson looked back down at the paper in his hands and continued writing. With a click of the pen, he placed it back in his coat pocket. When he looked back up at Kent the smile, he had on his face seemed more genuine.

"She has started waking up and is asking for you, Mr. McPherson."

Kent felt like a jolt went through him at that news. He was thrilled and his brothers must have felt the same way because hands clapped his back. Kent couldn't stop smiling. Dr. Larson's hands fell to his sides, the chart dangling from his fingers.

"Can I see her?" Kent was looking behind the doctor at the doors. His mind was expecting to see them open and Aaralynn to walk on out. In his subconscious though, he knew that wasn't possible.

"Soon. But before you go back, I need to go over some things."

****

"There now. Is that better?" Nurse Crystal asked as the lights were dimmed in the hospital room.

"Much. Thank you." Aaralynn's voice came out low and croaked. Her throat was dry and it was hard to speak. The lights had been increasing her already major headache and she had to squint to keep from feeling like she was going to vomit.

"Now let's get you some ice." Nurse Crystal walked over to the tray that had been placed on the sink counter and put it on the roll-able tray next to her bed. When she had woken up a team of nurses and doctors had swarmed her room. Checking every machine and asking so many questions that she screamed to make them stop. At least, she felt like she screamed. What came out was raspy, gurgled noises, that even she wasn't quite sure what you would call them. Her voice felt raw and her mouth felt like it was stuffed with cotton. She wasn't even sure what day it was. All she knew was she wanted Kent and had asked for him as soon as she was able.

The need to feel him against her so strong, it was palpable. He calmed her and right now she needed something to calm her anxiety and make her headache go away. Her bed moved in a sitting position as nurse Crystal presented a spoonful of ice out of a Styrofoam cup.

"Here you go sugar." Leaning over, Aaralynn gladly took the ice into her mouth. "Only suck on it, you hear? Your head probably hurts something fierce and chewing might make it worse." Her tone was so soft compared to the swarm of medical personnel from earlier. She didn't get nauseous every time Crystal spoke. Aaralynn was grateful for it. "That's it. Just like that."

Aaralynn closed her eyes, focusing on the ice in her mouth. The way the frozen pieces began to melt around her tongue. She leaned back against the bed again and tried to will the pounding to stop. Hands lifting to rub at her temples when she felt a slight tug on her right arm. With one eye slit open, she saw the IV line going from her arm to the saline bag hanging on the metal peg. Closing her eye again, she laid her hand back down.

"On a one to ten, how bad does your head hurt?"

"Seventy-five."

"Well, that's unfortunate." The familiar voice that floated to her ears was both wonderful and agonizing. *Did he have to be so loud?*

"What," Aaralynn said, trying to open her eyes enough to see him but failing. He was a big blobby blur since she was only able to slit her eyes open.

"If your head hurts at a seventy-five then I think it would have exploded." She could hear the smile in his voice. Knowing he was teasing her but she couldn't laugh, yell or even complain. The octave his voice had her head pounding.

She could see his figure moving into the room but nurse Crystal stopped him. At least she hoped it was nurse Crystal or the light blue blur was another person in her room she wasn't aware of. "Sir, I think you should go back to the waiting room." The firm, no-nonsense voice confirmed that it was her nurse.

"The doc came out and told me she was asking for me." Aaralynn saw a nod in her direction and she had to close her eyes to stop the room from spinning. Nausea hit her hard at that moment and she lurched forward. The motion pulled her IV line, made her headache worse which in turn made her nausea worse too.

Kent was by her side in an instant. His hand cool against her neck as something was placed in front of her face. She hoped it was a basket but it didn't matter. Whatever was in her stomach for the day was coming up either way. As she heaved into the container, his cool solid hand rubbed her back and neck.

"Shhh," he soothed. His voice much softer now. She could sense his worry for her and that helped calm her nerves too, even though she was embarrassed for having thrown up in his presence. "Sweetheart, it's ok. Everything is going to be ok."

Tears stung at her eyes and she felt even more uncomfortable. Kent was being so nice to her. She very well could have puked on him, but he didn't seem to mind at all. She heard the nurse rushing around and things being moved, as the container was taken away. Leaning back, a washcloth wiped at her face. A cool, damp cloth covered her forehead, and the relief she felt was like heaven. She moaned slightly at the sensation.

"I am going to check your temperature then call in the doctor to check on you before I give you any pain reliever." Slitting her eyes open again, Aaralynn could see nurse Crystal on her left side, while Kent sat in a chair to her right. He was holding the cloth to her forehead. Her mouth lifting at the corner in a small smile. His hand covered hers, squeezing slightly as the nurse ran the thermometer across her forehead down behind her ear. At the beep, Aaralynn turned her attention to her nurse.

"101.2" She heard her say before checking something on the monitor and walking out of the room. Kent leaned over and rubbed the back of her head as he kissed her cheek. She sighed and tried to relax but her pulse quickened again when a doctor came in to check on her.

Kent stood up and greeted, "Dr. Larsen."

The Dr. just nodded and flipped through a chart. After a few seconds, Dr. Larsen looked up at Aaralynn, moving towards her head. He grabbed something off the wall behind her and then leaned down face level with her.

"Now the nurse tells me you have a bad headache and a fever."

Aaralynn croaked out a reply that resembled a "yes" and Kent squeezed her hand again.

"Now I am going to check your eyes for a second. This may bother you but I need to make sure your pupils are ok."

A light came on one second and the next her eye was being opened to flash a light on it. He did it to both eyes. Her head was pounding so hard from the bright light that she dry heaved. Another cool cloth was pressed to her neck this time since the one on her forehead fell off with her retching.

"Ok, the nurse is going to give you some pain medication through your IV. It should kick in within five minutes and you should be getting some relief from that. Your pupils seem to be functioning fine." Dr. Larsen stood up, replaced the light back on the wall, and turned to write some notes down on a chart. "Your concussion seems to be mild but we did note very little swelling on your MRI. I see nothing else wrong but we need to wait for the swelling to go down to discuss releasing you." He clicked his pen and closed the chart to look at her. Aaralynn's vision was cloudy but it seemed to calm down some now that she didn't have the bright light shining in her eyes.

"When do you think she can go home doc?" Kent moved closer to the side of the bed but never let go of her hand. She felt reassured at that small notion.

"If everything goes well, we will try for tomorrow but I will need another scan done in the meantime to make sure the swelling goes away. She will also need to keep fluid and food down before she can be released. I want to monitor that headache closely too for any signs it could turn into something else, like a blood clot. I highly doubt that will happen

but we don't want to take any chances, now do we?"
His head tilted down. She imagined the doctor giving
her a pointed stare.

"No sir," Kent answered for both of them.
Aaralynn attempted to shake her head but the motion
made her queasy again and she stopped abruptly.

"Good."

Nurse Crystal walked from behind the doctor
with a syringe in her hand. She typed something into
the portable computer screen and checked her IV line.
"Here are your pain meds now. After they kick in, we
will try to see how you feel about getting something
into your system. Liquid first, then we will move up
from there."

Nurse Crystal injected her IV line with the
needle.

"Let me or your nurse know if something
changes. Blurry vision, increased pain, pain anywhere
else, funny feelings in any body part, or anything else
that makes you question it. If nothing happens by the
time, we do another scan tonight, we will look into
getting you out of here tomorrow but Ms. Gravella…"
The doctor paused until her eyes tried to focus on him.
"You will have restrictions when you leave. No loud
noises, no bright lights, no being alone, and no quick
movements or jostling. You will need to calm down to
make sure you heal properly." He patted her foot
before turning around and walking out the door.

"Now," Nurse Crystal started, "your
medication is all in and you should be feeling better
soon." Aaralynn closed her eyes again and listened to
the noises in the room. Kent was breathing pretty
heavily and she could feel his hand warming hers. His
callouses felt good against her soft skin. She heard

shuffling and things being moved about on her other side. Her nurse was very nice and made sure she had everything she needed. "Now, Mr. McPherson. No loud noises, this includes your speaking. She needs everything to be soft or quite for now." More rustling sounds. "Aaralynn honey, you may get drowsy when the med's kick in so I want you to suck on some ice chips while you can. This way your throat and mouth won't feel so ruff later."

"Yes, ma'am," Kent replied and, in her mind, she could make out him tilting his hat to the other woman, if he had one on. He didn't when she saw his blurry figure earlier.

"Alright."

Aaralynn heard the woman leave as she opened her eyes. She turned to Kent, who already had a spoon full of ice chips in his hand and holding it out for her to take. Opening her mouth, she accepted the cool cubes. Slowly, she sucked on the chilled pieces. Delight filled her mouth at the moisture it was giving her.

"I'm so sorry baby." His face was turned down in a sullen frown and she felt her heart pull in her chest.

"Sorry for what?" she tried to get out but it was so ruff coming off her lips that she didn't know if he heard her.

"I shouldn't have left you alone. I should have gotten to you sooner. I'm sorry I failed you. I hate that you're in here." His voice broke on that last statement and she made out the ticking of his jaw.

How could he think he was to blame for any of this? He didn't do anything wrong. In fact, he saved her and she told him as much, but he just shook his head at her response.

"I shouldn't have let it get that far. I won't ever let that happen again. I will make sure you are protected, always."

Is he saying what I think he is saying? He said always and she didn't want to get her hopes up. It could be the medication kicking and this could all be a delusion. *What did the nurse give her exactly?* She cleared her throat. "What are you saying exactly?" He leaned down to stare her straight in the eyes.

His breath mingled with hers he was so close. She tried to hold her breath, but that made her headache worse, making her flinch slightly. "No need to be afraid." He must have taken her flinch as something else. "I am saying I love you Aaralynn, sweetheart, and I am never letting you go. Not without a fight unless you don't want to be with me. I am saying I am yours and I am hoping you are mine because even if you say no, I will still think of you and protect you as if you are mine. I am not going anywhere. You are stuck with me." His words, every single one, was like a hot shower on a frigid December day after you have been walking miles in the snow. It warmed her and melted her in places she had never realized were frozen.

"Kiss me." Was the first thing off her lips and she was elated when his mouth lightly collided with hers. Her eyes shut and she moaned against him. The kiss was soft, claiming. The feel of his tongue grazing her bottom lip had her parting them but he pulled back. Her eye's fluttered open.

"So, what do you say?"

Without having to think, "I love you too." Rushed out. She could make out his mouth moving upwards and she knew he was smiling. Even with her voice still hoarse, she spoke again. "I have for a while now; I just didn't know how to say it." She closed her eyes and leaned back against the bed as her body started feeling tired. *The medicine must be kicking in*, she thought. "I don't want to go anywhere, but I am also scared. The last time I jumped into a relationship it didn't turn out so well."

The bed dipped on one side and she felt his body lean into hers. Moving over she gave him more room on the bed next to her. "We can take it slow sweetheart but I promise you, you don't have to worry about being hurt with me. I may be an ass sometimes, I am a man after all, but I will never be careless with how you feel." His arm wrapped under her neck and he laid down beside her. She heard a mechanical noise right before the bed moved. Kent laying the bed back.

When they laid flat, he pulled her closer to him, and she was able to lay her head in the crook of his arm and chest. His arm possessively wrapped around her, rubbing her lower back and hip. The movement had her mind getting fuzzier with the need for sleep. She went to say something but it came out all muffled. "Shhh," he said into her hair. "Get some sleep. I am not going anywhere." A kiss on her head was the last thing she remembered before drifting off into peaceful slumber.

****

Chapter 17

Aaralynn could feel a slight breeze hit her skin and she shivered. The chill in the air promising more snowfall. Her hair fluttered around her face and she used her hand to brush it back. It had been two weeks since the incident and sometimes she still got headaches but the doctor assured her it was normal. Her brain needed time to heal and she had done nothing but rest since she had been back. She even had to miss out on the wedding. Although, Annette, Molly, Gran, and the two adorable little girls got ready at the cottage so she could be as included as much as possible, but she still felt bad about missing the ceremony. All of them, even Kent had assured her it was ok.

Kent spent most of his time trying to cater to her. Aaralynn both loved the attention and hated it. The thoughtfulness of it had her heartwarming but she also didn't want to take up all his time, knowing he needed to spend some of it with his friend Tanner, who had come into town just to see Kent. Tanner was a little younger than Kent but from what Kent had told her, he was mature for his age. The two had met when Kent was doing a job over in Guam. Tanner had been a new private and assigned to aide them in their intel. They got along so well they stayed in touch and Tanner soon after asked to be transferred into Kent's unit.

At the wedding, Tanner had met one of Kent's cousins that lived in Virginia and the two had spent most of the night together. The cousin was only in town for a few days to catch up after the wedding. Most of that time Tanner spent his time getting to know her, from what Aaralynn had been told.

Kent did spend a few days with Tanner after his cousin left but it was short-lived. Kent spent precious time he should have been spending with Tanner on her. Always worrying and fretting over her. It as silly in her opinion and seemed that Kent barely hung out with his friend before he had to go. Tanner wanted to visit with his 'other family' too. Aaralynn still wasn't sure if he meant actual family or his military family.

Now, she was walking to the barn, in her dress the girls picked out for her for the wedding. She thought it was odd that the girls came over, huddling around her and making her get dressed up just to go to a barn. After hair and makeup, she felt anxiety creep up. She was only told that it was a surprise. She never liked surprises because of how she grew up. Her mother was a prime example. When she had come home from the hospital Ray called her to inform her that her mother was now reported as a missing person. She felt a tinge of worry but not as much as she figured she should. Knowing her mother, Aaralynn was surprised the woman had lived as long as she had without incident.

However, now was not the time to think about such things. Her heart was fluttering enough as it was and she didn't need to think of anything else. Pulling up her wool jacket helped to stave off the cold of the evening. The sun was falling and casting an orange luminesce across the fields covered with icy snow from the last two nights. The light shimmered on the surface to make it look like glass.

"You will be fine," Annette said pulling Aaralynn back to herself. "Just breath." Annette got back from her honeymoon a few days ago and Molly had stayed on at the ranch with Krissy. Gran insisted they stay as long as they wanted. She was probably the reason Reed had come back a few times to the ranch already but nothing has been outright stated about it. Aaralynn could tell Gran loved seeing her eldest grandson so often.

Aaralynn let out a breath that she wasn't aware she had been holding. "Sorry, I was just thinking." Another shiver. "It's cold enough to freeze a pipe out here." That statement got her a few giggles and she smiled in response.

"Yes, it is, but I think we will manage."

"So, are you ever going to tell me why I am walking to a barn?"

"You'll see for yourself in a minute," Annette replied while pushing the barn door open.

The barn lit only with candles and twinkling string lights. An intimate table sat in the center, with a white cloth and set up for two. Kent stood next to it, clad in a pressed long sleeve button down black cotton dress shirt and dark washed jeans. His black Stenson sitting on his head. His accessories of a brown leather belt, a moderate belt buckle, and brown boots completed his look. The sight had Aaralynn's breath catching in her throat and her mouth growing dry. Her eyes following as Kent moved toward her, his beats matching the beating pace of her heart.

"You two have a nice night," Annette said with a wink before turning around and shutting the barn door. The click of the door closing echoed in the space.

"You are the most beautiful creature I have ever seen." Kent's words had her knees feeling weak. Taking her hand, he pulled her towards the table. "I figured since you were so upset about missing the wedding that we'd have a dinner of our own."

They stopped at the table and Kent walked around her to take her jacket. When the garment fell from her shoulders to reveal the pink silk empire dress underneath, she heard a sharp intake of breath and her eyes lifted to his. The look in Kent's eyes was one of appreciation and desire. His gaze roamed her body, lighting her with fire everywhere they reached. When they fell back onto hers, they stood there staring at each other, everything else fading away. She would have given in to the pull of her need for him, but the sound of someone clearing their throat had them both turning their attention. A man in a black penguin suit stood off to the side, his hands behind his back. Kent smiled and pulled out her chair, motioning for her to take a seat.

She blinked a few times trying to get her wits about her. When she finally calmed down enough to move, she smiled at him and went to take her seat. Kent pushed her seat in as the man moved over to the table.

"Good Evening. I am Mark and I will be waiting on you tonight." Aaralynn felt a blush creep up her neck and she couldn't help feeling like this was too much just for her. She was grateful but no one ever went through this much trouble only to take her on a date.

Kent took his seat opposite her when another person walked in with a pushcart. Mark began to speak as the young man placed two covered trays in front of them. "Tonight, we have pecan-crusted flounder with a side of mashed sweet potatoes and a medley of vegetables." The boy pulled the lids off the plates and the most mouthwatering smell from the steam coming off the food reached her nostrils. Closed her eyes, Aaralynn breathed it in.

"Now, we have water, sparkling berry, or red wine. Which would you prefer on this fine evening?"

Kent tilted his chin at her, "I'll have whatever she is having."

Both men stare at her and for a moment she felt her normal anxiety creep up. Taking in a breath and blowing it out, her anxiety seemed to dissipate. "I'll have the sparkling, thank you." After their drinks were poured, Mark excused himself and the young man pushed the cart away. Dinner was an easy flow of polite conversation. Aaralynn found herself laughing and genuinely enjoying herself. She had never been on a date that felt so normal and at ease as this one. Silently, she hoped they had more of these.

Just as she put down her fork and wiped her mouth with her napkin Mark came back out to clear their plates and refilled their drinks. The young man returned with their dessert, sitting the plates down in front of them before he turned around and left again, this time with Mark.

She went to take a bite of her frozen treat but Kent placed a hand over hers before she dipped her spoon in. "Let me do that." He leaned over the table, dipped his spoon in, and held it to her lips.

An anxious smile touched her lips. She had never had anyone feed her before and she felt a little uncomfortable with it but decided it. Pushing the uneasy feeling down she leaned over and took the bite he offered. "Mmmmm," she said. Her eyes closing to take in the taste of vanilla and berries. It tasted like heaven.

"Stunning." His husky voice so close to her ear, had her eyes popped open in surprise. Her vision filled with him. His tall muscled frame stood next to her chair. With a tug, he turned her seat to face him. In one swift motion, he was kneeling in front of her with a red box in the palm of his hand. Her rushing heartbeat filled her ears so loud that she was amazed she could hear anything he was saying.

"Aaralynn, my sweetheart, I know it hasn't been years since we have known each other and I know what some people might think about this. The fact is, I am not willing to live without you. The time you were in the hospital, I have never felt more helpless and scared in my whole life. Like losing you meant I was losing myself." He cleared his throat. She saw unshed tears glittering his eyes and knew he meant every word he was saying.

The prick of her tears in the corners of her eyes made the swelling of her heart in her chest more prevalent to her. "I promise to do everything I can to protect you and to be there for you as long as I live. I know I love you with my whole heart." He reached over with his other hand to open the small box. With a click, a thick carved band with a green emerald and two small diamonds glinted in the candlelight. "Sweetheart, will you make me the happiest man in the world, promise to never give up on me or us, and marry me?"

Tears were streaming down her face. Her vision blurred. She never imagined she could be this happy about anything ever again. All her fears and anxieties, all her pain and heartache seemed to melt away as she nodded her head at the man she loved. Her throat constricted. Words failing to come. Kent smiled brightly and took her hand in his, placing the ring on her ring finger. Kissing her hand, he stood, pulling her with him. Her arms wrapped around his neck and he molded her body to his. Breathing her in, he buried his face into her fiery hair.

"I love you." She choked out into the crook of his neck.

"I love you so much, sweetheart."

****

Epilogue

"Have I ever told you how wonderful you are?"

"You have told me how annoying I am. Is that the same thing?" Kent replies as he pulls his fiancé in for another kiss.

Aaralynn pulls back after he finished his assault on her lips. "Maybe." The flitter of her eyelashes and the beginning of a smirk on her face tells him she is teasing.

"Why am I wonderful this time?"

They just got done having lunch and were standing outside the Sheriff's station. Kent had started on as a K-9 Operative for their brand-new K-9 unit within the force. After a month of going back and forth over what the department was looking for, salary ranges, and other tidbits, he finally agreed to come on board to spearhead the program. The only specification he would not budge on was he would have Ash as his partner. After getting over the initial shock of the request, Aaralynn thought it was a fantastic idea. The Sherriff had no problem agreeing, but the Mayor took a little longer to persuade. Ash was a wolf after all. Once he was able to start training her and prove to the Mayor that she could handle the work with grace and precision, the mayor agreed Ash would be a wonderful asset.

"For one thing, your ability to make me smile and laugh, even when I am mad. Especially when I am mad at you, for instance," A giggle slipped past her lips and she entwined both her hands with his, swinging them out and in.

Kent kissed the tip of her beautiful nose and waited for her to go on. When she didn't, he prompted her with an "And…"

"I just think it is wonderful how you planned a surprise party for your brother's birthday. The whole family able to make a weekend of it too." Her lips brushed against his in a chased kiss, "you are just amazing to plan it all." Still holding on to one of his hands, she released the other to swing around. Her arm outstretched to span the width around them. "I have never been to New York before. This park is amazing."

Kent smiled at her enthusiasm. The way she takes everything in and makes it into something fun. The world today is full of serious, unfun, and moody situations that if dwelled upon can bring you down in an instant. Their steps had them walking closer to the group in front of them near the pond.

"Your family looks like they are enjoying the day. It's nice now that it is starting to get warm out." Aaralynn waved to Holly, who was holding onto Gran's hand in the group in front of them, before snuggling into his side. He swung his arm around her shoulders to keep her close to him. They fit together like they were made for it. His lungs heaved in a big whiff of spring air. "I hope your brother likes his party."

He noted the nervous edge to her voice and knew she had been antsy on how Reed would take having everyone here for his party. Kent kissed the top of her head when they reached the group and stopped. "He will love it. Don't worry."

"I only wish Ash could have come." Those big green eyes tilted up to face him and he could see the tint of sadness in them.

He stroked the side of her arm in slow movements, "I know. I wish we could have too but it would have been too much. Besides, she is having a blast hanging out with the other K-9's at the unit. I got a text a half hour ago and they said she is playing with the new German Shepard puppy we got in." That had Aaralynn giving him a weak smile, but a smile nonetheless. "How about we bring her a doggy bag back? Maybe a big steak too?"

"That sounds perfect." She agreed, going back to snuggling into him.

The air swirled around them and he could smell the dew from the morning mixing with the smell of daffodils and other scents around them. Kent always loved the park too. It was the only big green space in the city limits and the only place that remotely reminded him of home. Apparently, his family loved it too because they have been walking around for over two hours and none of them look like they are ready to leave.

Holly ran over to them and Aaralynn bent down to scoop up the little girl. Her flowy yellow sundress with big daisies made the child look even more adorable. "Auntie Lynn," as Holly began to call her, "when will you have a little girl for me to play with?"

Kent watched as Aaralynn's eyes went wide and her whole body stilled. At first, he was amused because kids always say the oddest things at the most inopportune times, but then when he thought about it, he wanted to know what she thought about the idea too. They hadn't talked about kids, at all, but he always knew he wanted to have some.

Kent laughed when Holly crossed her arms and gave a frown while she waited for Aaralynn to finally speak. When she did, Kent knew she felt out of her element.

"Well," she cleared her throat, "I might need to talk to your Uncle Kent about that and get back to you." Holly looked back and forth between Aaralynn and Kent before nodding in agreement, swiftly wiggling to be put down. Holly waved as she went over to her mother and asked to be picked up again. Aaralynn sighed as she watched the little girl. Kent watched her face softened as her body began to relax again. It had him still wondering what she really thought of the idea.

"So," he began as she tilted her head up toward him, "are we going to discuss the topic of babies? I mean, when are we going to give Holly a playmate?" He grinned, knowing his remark had her when she smiled in return.

Aaralynn leaned into his side. The feel of her body pressed against his something he knew would never get old. Pushing up on her tiptoes, she whispered in his ear. "You may not have to wait too much longer."

Kissing his cheek, she rolled back on her heels to look up at him again. It took a few minutes for him to register what she had just said. Then, another second to understand the meaning behind them. When it sunk in, he blinked a few times.

"Wait? What?"

The smile she gave him said she has a secret she can't wait to tell. "Well, I was going to wait till the party tonight, it being a surprise and all. But I guess some things are too good to keep to myself."

She squealed as his pent-up excitement had him snatching her up and lifting her into the air above him. "I'm going to be a dad!" he shouted when his family turned to see what all the noise was about. Gasps, shouts of joy, congratulations, and murmurs floated to his ears.

"When are you due?" He asked while placing her firmly back on the ground.

Her red curly hair shook around her face. "I don't know. I just found out last night. I need to call and schedule an OBGYN appointment when we get back."

"As soon as we get back. Or how about tomorrow morning? I think the sooner the better." His words rambling together but abruptly stopped by a finger pressed to his lips. Aaralynn's finger shaking with a slight tremor and Kent noticed she was trying to hold in her laughter at his onslaught of words. Shrugging he gave up. He pushed aside her finger and pulled her to him, ignoring the fact that their family was now circling them and speaking. "I love you and as soon as we get back, we are getting married."

"But- "

Her words were cut off by a searing kiss. All of his desire for her and the excitement for their growing child poured into that kiss. Everything around them fading into the background for a few seconds. Kent pulled back, leaving them both panting.

As they caught their breath he went on, "I love you and can't wait to start this family with you, Mrs. McPherson."

"I am not a McPherson yet," she corrected him.

"Sweetheart, paper or not, you are mine. You will always be mine and I will always be yours. That makes you a McPherson with or without that paper. Although, we will have those legalities taken care of as soon as we get back. I assure you."

"I love you Kent. All of your annoying, arrogant, sexy self."

He wrapped his arms around her waist. "And I love you. You may be a Hellfire and trying at times with your sexy ass but I wouldn't have you any other way."

The End

Look for the next installment of the Rayne Falls Ranch Collection: **Their Saving Indelible Love**.
Coming soon. Till next time remember....
"You can't have history without a story in it."

If you feel you are in a bad situation, please reach out to someone. Your local authorities are a place to start but sometimes that is not always an option. If you feel uncomfortable doing so, please reach out to a hotline. One hotline is the National Domestic Abuse Hotline: 1-800-799-7233 (www.thehotline.org). The National Sexual Abuse Hotline: 1-800-656-4673. Or also reach out to www.childhelp.org if you need help with children. Please know there are resources to help if you need it. Always stay safe my readers. You are all important.

www.ingramcontent.com/pod-product-compliance
Lightning Source LLC
Chambersburg PA
CBHW030241200626
46816CB00002BA/457